Destined for Temptation

USA TODAY BESTSELLING AUTHOR
ALLYSON LINDT

For my eternal dragon

HEARTS
IN THE
SAND

A
VALKYRIE'S LEGACY
PREQUEL

CHAPTER ONE

Even the gods weren't meant to fight one war after another, in a string of unending battles, for eternity.

Gwydion watched the water run over his hands. It wouldn't rinse away blood that wasn't there. He couldn't erase the centuries of memories. Of death. Of the soldiers who had died on his operating table.

His hands were red from the heat and scrubbing. Unlike the men he treated who lived out their final hours attached to a morphine drip, Gwydion would heal the instant he shut off the water.

Immortality wasn't always the gift people expected. While he was never grateful for war, he was glad this one had a much lower mortality rate than most.

He turned off the faucet. He should call it a night. The second shift surgeons were in, and he needed to cleanse his mind. As much as that was an option.

He headed toward the exit of the hospital tent he worked in.

His blood ran hot and cold at the same time—a woman's voice, irritated but familiar. A voice he hadn't heard in nearly half a century.

The woman at the front desk bed wore the same BDU's that everyone on base wore. Captain bars and a black cross graced her collar, and a purple band circled her arm—she was clergy.

"I was told an evening appointment wouldn't be a problem." The thread of tension running through her voice betrayed her otherwise calm tone.

The flustered private at the front desk flipped through a stack of papers that had nothing to do with appointments. "I'm sorry, sir. I don't have a record of that, and we don't do evening physicals."

"Who did you make the appointment with?" Gwydion tucked away his reaction. Maybe it wasn't her. He was tired. It was late.

She turned, and Gwydion's heart paused when he saw her face. He should have expected it. He'd know it was her the instant he heard her. But seeing the confirmation.

Kirby. He'd found her.

The irritation in her face faded to a light smile. Either way, she was stunning. But no recognition flashed in her clear blue eyes. "A Private Johnston. He told me they could make an exception for my schedule."

He'd make an exception for her schedule. He'd be happy to pull her into an exam room right now and give her a full-body whatever she wanted.

Gwydion mentally winced at the tacky proposal. He'd loved her across several lifetimes, but she didn't know that yet.

As far as she knew, this was her only reality. At least until her memory came back.

"Private, put Captain..." He paused for her last name.

"Pastor Kirby is fine. Rank only matters in the appropriate situations." Her smile grew.

"Pastor Kirby on the schedule with Dr. Gregory first thing tomorrow morning. I'm sorry," he said to her. "We don't do evening physicals."

Her sigh was exaggerated, and it took a great deal of willpower to not watch her chest rise and fall. BDU's had never looked sexier. "All right. I guess I'll have to play by the rules. I just wish someone had explained that to me the first time around. Thank you, Captain..."

"Gibbons. But Gwydion is fine." He'd love to shrug off rank the way she had, but some things were ingrained in him.

"Gideon? How biblical." She never quite got his name right when they were re-introduced.

"Real close. Put a faint *W* after the G. And it's Welsh."

She furrowed her brow, and mouthed the name a few times.

He did love watching her lips move. And he wasn't going to stare. Instead, he turned to the private, who watched them silently. "Is she all set?"

"Yes, sir."

Fantastic. He should send Kirby on her way, and head to his cot. "Can I walk you back to your chapel?" The question came out without his permission. He wasn't interested in taking it back. He'd seen the tent several times, but never gone in. Like most gods, he preferred not to pay tribute to other deities.

"That does seem safest." Her smile had turned almost playful.

How did she undo him every single time they met? The desire that pulsed through his veins was hotter than the sand outside on a scorching day.

She fell into step beside him, and they strolled into the warm night. She was almost his height, and her blond hair was just long enough to pull into a ponytail at the base of her neck.

He couldn't keep from glancing at her every few seconds. It was really her. Moving with the grace of a panther. Looking up at him with a gaze that stole his breath.

"You haven't stopped staring at me since we met," she said. "Do I have spinach in my teeth?"

"You've got stunning blue eyes." It was the first response that came to mind. "Like the sunlight hitting a frozen lake on a winter morning."

Pink dotted her cheeks. "I bet you say that to all the pastors you walk home at night."

"I don't. It's been decades since I met a woman as beautiful as you." Which was a half-truth. The last time it had been her, in a previous incarnation. No one ever caught his eye the way Kirby did.

"It's a good line, but I'm not that easy."

"It's not a line, and I'd never dare to assume."

They strolled in silence for a few minutes. Shouts echoed in the background, mingling with the roar of engines. Sand kicked up around their feet. Now that the sun was down, the heat wasn't so stifling, but it was still too much for him. Nights like these, he missed the weather of Wales.

"Why clergy?" Gwydion asked. He'd tell her anything she wanted to know, but he had to be careful with the way he framed it. He didn't want to lie to her, but some things wouldn't make much sense until she got her memory back. In the meantime, he wanted to learn where she'd been in this life.

Like most of the troops deployed to Iraq and Kuwait, she looked to be in her twenties. The few times he'd seen her start to become a Valkyrie, she'd been about this age. Given he was almost two-thousand—and the youngest of the men who had loved her in past lives—that made him quite the cradle robber.

She let out a long breath. "It's complicated? Or rather, it's hard to explain without sounding wacko."

"No judgment from me."

Her laugh was hesitant, but still an amazing sound. "My father is a pastor. Unitarian. The whole worship thing never really spoke to me. I was JROTC in high school, majored in anthropology in college, and when it looked like we were heading to war... You don't want to hear my life story."

"I don't mind. I'd bet you listen to people all day every day. Let me return the favor."

She gave a tiny shake of her head. "War is its own religion. Suddenly I understood where Dad's faith came from, and I'd found my own. Warriors riding into battle on metal steads. Defending the things they love. The things they believe in. It called to me. Like I said, it sounds wacko if you can't feel it for yourself."

"No it doesn't. I get it." And he wouldn't expect any less from a Valkyrie. "What's your least favorite part of the job? Besides the celibacy." He didn't know if her current faith required it, but this was an easy way to find out. Being this close to her after too much time, walking near enough their arms brushed, sang to his senses.

"Oh, I'm not celibate." Her chuckle was lighter this time. More carefree. "I love fucking way too much to serve a god who doesn't approve of it."

He couldn't fight his grin. "That's a hard stance to argue."

"You'd be surprised how many people see the cross on my collar and try to do exactly that. But to answer your question, the hardest part is probably..." Another long sigh. "Seeing the people this breaks. Soldiers who become lost souls. Wandering. Looking for peace they'll never find."

He knew that feeling. She might as well be describing him.

"If it was in my power, I'd given them their own kind of rites. Not a prayer to see them to the afterlife, but one that carried them through the rest of this one. A blessing for them to have more."

The sentiment and the idea itself hit hard, squeezing his chest. "I should have stuck to the tangent about sex."

"It's never too late to go back."

Her words struck another dark chord inside. With Kirby, it was always too late to go back. There was only forward, to try to save her the next time. "I'd hate to force it. Unless that's your thing."

"Hmm..." She twisted her face into exaggerated contemplation. "I've been known to kneel in the right circumstance, but I've also required the same."

Her innuendo was enough to break down the dam struggling to contain his memories. The past flooded in, complete with visuals and every other sensation. Her lips wrapped around his cock while she looked up at him with wide, hungry eyes. Him in front of her, worshipping her pussy with his tongue.

Scents. Sounds. Sensations. It was all there. Here they were talking about faith and fury, and he was fantasizing about fellatio.

"I wouldn't mind bearing witness to either," he said.

She licked her lips. "Are you one of those people with deep-seated religious fantasies? Fucking the priest on the altar kind of thing?"

"No. Definitely not. These are all right near the surface." If they were throwing vagueness out the window, in favor of being direct, he was taking advantage of it.

She laughed lightly, and the music drove straight to his cock. She turned to face him. "I offer services to any faith, including hearing confessions, if you're feeling the need to unburden your soul."

They were paused outside the tent designated as the chapel, near the back side where her room would be located.

A reply hovered on the tip of his tongue, flavored with need. The need to taste her again. To feel every inch of her body. To inhale her familiar scent, and tell her everything he wanted to do to her.

He stepped closer, and her breath caught. She watched him with wide eyes, but it was anticipation rather than fear that stared back. He dipped his head to hover his mouth near her ear. "Good night, Pastor Kirby."

"Pleasure to meet you, Captain Gibbons." Disappointment lingered in her words.

He knew the feeling. Why did he do that? Why hadn't he taken advantage of the moment?

She gave him one more glance and disappeared inside.

Because the pull to her was stronger than it had ever been. If he gave in now, he wouldn't want to let her go. And until she knew more about herself and him, his affection might come off more as obsession.

Whom was he kidding? It was completely obsession. Strong enough it had lasted for centuries and so potent that if she'd nudged him one more time, rather than walking away, he wouldn't be able to turn her down.

CHAPTER TWO

Kirby didn't know what it was about the man outside her tent, but in the short time since she'd met him, her pulse hadn't stopped screaming, and her heart kept racing. She unlaced her boots and set them in their spot.

She'd never seen the man with the reddish blond hair and piercing hazel green eyes before. But it felt like she'd known Gwydion for a lifetime. Or longer. If she closed her eyes, she swore she could picture exactly where to touch to make him groan. Exactly how it felt to have his hands roam her skin.

She unbuttoned her BDU top, and shrugged out of it, leaving her in just a black tank top. The cooler evening air rushed in, kissing the moisture from her skin, but not soothing the heat that rushed through her veins.

He was interested. He didn't make any secret of that.

She shouldn't even be considering hooking up with him. Their conversation was somber, rather than arousing. And for discretion's sake, she needed to be careful whom she slept with.

Gwydion though... She'd never seen sex as dirty or sinful, but right now her body screamed at her to let him do anything and everything filthy to her that he could imagine.

There was one guaranteed way to cure the feeling.

She tugged her tent open again, to find him loitering just a few feet away.

"Do you want to come in for a glass of wine?" she asked. "I know, it's a dry country, but this is communion wine, and I won't tell if you won't."

He shook his head. "I don't drink." Yet, he was still here. So that wasn't a brush-off.

She stepped aside enough to hold the tent open wider. What was she doing? She had zero desire to stop, whatever it was. She needed him here. Fuck that. She just needed him. He obliterated her reason until the only thing she could focus on was him. How irrational was that? She didn't care. "Coffee then? Cookies? Sex?"

"All right." He stepped inside.

She zipped the flap shut behind him. "To which one?"

"All of the above. But not in that order." The gravel in his voice made her breath catch

She whirled to find him watching her with that same heated gaze he'd traced over her since they met. "Where would you like to start?"

In response, he knotted his fingers in her hair, under her ponytail, and crushed his mouth to hers. She swore lightning spilled between them, dancing on her skin and sparking in her thoughts. She groaned against his lips. He deepened the kiss, driving his tongue into her mouth to dance with hers.

The entire world faded into the background until there was nothing but him. His touch. The intoxicating sound of his groans.

She wanted to wrap her arms around his neck, and her legs around his waist, and fuck him right here and now.

Her thoughts, her body's response, none of it made sense. She shouldn't be throwing caution to the wind because a smooth-talking doctor made her panties damp.

She wasn't in the mood to listen to reason. She felt frantic and desperate and unhinged.

The way he dragged his mouth along her jaw, to suck on her neck, implied she wasn't the only one.

Kirby needed to be closer. She pushed his shirt up.

He broke away from her long enough to tug his top off, then scraped his teeth along her shoulder. He bit the strap of her tank top and dragged it down to expose more skin.

She licked up his chest. He tasted faintly like sand and sweat and desperation. Or that last one was her.

He barely had her pants unzipped before he shoved them to the ground.

She undid his belt and worked him free. He bucked against her hand when she wrapped her fingers around his shaft. He was as hard as she was wet. She draped her arms around his neck.

"You should know," he murmured against her lips, "I don't make a habit of this."

"So I should feel special?"

He glided his hands down her back, to cup her panty-clad ass. "You're better than special. You're exceptionally extraordinary."

It was a cheesy line. But the sincerity in his throaty answer stole any witty response she had. "Okay."

He turned them both so her back was to the bed. He lifted her enough to steal her balance, but managed to gracefully lower her onto the mattress, leaving her legs hanging over the edge.

Gwydion knelt at her feet.

Anticipation jammed her heart in her throat. She hadn't expected him to take the kneeling thing so literally. Not that was complaining.

Especially when he kissed the inside of her knee. The feather-light brush of his lips skittered over her entire body. He nibbled up the inside of her thigh. There was just enough of a five-o-clock shadow on his chin to add a delicious burn. He scraped his teeth over her panties, the licked along the cotton covering her mound.

The build-up was enough to make her squirm. With him so close to the core of her need, so attentive, but still so far away.

He nibbled, nudged, and teased through the thin cotton covering her mound for several minutes.

She grabbed fistfuls of her blanket, and her hips thrust in time to his licks. She wanted to squeeze her thighs together to mute the pulse, but that wasn't happening with him between her legs.

He hooked his fingers in the elastic of her underwear and dragged it off.

The warm evening air against her damp skin was another layer of sensation, adding to a build toward overload.

When he slid his touch along her slit, she groaned in anticipation. He wrapped one finger on either side of her clit, the licked across the head.

Sweet mother of all that's holy. She raised her ass off the bed to get closer.

He licked and sucked and squeezed.

She bit the inside of her cheek to keep from screaming out. Tent walls weren't exactly known for their ability to mute sound. Pleasure built in her skull, swelling until it forced out everything else. Lightheadedness swam in, and a rainbow of sparkles danced behind her eyelids. She came hard, pressing into his mouth.

As she hit the peak of her orgasm, he pulled his hand away, still sucking on her clit. He slid two fingers inside her without warning. He hooked his touch up, and struck something inside her that nudged her headfirst into another climax.

She clenched around him, and thrashed against his touch, not sure if she wanted more or if it was too much.

When her body decided for her, shuddering and pulling away, he eased up.

Her head was still swimming when he stood, leaned over her, and crushed his mouth to hers. She dove into the taste of herself on his lips, not caring that he'd knotted slick fingers into her hair.

This was incredible, and she needed more. Her body sang to be wrapped up in him.

"Condom?" she asked breathlessly. She hadn't completely lost her reason. Just mostly.

He groaned and rested his forehead against her, where her neck met her shoulder. His breath was hot and tantalizing on her bare skin. "Don't have one."

Praise the Slain God one of them thought ahead.

She rolled on her cot enough to reach the bedside table, and plucked a condom from the nightstand drawer.

She held it up, and he nipped at the foil with his teeth, tearing the package open. Playful in the midst of frantic need. Apparently, he could get hotter.

She rolled the protection onto his thick shaft, reveling in his low groan.

He shifted them both on the mattress, so she was completely on the bed, then knelt between her legs.

How were they going to keep the springs in this thing from squeaking? Did she care? At this moment, she'd do anything he asked of her, no matter how depraved. He could fuck her in front of the entire battalion. Let every single one of them use her mouth and come on her bare skin. As long as she got to feel him buried inside her.

Gwydion nudged her opening with the head of his cock, and slid in enough to stretch her open, before withdrawing again.

She wrapped her legs around his ass, and tried to coax him forward.

He entered her slowly, with drawn out strokes, until he was buried inside her. His pause and low groan confirmed she wasn't the only one on the edge of desperation.

He gripped her thighs and pushed her knees back to her chest. And then the teasing was over. He hammered inside her hard and fast, his face screwed up in ecstasy.

She swore a tangible energy flowed between them and wrapped around them. Tendrils of power and desire, wrapping their bodies together with hunger and need. The frantic pace of his thrust pushed her into orgasm a third time. She came hard, squeezing his cock, her mind floating on an impossible sea of cotton.

His soft grunts and stuttered pace told her he was close too. He paused for a heartbeat, and then slammed harder against her, stuttering and finally slowing to a stop.

The outside world filtered into the edge of her senses as the world swam back into focus. The distant roar of engines. The scent of sand mingled with sex and sweat. Their heavy breathing.

He let go of her legs and dropped his head onto her chest.

She wasn't sure how long they remained like that before he rolled to her side. He stripped off the condom, disposed of it, and stripped off the rest of his clothing.

Then he lay down on the cot and pulled her into him to spoon against her back.

The bed was a tight fight. She didn't care. Even being wrapped in his arms, feeling his heart beating through her back, was its own kind of wonderful intensity.

She didn't realize she'd fallen asleep with Gwydion pressed against her until she woke up. The frantic hunger that drove her last night had faded. There was still a soft voice, telling her to stay here. Whispering she should curl up next to him and go back to sleep. Or wake him up for early morning sex.

She had things to do, and so did he. This needed to be a one-time deal.

In the creeping light of dawn, he looked peaceful and fierce at the same time. Tattoos decorated his chest and upper arms. She hadn't seen him properly last night. A lot of the soldiers had ink, but on Gwydion, the scrawling letters and patterns were more than just art. Though that had a lot to do with the canvas.

Kirby pushed aside the desire to steal one more kiss. She scribbled him a short note, dressed enough to be presentable, grabbed her things, and headed for the showers.

Last night was incredible, but it was time to get back to reality. The ache in her chest, telling her not to walk away from him, was because the sex was so good. Nothing more.

CHAPTER THREE

Gwydion was disappointed to wake up alone in Kirby's cot. Memories of the night before teased his senses. The faint scent of poppies and copper—distinctly Kirby—clung to the sheets and his skin.

Gray peeked in from outside. It was near dawn. He'd slept through the night. That hadn't happened in ages. He needed to get back to his tent, and then start his shift.

Voices carried from the next room. Kirby and someone else. She was already working. No time for a round two of last night. Or maybe something a little slower, and less frantic. Either way, it was probably for the best that they put a little breathing room between them. He didn't expect last night to end on that note, but the stress relief... the connection... having Kirby again... it all undid him.

Now that he'd sated the urge, he could step back a few paces. Focus on protecting her until she came into her own immortality, and woo her at the same time. Every time they met, she fell in love again for the first time, and he adored seeing that through her eyes.

He forced himself out of bed. His clothes were folded on a nearby chair. The note on top was scrawled in a flowing script.

Thank you. See you around the base.

He folded the brief letter, and tucked it into his wallet.

Gwydion was cautious emerging from her tent. He didn't care about rumors—this was another chapter in a never-ending life—but she didn't need them.

He headed back to his own bunk. Even in the pre-dawn light, the base buzzed with activity.

He needed to call Min and Starkad. Let them know he'd found her. There was a sliver of temptation, a tiny voice, that insisted he keep Kirby and the news she was alive all to himself. He wouldn't be happy with that, and neither would she.

Kirby was one of Odin's original shield maidens. Created to decide which warriors would be carried to Valhalla when they fell on the battlefield.

But she'd betrayed Odin, at least in his mind. Extended her reach to other warriors, who worshiped other gods. So Odin cursed her to never know peace, until she learned what true loyalty was.

That had translated to her being reborn each time she was killed. But she never came back with her memories or Valkyrie strength intact. Those rushed back in when she was older. Leaving her mortal and mostly helpless until that point in her life.

Kind of a bad thing when she was drawn to war even before she realized who she was.

Gwydion met her in life four or five. He was art, and pranks, and she was the antithesis of everything he believed. They fell in love despite—or maybe because of—their differences. He'd been devastated the first time she died, believing she was mortal.

When Starkad and Min arrived in his village just a few days after her passing, they explained her story. They'd both loved her in past lives, and searched for her across time and continents.

Gwydion thought the news miraculous at the time. He could have the woman he loved again. He didn't have a problem with her loving them as well, as long as he could find her.

Since then, he'd watched her die almost half a dozen times. Knowing she would come back, only to suffer again, was no longer reassuring. He—they—needed to ensure she survived this time. Whatever it took, they'd break Odin's curse.

He reached his bunk, and grabbed a towel and the satchel he kept his toiletries in.

A whisper of Kirby's intoxicating scent rushed over him. Memories rushed back full-force, of now and the past.

Knowing she was so close, combined with the images of their pasts together, flowed through him, and focused on his cock. After all these centuries, a hint of Kirby was enough to make him hard.

Last night should have been enough to hold him over until he could spend some more time with Kirby outside of the bedroom. But having found her again... Every time her name or her face or her taste rushed through his thoughts, his erection grew harder.

He brushed himself through his pants, and his dick jerked at the light contact. He could try to think about baseball and cold showers, and hope that kept him from walking into the showers at full mast, or he could take care of the distraction.

Gwydion worked his cock free, and wrapped his fist around it. If he closed his eyes, he could almost picture Kirby in the room with him. He stroked as he let the memories dance through his head. Her light voice. Her tight, slick pussy. The way her lips felt wrapped around him. Her throaty cries when she came.

He fell into the phantom sensations, and straight toward orgasm. His balls tightened. His gut clenched. He gripped himself harder and stroked faster.

He came hard, coating his hand and an unfortunate sock with thick streams. He pumped until his dick was raw and his arm ached, and even then he didn't want to stop.

As a trickle of reason flowed back in, he took several deep breaths to center himself. She was here now. The only thing he had to rush was making sure she stayed alive.

If that happened, they had eternity together.

He cleaned himself up enough to not be lewd, and headed to the shower.

Fortunately or otherwise, the crowded communal tent made another round of Kirby-induced masturbation a bad idea. He bathed quickly.

After he was dressed, he had enough time to make a phone call before his shift started.

Gwydion didn't know how to find Starkad. The berserker moved in some interesting circles. Most of which were dedicated to stopping the gods from killing each other.

He called Min.

"Yes," Min answered almost immediately. No one else had this number. He kept it specifically for this purpose.

"She's here."

"I'll be there by this weekend." Min disconnected. He knew where Gwydion was. On the front lines, where Kirby was most likely to appear if she was alive.

It was going to be difficult to work. Gwydion had a job to do, though, rediscovered lost love or not.

He slid into his morning, making his rounds, checking up on patients.

He was a half an hour into his shift when someone called his name. "Dr. Gibbons, you've got a patient in exam room one. Physical."

"Who?" He didn't have any appointments.

"The priest. Gregory is finishing up in surgery."

Concern spiked through Starkad. Why was he wandering the floor if they didn't have any patients? "Any casualties? How many injured?"

"Appendectomy."

"Ah." His heart rate could return to normal now. Any minute that would be fine. He grabbed Kirby's chart and headed to the exam room. He knocked once, heard her call *yeah*, and pushed inside.

She sat on the table, cotton gown tied in the front and thin blanket draped over her legs.

Yeah, his pulse wasn't returning to normal anytime soon.

CHAPTER FOUR

Kirby's mouth went dry and her mind blank when Gwydion walked into the exam room. She swallowed hard when he locked the door behind himself.

"Dr. Gregory is in surgery." His tone was cool as he flipped through the folder in his hand. "You're stuck with me this morning."

"There are worse things." Like just being in the same room as him, remembering the intensity that flowed between them last night, made need throb between her legs. It was a distinct reminder of how much she wasn't wearing. She was going to leave a damp spot on the paper beneath her if she didn't calm down.

"Looks like your past history is all right. Nothing abnormal. Your temperature, pulse, and blood pressure are good." He still wasn't looking at her.

She was grateful they'd checked her before she found out he was her doctor this morning. Otherwise they would have hospitalized her for her heart rate. "That's good." Brilliant response. Not.

He fitted the stethoscope into his ears and stepped up next to her. He was close enough the faint whisper of aftershave teased her. "Breathe normally."

She was trying. The device was cold through her thin robe.

He raised an eyebrow, and moved to another part of her chest.

This was killing her. She didn't know what it was about this man. She didn't know him. But all she could think about was how close he stood. How almost-naked she was. How incredible things were between them last night.

He finally met her gaze. "Your heart rate is elevated. Are you all right?"

How the fuck did he say that with a straight face?

"I have a confession." She trailed her fingers along the edge of her gown, below the first set of ties. What was she doing? Sating an intense craving. "I have this naughty doctor fantasy."

"Hm." Gwydion's tone didn't change, but one corner of his mouth twitched up. He set the stethoscope aside. He tugged the top tie on her robe, and the bow slipped loose. The fabric fell to each side, exposing the middle of her chest, but still covering her breasts. "That could be problematic."

"How so?"

He undid the next tie, and tugged her gown open further. "That's the kind of distraction that makes it hard to focus on conducting a physical."

"How hard?" She let the playfulness slide into her question.

He traveled his fingers along the inside of her arm, tickling the sensitive flesh, grabbed her wrist, and brought her hand down to cup his erection through his scrubs. "You tell me."

"That's pretty hard." Kirby stroked him through fabric, reveling in his low groan. She was done with questions like *what am I doing?* She was looking for another high. That rush of passion and power and union they'd shared last night.

"Do you have any allergies?" His professional tone wasn't so steady now. "Latex? Anything like that?"

Not the sexiest question. "No."

Gwydion broke the contact between them.

Her disappointment mingled with swelling anticipation.

He tugged a pair of gloves from a box on the shelf, and snapped them on. "If you're going to live the dirty doctor fantasy, you might as well do it right."

He rested his hands on her thighs, heat searing through the thin sheet that covered her lap, and nudged her legs open, so he could step between. He tugged open one side of her gown, to expose her breast.

She couldn't squeeze her legs together like this, which made it harder to ignore the throb between. The line about the fantasy had been a joke, a throwback to last night, but now the scorching hot taboo of being fucked on an exam table was all she could think about.

He dragged a latex-covered thumb over her pert, tender nipple. The texture was unique blend of smooth with a hint of stickiness.

She clamped her jaw shut to keep a groan from escaping. If they kept this up beyond today, their next time needed to be someplace she could be loud.

And if she had anything to say about it, they were definitely keeping this up.

Gwydion opened her gown wider, exposing her breasts. He cupped one, kneading then rolling her nipple between his fingers. He moved to the other side, and repeated the gesture. His light touches were enough to light her senses up.

"Everything checks out." Despite the clinical words, his voice was a throaty grown. He dipped his head and wrapped his lips around one swollen nub.

She swallowed a groan of pleasure and pressed into his mouth.

He sucked and nibbled and licked for several minutes, until she was sure she couldn't take anymore, and he switched sides.

The pulse between her legs was insistent. She reached to soothe it, and he grabbed her wrist.

"I'd like to give you a closer look." He nudged her shoulder and helped her lie back.

He glided his palms along her thighs, then lifted her legs, and settled her feet in the stirrups.

Her pulse screamed through her veins at how exposed this left her. The feeling was dangerously incredible.

He traced circles around her clit, drawing tighter then moving in a wider path. He drew away each time her breathing grew shallow, then honed back in the sensitive spot.

If she bit the inside of her cheek any harder, to keep silent, she was going to break the skin.

Still stroking her clit, he traveled his other hand lower, to dip his fingers inside her. She was so wet there was zero resistance.

He hooked his fingers up and pressed the tender spot inside. Holy hell he was good at that. A benefit to fucking a doctor.

Her pussy tightened around him, and orgasm spilled through her. She bit the side of her fist, barely smothering her screams.

Through the haze of bliss, she was vaguely aware of the sound of a zipper.

He nudged her opening with his cock, and thrust inside. At this angle, the sensations were unlike anything she'd ever experienced. And being held in this position was deliciously wicked. She was more exposed than just being naked. At his mercy. And her head was drowning in the haze of him gripping her thighs and pounding inside her.

He pulled her ass half off the table, putting her in a precarious position, but he held her so tightly she wasn't going anywhere. With each thrust, a new wave of pleasure rippled through her.

She wanted to watch his gorgeous face, screwed up with desire. But she was too lost in the sensations to focus on anything else.

Orgasm built more slowly this time. Holding her over a chasm. Promising amazing things below. And then she tumbled into climax. A night sky full of stars filled her thoughts. She was floating in a blissful sea.

Gwydion's grunts grew to staccato bursts. She was fading away from her own peak, and the sensation of him sliding out of her was light.

Something warm and fluid hit her stomach and mons. She lifted her head enough to see him fisting his cock as he came on her exposed skin. His groans were as delicious as seeing him lost in the moment.

He finished with a breathless pause, resting his forehead lightly against her leg.

"Fluid spill in exam room one," Kirby teased.

Gwydion laughed. "Don't move."

She wasn't sure she could. Not easily, anyway. The strain of her pose, combined with the pleasure he'd administered, pulsed in her thighs. Not that she minded the pending wobbliness.

He used wipes to clean her. The cool touch made her gasp, but his tender ministrations were their own flavor of erotic. He eased her feet from the stirrups, helped her sit, and pulled her gown closed together in the front. "There. All proper again."

"Nothing about that was proper." She was smiling. The happy sparks that danced through her would linger for a while.

Gwydion pressed between her legs and hooked his hands at the small of her back. "If we're going to do more of this, I should at least buy you dinner."

She shouldn't, even though she'd already decided otherwise. Mostly because she didn't know why her body and head reacted to him this way. Then there were the rumors, and the rules... Did she care about either? "As in, an actual date?"

"As in."

Underneath all her other concerns, there was a thread of fear. Not of him. Of something she couldn't name beyond the ridiculous label of *impending doom*. And it was as intense and irrational as her attraction to Gwydion.

"Dinner sounds wonderful." And maybe in public, they could keep from tearing each other's clothes off long enough to have an actual conversation.

CHAPTER FIVE

Gwydion didn't know how he made it through the next couple of days. His thoughts drifted toward Kirby a dangerous number of times. He managed to keep his attention on work when needed, but it was fortunate the need was infrequent.

So many thoughts played through his mind. There was the question he always asked himself—what was the best way to tell her *I've loved you in so many past lives. Does that make my infatuation with you any less creepy?*

It didn't matter he'd had several chances at that moment. He'd never quite figured it out. Once again, he'd play things by ear.

And then there was the explosion that she and everyone around her lived through. That had been her doing—he had no doubt. As a Valkyrie, she didn't just escort warriors to Valhalla, but she decided who lived and died in battle.

She hadn't wanted those innocent people to die, and part of her knew how to prevent it. She was getting closer to realizing who she was.

If she hit that point without being mentally prepared, it would be horrible for her. It wasn't a great experience anyway. He'd witnessed it twice. All of her memories, from all of her past lives rushed back. Including each and every time she died.

She'd be forced to relive that, and if she was this close to the discovery, he wanted to prepare her.

The evening of their date rolled around. They'd picked a night where they could both request a little free time the next day. They tried to choose when several soldiers were heading into Kuwait, but not so many that they'd leave stations unattended.

She would meet him there, to draw less attention than them riding into town together.

During the last hour long stretch before he saw her, he fidgeted like a schoolboy. He arrived early at the restaurant another doctor recommended, unable to wait any longer.

Kirby was already there. She wore a loose cotton blouse that covered her arms, and beige slacks. There wasn't an official dress code in the city, but they'd been asked to be respectful of the local culture.

It didn't matter that her clothing hid her figure. She was captivating.

"Shall we?" He nodded toward the entrance.

She joined him inside.

The lighting was dimmer in here, with shades covering the windows, and dark wood adorning the dining room. He told the host they had a reservation, and they were seated immediately.

Most of the cloth covered tables were empty. Even in the nicer parts of town, businesses suffered from the war.

"You speak Arabic?" Awe filled Kirby's question.

"You thought my tongue was only good for one thing?"

"I figured it had other uses... But bilingual."

"And then some." He'd lost count of how many languages he spoke. He itched to reach across the table and touch her. Hold her hand. Run a foot up the inside of her leg. He should really let his dick stop thinking for him, and use this opportunity to get to know her again. "Is this public meeting place your nefarious plan to get me to keep my hands to myself?"

She looked at ease here. All easy smiles and light laughs. "Nefarious? If we're pretending you didn't suggest the restaurant, then yes that's exactly my plan. But I have to admit... I'm getting worried."

The waiter interrupted with two bottles of sparkling water, and to explain the specials.

It was tempting to send the man away, so Gwydion and Kirby could keep talking. On a more practical note, the sooner they finished their meal, the sooner they could walk across the street to the hotel.

Waiting fifty or more years between each meeting hadn't taught him any patience. He looked at Kirby, who watched him with a lost look. "Do you like spicy?" he asked.

"Innuendo aside? Yes."

"May I order for you?"

She furrowed her brow, and then nodded. "Please."

Gwydion told the waiter they'd like the *kebabs* and *biryanis*, and the man left them again.

"Worried about what?" Gwydion gave Kirby his full attention again.

"That my plan to keep your hands off me might actually work."

He chuckled. "Would you be less concerned if I told you I have a reservation across the street?"

"In the stunning five-star hotel?"

"That's the one." He didn't care about the luxury for himself, but she deserved the best.

She raised her eyebrows. "On an Army salary?"

"I come from money." His own.

"Noted and I'm coming back to that. As for the hotel, presumptuous much?" Her tone was playful.

"Always, but especially after the conversation where we agreed *Let's pick a day where we no one will miss us if we don't come back the next morning.*"

"*So many* assumptions." Her smile grew.

"The way I see it, we've only hit the tip of the iceberg for fantasies, and we've got all weekend to tick a couple more items off."

"How long is your list?"

Growing longer with each second I talk to you. We've got preacher's daughter... Taboo workplace hookup..." He ticked each one off on a finger.

Her laughter, light and carefree, sang to his soul.

"Excuse me. So sorry to interrupt, my huntress. Gwydion, it's been a long time."

Ambivalence washed over Gwydion at the familiar voice. He knew exactly who he'd see when he looked up. He turned to the new arrival. Talk about shitty timing. Not the worst, but close enough.

"Min. Wonderful to see you again." He forced himself to sound sincere.

Min tasted the passion and sex in the air before he even walked in the restaurant. One of the gifts that came with being a god of pleasure.

He didn't need to see Kirby to know exactly where she sat.

He strode past the host without pause, toward his huntress. Kirby watched Gwydion with adoration, unaware of Min's approach. The two had already slept together at least once.

Gwydion hadn't wasted any time. Not that Min blamed him. His huntress could love whomever she wanted, as long as he and she were side-by-side. A woman as fierce as Kirby should never be bound without her permission.

When he interrupted, he didn't miss the ghost of irritation that passed over Gwydion's face. This wasn't a dinner between colleagues; it was a date.

The way she watched Min stole his thoughts. It had been too long since he'd seen her stunning face in person. Tasted those full lips. Heard that melodic voice.

He pulled out a chair. "I'll only join you for a moment, and then I'll leave you two to your evening."

Gwydion clenched his jaw.

Kirby furrowed her brow. If she said *no*, Min would leave.

He very much wanted her to accept his self-invitation.

Kirby didn't know who this arrogant man was. This gorgeous, sultry-voiced, arrogant man. His ebony skin was a stark contrast to his white suit, and if she stood, he'd still tower over her by at least six inches.

He'd interrupted their evening. He showed no remorse. And Gwydion hadn't told him to fuck off yet. Then again, the men appeared to be friends, and until Kirby got to know Gwydion better, she was a fuck buddy at best.

Given all that, why couldn't she stop staring at this Min? Her body was reacting the same way it had to Gwydion, with desire pulsing under her skin, and an irresistible pull that made her wonder if what they said about men with big feet was true.

"It sounds like you two need to catch up," she heard herself say. What was she doing?

"Only if you stay." Gwydion grabbed her wrist.

She sucked in a sharp breath at his grip. It wasn't a request on his part, but she hadn't planned on leaving anyway. "Of course. We've got that list to go through."

Gwydion smirked.

Min raised an eyebrow, but didn't look bothered otherwise. He settled into his seat, waved the waiter over, and ordered himself a sparkling water. Then he turned to her. "I'm Min." He grasped her fingers and kissed the back of her knuckles.

"Kirby." She was just put off enough by his assumption that she was able to ignore the twittery, swoony voice in her head.

"A stunning name for a fierce huntress." It was the second time he'd called her that.

The way he studied her with eyes so dark they were almost black, sent delicious images dancing through her mind. Things she'd never tried. Never enjoyed the thought of—of him binding her. Spanking her?

She could almost feel the sting of his palm on her ass, and the phantom sensation reverberated along her skin.

She found the willpower to tug her hand away. "I've never hunted anything except the perfect slice of mall pizza."

His lips curled into a hungry smile. "There's time."

Kirby's senses were frazzled. She didn't want to be interrupted. She wanted this weekend to get to know Gwydion, and find out what this pull was. She wanted Min to stick around so she could figure out what the fuck was going on there...

Despite Gwydion and Min's familiarity, neither of them spoke.

The silence spurred her mind to bounce from one idea to the next. She drifted back to the simple first—wrapping her legs around

Gwydion's waist as he pinned her to the wall and drove inside her.

The imprint of brick ghosted on her back, but was washed away by the thought of Min blindfolding her. Stealing her sight so his smooth, seductive voice drilled deeper into her thoughts. Making the lack of touch as enticing as those sharp sparks where he licked along her neck, or took a belt to her backside.

She mentally cleared her throat. "How did the two of you meet?" She needed someone to talk, or she'd tumble into lust and never climb out.

If they joined her, that might not be a bad thing.

The men exchanged a glance she couldn't interpret.

"That bar in... Where was it?" Gwydion said.

Min didn't blink. "Belfast."

"Right. It seems like centuries ago."

"It was."

They almost sounded like they believed that. For two people who had so much past, they didn't seem to have a lot to say to each other. Maybe they'd already both said it all.

From the glances they swapped every few seconds, she doubted it.

CHAPTER SIX

Min didn't care for this place, surrounded by these rules and people who suppressed his ideals. But it seemed the most likely spot to introduce himself into Kirby's life again.

The way she studied him, gaze intense and skeptical curiosity dotting her features, was enthralling. "The two of you know each other, but you're not friends. Not best buddy dudes." The turning gears in her head were almost audible. "Was it for business reasons?"

He loved her analytical mind as much as he did the rest of her. "Do I look like military to you?"

"No. You look like a wealthy businessman who's used to getting his way regardless of the situation." As direct as always. Stunning. "But he mentioned he comes from money, and his past haunts him, so there's more to him than being an Army surgeon."

"You assume," Min said.

Her smile was dry. "I do. But I was hoping to confirm over the next couple of days. It was a woman, wasn't it?"

"What was?" Gwydion asked.

"The thing that you have in common. How you two know each other. I bet it was a rivalry."

Min was captivated by the conclusions she was drawing. In a way, they were logical, but they also took overlooking several other possibilities. Did he dare hope she was close to remembering? "It was a woman, but it wasn't a rivalry."

"She doesn't want to hear about your past conquests." Gwydion didn't seem to be enjoying this as much.

Of course he wasn't. He'd had the Valkyrie to himself.

Kirby reached across the table to brush her fingers over Gwydion's arm. "You don't speak for me."

Sparks. Delicious.

She looked at Min again. "What was it, then?"

"We loved her, and she loved us." He didn't care for speaking of this in the past tense, but some concessions had to be made.

Kirby's lips parted slightly, and it was a moment before spoke. "At the same time? Are you like... reverse Mormons?"

Min swallowed his chuckle. What he represented was older than any other faith, ancient or modern. "The only worship—the only loyalty—we gave was to each other. Our universes revolved around her, and hers, us."

"At the same time?" A flush crept over her skin, and her pulse raced.

He heard it from where he sat. He smelled the desire spilling from her. "Frequently."

It was surprising Gwydion was quiet during this exchange. However, they had similar goals—Kirby becoming—and this seemed to be getting them closer.

Kirby licked her lips, leaving a tantalizing shine behind. "To be clear, we're talking about sex, am I right? Both of you, plus this amazing woman from the past?"

"We're talking about so much more." Min traced a finger along her bottom lip, pulling it into a pout before releasing her. Her quiet gasp flooded him like a fine wine.

"But yes, sex is on the list," Gwydion said.

The man never had been a poet. However, Kirby loved every time she met him, and Min had nothing but respect for him.

Kirby glanced at Gwydion, then back. Her mouth was quirked in disbelief, but lust and discovery still radiated from her. "Men don't share. There's no way that works. No wonder you hate each other."

"We don't hate each other." Gwydion's sincere denial came quickly.

Min nodded. "No, we don't. You obviously haven't met the right men. I'm not talking about jealousy or trying to possess another soul. I'm talking about union. Joy. Wonder. Singing your praises. Each of us tasting your skin. Drinking your honey. Setting you on a pedestal so the world knows you belong to no one.

"I'm talking about endless nights and countless days of discovery. Diving into your depths. Coaxing you toward pleasure until you sing the most beautiful songs. Then sliding into security, to begin the process anew when we're rested." So much for keeping things in the past tense.

Kirby's pupils were wide. Her breathing shallow and her lips flushed. "Who are you?"

Min covered her hand and leaned in. He held her gaze. "I'm Min. I'm an ancient, powerful god of lust and sexuality. I've been worshipped by more people in my existence than currently walk the earth. I can make my lovers quiver with a single touch or whisper. And none of that matters unless I have you ruling by my side."

Gwydion coughed.

Kirby stared back, unblinking. Would she laugh in his face? Call him insane and walk away?

Kirby's heart hammered against her ribs, and she was pretty sure Min could hear it.

The flowery words were pretty, but the man was fucking insane. A god? He wasn't just saying it. He believed it.

And she was scared. Not of him. Not the way she should be, if she were any sort of rational. There were two branches of fear inside. The first was that same sense of dread she had around Gwydion, but Min amplified it. It wasn't because of them, but it related to them being in her life.

The second was more immediate and tangible. The longer the three of them sat here, the stronger her impulse became to surrender to this stranger. To believe him when he said he was a god. To beg him to bring his words to life, using her as a canvas. To bow down and give him anything he demanded.

The impulse thrummed in her thoughts. Each time he spoke, his meaning splashed across her skin like a memory. As if she were this woman he described.

That fucking terrified her.

No one could have her surrender. Especially not an arrogant stranger in a random restaurant in Kuwait.

She turned to Gwydion. "I don't think I'm hungry. I'd like to go." She shouldn't have a problem keeping her tone firm, but Min had thrown her so off balance, she wanted to pat herself for her voice not cracking on the request.

"Of course." He already had his wallet out, to set a short stack of bills on the table. He stood and extended his hand.

She wouldn't look back at Min. She couldn't. He'd unravel her in with a glance.

She took Gwydion's hand, gripping tighter than she intended, and strolled with him onto the street.

Kirby couldn't get rid of the tremble that ran through her. It wasn't a fear of Min... Not that he would cause her harm. But her own irrational thoughts terrified her. Especially the thought that was happy he followed them from the restaurant.

"Why is he behind us?" Kirby asked.

"He's probably staying at the same place."

That made sense. More sense than anything else about him. Kirby and Gwydion walked into the hotel, and the world vanished behind them. Despite the chaos in her thoughts, she stepped aside and paused in the lobby, trying to take it all in. Gold and marble and leather stretched as far as the eye could see. Wide, mirrored columns raced to high ceilings.

It was more stunning and opulent in person than any Hollywood production made a high-end hotel appear.

She swallowed her awe and loosened her grip on Gwydion's hand. The pause was enough to reset her brain. It gave her time to be more rational. She couldn't blame her overreacting on a random stranger.

"The woman he was talking about. The one you both loved, who was she?"

Gwydion met her gaze with a sigh. Pain and sincerity reflected back. "You."

Bullshit. She should slap him and stalk away with an answer like that. He was insane. She barely knew him. She hadn't loved him or Mr. Very Tall Dark and Handsome. This was where she should walk away from Gwydion and straight toward the embassy. She'd demand to be reassigned. Sent to the front lines where soldiers needed her faith.

Instead, a whimper escaped. "I don't know you. Either of you."

"Come upstairs. Let him join us. I'm not talking about sex. This is about explaining things."

"No." Kirby stepped back from Gwydion. She wasn't trapping herself in a room with two men she couldn't control herself around. Who, as far as she could tell, were stalking her and thinking she was someone else.

Gwydion didn't close the distance between them. "He's not going to hurt you. Neither am I."

Why did she believe him? Because she was a horny idiot? "Just because you say it doesn't make it true."

"You can say *no* at any time," Min said from behind her. "Right now. Five minutes from now. Two hours from now. Any time."

She believed him, too. She was a freaking idiot.

Whispers of memory flitted through her, of times and places she'd never been. She shouldn't recognize the World War II uniforms from England, but she did. The French Revolution. The Hundred Years War.

Gwydion and Min were there in each instance. This wasn't sensual like when Min had been speaking. It was war. They were fighting. Both of them soldiers.

And Kirby saw it in her mind as clearly as if she had watched it happen. Her heart felt the reality and her brain argued she was losing it big time.

She took another step back. "This is all insane. Both of you. What are you doing to me?"

This time Gwydion approached her. He lifted her chin to look her in the eyes. He studied her with stunning green eyes filled with affection and concern. He brushed his lips over hers.

Her thoughts quieted, and her fear was muffled under a heavy blanket. How did he do that with a touch?

"We're taught so many things as children." He dropped his hand, breaking the contact between them. "We're indoctrinated form the second we're born. The lessons have changed over time, but beliefs are always drilled into our thoughts until the becomes the cornerstones of our reality.

"You were raised to worship a god who can do see everyone and is capable of anything. But you were told magic isn't real. Experience has drilled into your head that you can only trust yourself, but the world tells you that same instinct is a lie."

"We're telling you the opposite." Min's tone had shifted. It was still deep and sensual, but the seduction had been replaced with matter-of-factness. "You *can* trust your instinct. Believe your heart. Stop listening to everyone else's reality, and hear your own."

"And I do that by letting the two of you speak?" This was too much. She didn't want to rewrite her faith. There was no reason for her to dismantle her entire core. This weekend was about getting laid.

"You do that by listening to yourself after you hear us out," Gwydion said.

A switch flipped in her thoughts. Whatever they were talking about, whatever they were getting at, she didn't need to jump through those kinds of mental hoops. "I didn't come here to rearrange my universe. What if I just want to get laid?"

CHAPTER SEVEN

It was easier than Kirby expected to sweep aside doubt and focus on desire. Want already thrummed under her skin, and now it was unleashed.

"If that's what you want, that's what you'll have," Min said.

Kirby couldn't think about this anymore. The conflict between head and heart was making her dizzy. She had to do something, and her body was currently the easiest to listen to. She grabbed Min's lapels, stood on tiptoe, and crashed her mouth against his.

More of the chaos faded, and her veins hummed with the beat of her hammering pulse. The memories that weren't hers intensified. She tasted his skin and his sex. Felt his hot breath and his mouth between her legs.

It was as if she lived half a dozen lifetimes simultaneously, all of them frozen on a moment where she was wrapped up and consumed by him.

Fuck logic or indoctrination or reason. "I don't care whose room, as long as we get there quickly."

Because kissing either of them was life. Breaking that connection or thinking for too long meant surrendering the ability to breathe.

She half-expected Min to scoop her into his arms. He'd done that so many times.

No. That wasn't right, because she'd just met him.

She also wasn't thinking about that right now.

Instead, he rested a hand at the small of her back, while Gwydion took her hand again, and they headed toward the elevators.

Apparently that was where half the people in the hotel currently were.

Gwydion dipped his head to hers. "Do you want to wait for an empty car?"

"No. This is fine." Waiting meant more time passing. And thinking. She didn't want either of those. There was still a tiny voice telling her she was being irrational.

And another argued with it, that if she didn't do this now, she might miss her chance this life. It was carried on a sliver of dread that outweighed anything besides her desire.

The three of them packed into the elevator like sardines from one of those old Tex Avery cartoons. Gwydion and Min kept her between them, heat seeping deeper into her joints than any desert afternoon.

She wanted more of this. With fewer clothes, and no other people.

They reached their floor. Every step toward the room clashed with her need. Waiting for Min to fit the key in the lock and rattle the old door into submission was delicious agony.

She'd embraced impulsiveness twice with Gwydion. Is that why this kept getting easier? No. If she ignored what she'd been taught, as Min said to, none of this felt wrong. And then they were in the room, closed off from the rest of the world.

Gwydion cupped her face and brushed his lips over her.

"I want both of you," she murmured against his mouth. She was allowed that, right? That was implied by them both being here? Her heart and the images in her head said *yes*.

He playfully bit her bottom lip. "Another tick off the list?"

"Something like that." But whatever part of her knew this was safe still had reservations about Min. Insisted she could have him, but not give him everything.

Kirby turned back to Min. Gwydion never let go of her, sliding his hands up her sides and kissing along the back of her neck.

More of her trepidation had faded. She felt stronger. Bolder. And that she needed to make up for lost time.

She crushed her mouth to Min's again.

He rested a hand at the small of her back, drawing her body into his hard, thick, muscled form. His erection, definitely larger than she was used to, dug into her stomach. How did this two-guys-at-once thing work? Because there was no way in hell he was sticking that her ass.

With their hands roaming her body, it was easy to set aside that concern. She lost track of who was touching and kissing and caressing where. Groping through clothes. A jumble of hands and mouths for her to lose herself in.

Kirby'd only taken off her shoes, and the desire was already clenching in her core, making her thirsty for more. She broke away from Min, and held his questioning gaze as she fell to her knees in front of him. She dragged down his zipper.

He groan rumbled through her, and she licked her lips in anticipation.

She worked him free from his slacks. His dick wasn't impossibly huge, but she'd seen smaller novelty dildos. She continued to watch his face as she traced her tongue along the head of his cock. The slight part of his lips, and the hunger written across his face, was as tantalizing as any touch.

She took him in her mouth, as much as he was able. His growl was delicious. Even better, Gwydion echoed the sound. She didn't know where he was, but the buzz on her skin said he was close.

Kirby sucked and stroked Min's shaft. His mounting arousal amplified her own. She'd never realized it was possible to be so turned on without being touched. It drove her to dive into the moment with enthusiasm. Licking. Stroking his soft sack.

He gripped her hair, holding her in place, and fucking her face. Each time he struck the back of her throat, reflex kicked in and she ignored it. She wanted to consume him. To please him. To become one with him.

"My huntress, please." His voice was dry croak. He tried to tug her to her feet.

He was close, and she wasn't interested in stopping. She tightened her grip, and set a pace in time with the thrust of his hips. She needed to taste him.

And then the salty fluid filled her mouth, some dribbling free and down her chin. She licked him clean, smiling in satisfaction when he shuddered at her touch.

Surprise filtered through her when he knelt as well. He kissed her face, licking himself from her skin, before moving to claim her mouth. His touch consumed her.

He broke away to look her in the eye. "You're my huntress," he said. "From now until eternity. And I'm your servant for as long if not longer."

The intensity of his words, of his promise, should have terrified the hell out of her. Instead it was a soothing promise. It brought back Gwydion's words about what she believed in. She was starting to understand.

Min rose, and helped Kirby to her feet. He was gentle and meticulous as he stripped her clothing off. It was the most tenderly intimate thing she'd ever experienced, but it was also familiar. The way he looked over her sent chills and heat racing over her at the same time.

Gwydion pressed into her back, his bare skin contacting with hers. Apparently she wasn't the only one who had lost her clothes.

"You don't have to be quiet in here," he whispered, his breath teasing her cheek. He snaked his palms up her stomach, and rolled one of her nipples between his fingers.

She half-squeaked, half-sighed at the sudden sharpness of his touch, and whirled to face him.

This was the first time she'd seen him nude in full light. She wanted to revel in his naked form—sculpted muscle, intricate tattoos, and girth where it counted. When did he put on a condom?

Gwydion had other plans. He settled his palms on her cheeks and captured her mouth in a hungry kiss.

She roamed her hands over his body, memorizing each contour, and trying to feel everything.

He stumbled back to the bed, and pulled her with him. "Did you know..." he said between light bites along her neck, "... you make the most stunning faces when you come?"

If her skin got any hotter, she'd combust. "I can't say I spent a lot of time watching myself."

"No?" Min molded his body to her back. He was naked now too, and his half-hard cock pressed into her. "You deserve to be watched and worshipped. Your room covered in mirrors to display the beauty that is you."

He spoke as if he knew from experience. According to their wacky story, he did.

She almost believed it. Not quite, but it didn't discourage her from being sandwiched between them.

Gwydion lay on the bed, tugging her down. When she lost her balance and landed on her palms, he gripped the back of her neck, leaned up, and crushed his mouth to hers.

"I want to see as much of you as possible, all weekend." His voice dropped an octave. "Beneath me. On top of me. Anywhere and everywhere."

"I like that idea." She crawled up his legs. When she lowered herself onto him, sliding down slowly, she moaned at the penetration. This was so much better when she didn't have to keep the noise down.

She tried to set a fast pace, needing release after the build-up of pleasing Min.

Gwydion tightened his grip on her hips enough to leave marks, slowing her down.

Maybe she could do slow. For a little while. This was good. Incredible even. Feeling him slide in and out, as he rocked against her.

Min moved in behind her again. His bare chest against her back wrapped her in ribbons of desire. He was attentive, rather than demanding. Kissing along the back of her neck. Gliding his fingers along the creases where her thighs met her hips. Teasing her clit, while Gwydion filled her.

She sank into the layers of touch and caress. It was easier to wind it all around her than try to pick one sensation that was her favorite. Lust and arousal mingled and grew, spreading from her core to reach every inch of her body.

Gwydion dragged his palms up her stomach to tease her breasts. When he rolled her nipples between her fingers, it was another flavor in an already intense parfait. Min circled her clit, and Gwydion thrust harder. Faster.

Orgasm engulfed her. The only thing she felt... tasted... smelled... was pleasure. Making her head light. Dancing like a million fireflies in her mind.

And then the sound of Gwydion's climax joined in. She floated in the intensity of it all, until the edge faded, and the world slowly drifted back in.

Kirby curled up against Gwydion, head on his chest, the hammering of his heart matching her own. She pulled Min's arm to cover her, sinking into the security of his being wrapped up in him.

This all felt so right. Like the memories really were hers. That she had centuries of love holding and comforting her.

She faded toward sleep, and a new warmth engulfed her. Vibrant and timeless. A part of her whispered these were her memories. She didn't care what they were or where they came from, as long as she could follow the sensation.

As she stepped into a new room, the edges of everything were fuzzed. There were voices. So many voices. And faces hidden behind masks. Min stood in the middle of it all. His face was hidden as well, but there was no mistaking his body or the way his gaze burrowed to her core.

He stretched a hand out to grasp her fingers, and pulled her to him. Some of the people watched. Others stripped bare aside from the masks. Hands roamed bodies, and talking blurred into moans and whimpers.

It all raced over her skin like a million simultaneous touches. Their desire and attention filled her and buoyed her. Min removed her clothing slowly. Sensually. Letting each piece fall aside, until she wore nothing.

People reached for her. For Min. But he held her away from them all. He roamed her body with his mouth and hands. Sucking on her nipples. Biting her shoulder. Dragging his nails up her back.

And then he held a flogger. Her anticipation spiked, and the need between her legs became impossible to ignore. As leather knots struck her behind, pleasure and pain spilled inside.

She lost count of how many lashes there were. All she knew was the euphoria.

Min returned to kissing along her skin. His touch was tender and soothing on the fresh marks. Envy and desire flowed over them from the crowd. They all wanted to be her or use her.

But she only belonged to Min.

He stroked between her legs, teasing her but never letting her come. He knelt at her feet, to kiss down her stomach. To part her folds with his tongue.

She lost track of where one orgasm ended and the next began, as she floated through countless nights of orgies.

And then it was Gwydion wrapping her in his embrace. Laughing with her. Falling into a pile of straw in a tangle of limbs. He knew where to kiss, to tickle, to stroke, to make her gasp. She returned the favor.

His open mouth was hot on hers. His touches the most delicious kind of fire.

And when he slid inside her, she felt like they were one.

The surreal wash of moments blended into an abstractly erotic burst, with her reliving each orgasm as if it were new. Her body sang from one climax after another, across centuries of attention.

Something lingered in the shadows, though. Growing stronger with each new scene.

Terror nudged her heart, carrying more pain than one person could be expected to endure.

She couldn't see a source, or give it a name beyond *really fucking bad*, but it came from knowing Gwydion and Min.

She forced herself awake. Her pulse screamed in her veins and her heart felt like it was going to burst.

She tore away from the bed, unable to shake the fear and lingering agony. What was going on?

CHAPTER EIGHT

Min saw the terror in Kirby's eyes as she stumbled from the bed.

"Kirby. Talk to me." Gwydion was by her side in an instant. He pressed a hand to her chest. "I need you to breathe for me, and tell me what's wrong."

She shook her head. "I don't know."

Min did. His heart shattered for her. She was remembering more than just the sex. It was all coming back to her, and she was unraveling in the process.

He didn't know how to lessen the pain. If she remembered more of the good, admitted it was real, before the intensity of the bad came back, it might help.

He rose from the bed, and approached Kirby and Gwydion. He held out his hand. "Come here."

Kirby rested her palm in his, and he wrapped her in his arms. Her bare skin against his was always tempting, but now it also amplified his desire to protect her. If he could hold her like this forever, maybe she wouldn't die again.

Gwydion stood close, hand on her back. The concern on his face matched Min's.

"Are you able to talk about it?" Min would let her do whatever she wanted, as long as it made her happy and kept her safe.

She shook her head. "I don't know what *it* was. But..." She shuddered. "I don't want to find out. And I definitely don't want to sleep again."

"I have a solution to help distract you." He wanted to help calm her. He crouched enough to sweep his arm under her legs, and lift her up.

Her chuckle was strained. She hugged his neck, and leaned into him. "Are you going to carry me away from reality?"

"Something very much like that." His desire was still there. A constant vibration that wanted more from her. To make up for all the nights they'd been apart. But his concern was stronger. Kirby needed to be looked after.

He carried her into the bathroom and set her on her feet by the shower. Gwydion joined them.

She hugged herself, and a tremor ran through her. Lingering traces of the dream, or an onset of modesty? The second one wasn't like Kirby.

Min turned on the water, and gave it enough of a magical nudge that it was the perfect temperature for Kirby—a hair below scalding.

He took her hand and they stepped over the lip of tile. When all three of them were in the shower, he slid the glass door shut.

She turned her gaze to her feet. "I'm not up for sex." Her voice was quiet.

"This is about comfort, not arousal," Min said. "But you don't have to stay. And if you don't like it, you can leave any time."

She looked up. Shadows of whatever haunted her marred her face. "You've told me that before." She was starting to remember.

"I always tell you that. And I always mean it. What do you need?"

"I need..." She let out a shaky sigh. "I need to not be alone with my thoughts."

"We'll help with that." Min grabbed the bar of soap from its dish, and a worked up a lather. He handed the bar to Gwydion, who stood behind Kirby, then glided his hands down her chest.

As he worked his fingers along her skin, he applied light pressure. Enough to gently massage. To keep her grounded. He washed her stomach and her legs. Caressed her arms and her shoulders. Gwydion performed a similar ritual.

Kirby's skin was soft under his touch. The flutter of her eyelids as she began to relax was a stunning tie to the past. He grew half-hard when he slipped a hand between her legs, to clean her.

But he didn't linger.

They stayed under the water until the knots faded from her muscles, and the fear vanished from her eyes.

When they stepped out, he and Gwydion gently patted her, and themselves, dry with towels, then wrapped up on white, fluffy hotel robes.

Min lifted her again, and carried her back to the bed. Feeling her cradled in his arms clenched like a vise around his heart. The familiarity of it all, and the lingering fear of what may come next, disquieted him.

But her calmness and soft body pushed that away.

Min sat with his back to the headboard, and Kirby lay with her head on his outstretched leg. He trailed his fingers through her hair. The blond strands were silken against his fingertips.

Gwydion sat next to Min, legs crossed. He stroked Kirby's hip with his thumb.

"The dream wasn't all bad." She spoke more calmly now. "Until the end it was... Wow."

Wow. Min appreciated the sound of that. "Would you like to offer more detail?"

She laughed, and sat up. "You were there." She pointed to Min. "And you were there." She looked at Gwydion. "Just call me Dorothy. Dreaming about guys in my life."

"Pretty sure the Scarecrow never seduced Dorothy," Gwydion said.

"I'd ask how you knew what I was dreaming about, but you lived it with me, didn't you?" She studied her hands. "It was so real. All of it. They're memories. Everything you said earlier was true. You're really a god?"

Min nodded. "I've been many things to you, as you have to me. However, I've never lied."

"Who are you?" she asked Gwydion.

"I'm a god of art."

"And a trickster god." Kirby furrowed her brow. "You... used to tell people you were King Arthur."

Gwydion nodded. "And no one believed that I wielded supreme power just because some watery tart threw a sword at me."

Kirby laughed. It was good to see her relaxing, despite what must be spilling through her mind. "It's all in there. Some of it's clear, and some of it's not there, but the more threads I tug, the more the knots unravel."

"Do you know who you are?" Min rested his palm on her cheek and pulled her gaze back to him.

She studied him, so many questions reflected in her blue eyes. "No. I remember you. Both of you. And someone else. I remember loving you all intensely. I feel that passion, bright and vibrant."

"You lived all of that," Gwydion said. "Several lives. Since meeting you, we've looked for you in each life. That love is real."

"What if I don't want to love you?" Her question cut Min to the core. But he heard it each time they found her. She wanted to choose and love for herself, not for some past life iteration.

Gwydion's expression remained neutral. "Then you don't have to. You're not a separate person. It's a new body, but every life is you. That doesn't mean you can't change your mind, or grow in a different direction."

She pulled from Min's touch, turning her gaze back to the blanket. "What if I don't want you to hurt me?"

"I would never..." Min stalled on her question. "Why do you believe that's a possibility?"

"There's something else in my past, the thing that scared me in my dream, it's tied to knowing the two of you. It always happens after I meet you." Her voice had gone quiet, and she clenched her hand in tight fists.

Kirby was conflicted. Her memories said both of these men were good and wonderful. She felt their love for her, and her adoration for them in return. It was so potent it threatened to stop her heart. Lifetimes of love and affection.

But there was also pain. Terror. A shape she couldn't define, but that cut through her soul like razors.

"Do you trust me? Us?" Gwydion asked. He didn't look upset by her revelations. Min tried to hide his reaction, but she saw his hurt. "Nothing we say will matter unless you do."

"Yes." Kirby didn't know why, but she did. Her mind insisted she was an idiot, and her heart sang a beautifully persuasive song that she was right to give them her faith.

"I can't say for certain what's there, but I can guess."

I was a starting point. "Tell me."

Min frowned and worked his jaw. "In order for you to have lived so many lives, you've had to die that many times. We always look for you. To help you remember. To save you."

"We always find you before you die, but we've never been able to save you," Gwydion said sadly.

"Oh." It made sense, but it was still difficult to process. Hearing that she'd died... How many times had it been?

"Twice now we've seen you remember everything." Min's voice was thick with regret. "It's never easy on you to go through that. Considering the past is coming back to you again, the death is probably what's threatening your dreams."

Kirby thought she understood, but didn't want to put it to words. Because it was one thing to accept she'd lived before and was remembering loving two gods, but it was a whole new universe to relive what killed her. "But you try? To save me?"

"Of course we do. Always." The way Gwydion watched her, concern in his eyes, reinforced the words.

And she saw the reality of what he said. The memories were there. Fifteen hundred years and they'd never given up on her.

"We fall in love with you again and again," Min said. "You're the same person, but each life teaches you more. Enhances how distinctly *you* you are."

Kirby focused on him. "But some things about me, and you, are always the same." She could almost grasp this sensation. It was that second fear that only came from knowing Min. It wasn't the same kind of suffocating terror. This was a gnawing sensation that made her question who she was.

"It's true." Min let out a long sigh. "The person you are at your core never changes. And that means each time we meet, some things keep us apart at first. What else did you dream?"

She wouldn't be distracted by his question, but she needed to better put her thoughts together. "Passion. Love. Desire. Decades of it. Over centuries."

"What else?" The way Min watched her, he was waiting for her to pick at and delve into whatever scared her when it came to him.

CHAPTER NINE

Min expected this, but that never made it easier for him to hear Kirby was scared of any part of him. "You fear me because I demand things of you that you're reluctant to give."

And as much as it was in her nature to hesitate, it was impossible for him to not require it.

She frowned. "*Demand*? Totally sounds like something I'd be opposed to. What are we talking about? That I walk ten paces behind you at all times? That I surrender my life to live the one you choose for me?"

"Something far simpler, and much more complex."

Her scowl deepened. She was getting impatient.

"Everything," Gwydion said. "He demands everything."

It was blunt. Not nearly as eloquent as Min would prefer. But it was honest.

Kirby scooted back on the bed and pulled her robe tighter around her. "What does *everything* mean? You're okay with me loving others. So you must define the word differently than I do."

Min ached to reach for her. To kiss the back of her knuckles. To brush her hair from her face and worship her—mind, body, and soul. He'd settle for explaining. "It's true; I don't have a problem with you loving Gwydion, or anyone else. But in the part of your heart that you set aside for me, I want it to be all for me. I don't want there to be a disclaimer or an exception on it. If you love me, I want you to completely love me. To completely give that part of yourself to me. And I offer you the same in return."

"That's a lot to ask."

"It is." Hence the term *everything*.

She flexed her fingers and worked her jaw. "I remember loving you. I feel those same emotions. And I know you say I'm still that person, but I still feel a divide between those lives and this one. Right now, I can't give you that." Her voice cracked. "Does that mean I lose you?"

"No, my huntress." He hated the ache in her voice, but he loved the strength that required her to choose her independence over all else. "I'm not demanding that you offer yourself up to me right this moment, or else. My requirement is that when we do reach that point, when you're able to say sincerely that you love me, that we both give it our all."

Some of the tension drained from her shoulders and she slumped. "Until then?"

"Until then, and after, and for as long as I have you, I show you what you mean to me."

"That's almost sweet and awe-inspiring." Teasing sarcasm lined Gwydion's voice.

Min shook his head. "I am always awe-inspiring, and have rarely been accused of being sweet." He moved to Kirby, and grasped her fingers. "Let me worship you, my huntress."

Kirby didn't expect Min's explanation to alleviate her fears, but his words rang true. They tied to the bits of her past she remembered. And the men were right. The images that danced in her mind, the vivid splashes of pleasure, didn't feel like separate lives. They were more like one long life, with several intermissions.

She didn't see anything of herself in the past that she disliked. And everything she saw of Min and Gwydion floated to her carried on love and devotion.

Min's touch was light but deliberate as he removed her robe. As in the shower, he grazed his fingers along every inch of her body. But with her fear addressed and placed aside, arousal could rush in at the contact.

He stroked along the inside of her elbow. Kissed the soft skin where her neck met her shoulder. Nibbled down the inside of her thigh, to lick behind her knee. Everywhere he explored summoned a new spark of want. He drew gasps from her by teasing body parts she never knew were erogenous.

His attention was different that Gwydion's. While they both focused on her pleasure, she felt more frantic with Gwydion. It was intense, but light-hearted. Playful. Uncontrollable.

Was it because she'd found Gwydion first in this life? No. It had always been this way between the two of them. Unhinged in the best way possible.

Min moved back up her body, drawing his lips along her chest and then her collarbone.

"You're not always this gentle," she said between gasps. She'd expected that to be what would scare her, but the knowledge unfurled in her belly and tugged a cord that ran through every nerve ending.

"No." He cupped her breasts and grazed his thumbs over her nipples. "I like to leave my mark. But I enjoy everything we do together, as do you. Pleasure and pain are so intricately intertwined..." He shook his head. "We'll get there. Today though, I want to taste you, as I would honey. Sweet and pure."

He dipped his fingers between her legs, and brushed his mouth over hers. He swallowed her groans, stroking her clit, coaxing her toward climax until her head swam and her heart wobbled.

He circled her core until she came. The orgasm clenched through every inch of her, tingling in each spot he'd touched, drawing her into a tight line, until he eased away.

Gwydion grasped Min's wrist and drew a finger into his mouth, sucking her juices from Min's skin. She watched, captivated and hungry for more.

"If the two of you are gods, do you need condoms?"

They shook their heads.

"We do it for your sense of security," Gwydion said. "But we don't get sick. We don't carry disease. Pregnancy doesn't happen unless we will. Which would be never, without your permission."

Kirby liked the sound of that. "Neat trick."

Min lowered her back to lie on the bed. He spread her legs apart with his knee, and knelt between her thighs. When he penetrated her, she gasped silently at the way he stretched her out.

The way he glided in and out of her was as gentle and methodical as everything else he'd done today. It was a new level of teasing. A promise of what happened when he stopped holding back. A slow burn of anticipation that made her pulse race.

Gwydion knelt next to her, and lowered his head to her breast. He scraped his teeth lightly along one nipple, before nibbling harder.

She needed to feel more. To touch more skin. She wrapped her hand around his shaft and stroked in time to Min's thrusts.

When Gwydion sought out her clit, the new touch jolted through her entire body. His touch wasn't calculated. He circled her swollen nub with abandon, and she gripped his cock in response.

She pumped him harder, setting the pace for how he pleasured her. Their frantic exchange clashed and blended with the slow glide of Min inside her.

Gwydion came, squirting on her stomach. Coating her skin and hand. He didn't ease up on the attention he paid to her clit. He pressed his body into hers, getting cum everywhere.

She swore everywhere the slick stickiness touched she felt more... everything.

He coaxed her to orgasm, and she clenched as climax gripped her. She wasn't used to having something inside her as thick as Min, and her body hovered on the edge of discomfort and pleasure.

Her peak seemed to tear away his restraint. The slow, smooth strokes were gone, as he pounded against her. His passion was raw and all-encompassing.

He spilled inside her, and she felt it. Like his energy mingled with hers, and spread through every inch of her. The intense fucking slowed to a stop. He slid out of her, leaving her feeling oddly empty.

Gwydion caressed her side with a lazy touch.

Min kissed her still sticky stomach. The lack of shame in the room was another kind of desire. He licked a path up her chest, to press his mouth to hers. Gwydion's taste lingered on his lips.

She devoured his kiss.

If this was every life, no wonder she was terrified of losing it.

CHAPTER TEN

Knives shredded Kirby's gut.

Flame licked at her skin.

Water filled her lungs.

And fear stole her reason.

A sword pierced her heart. An explosion tore her to shreds.

Odin's curse echoed in her skull.

She was dreaming again. She had to be. It was the only thought she could grasp outside of agony. Death devoured her again and again. A dozen times or more. All compressed into the same bubble of time.

She screamed and forced her eyes open. Her skin was still hot. She couldn't see past the agony.

Someone touched her arm, and she swung wildly. Needing an enemy to fight. A way to stop the torture.

"Kirby." Gwydion's voice drilled through the chaos in her thoughts. He grabbed her wrists, holding her tight, despite her thrashing. "It's us. You're all right." His tone was cool. A salve on a million wounds. "You're alive. You're here with us. Focus on my voice. On my touch."

She was trying, but it was so hard. Death threatened to consume her.

"You're all right. You're here with us." Gwydion repeated the words until her terror faded.

She sobbed and jerked away from him.

He cupped her face and forced her gaze to his. His attention, his icy blue eyes focused on her, helped drive away more of the memories.

Min wrapped his arms around her waist and pulled her into his lap. He held her close enough his heart beat against her back.

She wanted it to be soothing. She couldn't completely shake the dream.

"Breathe." Gwydion kissed her palm. "Talk it out. If you can force it to become words, you can shove them away."

"You remembered," Min said.

She nodded, and tried to do what Gwydion told her. It was a struggle to process more than *I'm fucking dying*. "I can't put it into words. There's so much..." Pain. Love. Hate. Anger. Despair. It all clogged her lungs.

She couldn't think about it, let alone speak the horrors of her past.

And she had no doubt now that it was all her past. The love. The death. Everything.

"I can't. I need air." She broke away from them. Somehow, with trembling hands, she managed to yank on her clothes.

She stumbled from the room, ignoring their pleas to come back. Gwydion caught her in the hallway, and grabbed her arm. The pain of his grip almost dragged her back to reality, but it wasn't enough.

Kirby shook him off. "Let me go. *Now.*

He held his hands up in surrender, and stepped back.

She rushed for the stairs, not having the mental capacity to wait for an elevator.

And then she was on the street. There was no one else out here. Darkness covered the ground, and stars winked at her from above.

She should go back to their room, but she couldn't puzzle past the pain. Every inch of her throbbed in agony. Why did this hurt so much? Why did she always di so early in life? Right after she found them. Before she became anything. Before she could be who she was meant to be.

What was the point of Odin's useless fucking curse if she never lived long enough to learn and grow?

The longer she walked, the more the memories sorted themselves. As love and death split, it was easier to focus on the good. Sometimes she had months with Gwydion and

Min... and Starkad. He'd been her first love. He was part of the reason Odin cursed her. Would she survive this life long enough to find him as well?

She wanted to. She had to.

This wouldn't be like the other times. She'd have more than days or half a year to love. To grow. To reemerge as the Valkyrie she should be. She was going to survive this time. She didn't care what it took. No one was stealing her life again.

She wandered aimlessly until the sun crested the horizon. Her feet were sore. She'd forgotten her shoes. She wasn't in the nice part of town anymore. The buildings here were crumbled and in disrepair.

She was numb but every inch of her ached. She was exhausted and high strung

Kirby screamed into the dawn, pouring everything into the sound. Letting it tear from her until her lungs burned and her throat was raw. When she stopped, the silence rang in her ears. It was both soothing and disconcerting.

A low-pitched whistle greeted her, and then her world exploded. Pain engulfed her again. But this came from outside, and engulfed her in a flash of light and flame. An explosion nearby.

And it reached others. Death. Destruction. Lives that weren't meant to be lost. It all screeched together in an ear shattering crescendo.

It all bled into her, and tears spilled down her face, evaporating in the fire. These people weren't warriors. They were civilians. Innocent. They didn't deserve death any more than she had in her past lives.

As the fire and grief and death consumed her, she fell to her knees, and sobbed.

CHAPTER ELEVEN

Shouting punched through Kirby's unconsciousness. So much worry. What was wrong? She tried to open her eyes, but it burned. She couldn't see.

A pair of arms wrapped under her knees and behind her shoulders. Lifted her. *Min.*

"We have you. You're safe." Did he sound worried?

Why? What happened? She couldn't make her mouth form the words. The comfort of being held stole her thoughts, and she let everything fall away.

When she woke up again, soft blankets cradled her. She was in bed. Pain lingered on her skin, but it wasn't the intense, all-consuming agony she'd felt before.

She forced her eyelids open to see Gwydion sitting in a chair next to the bed, watching her.

"Hey." He brushed his fingers across her face. "How do you feel?"

"Am I gonna live, doc?" What she meant as a joke came out as a dry croak.

He kissed her forehead and laughed. "Yes. Most definitely yes."

Min moved into view as well. He set a glass of orange juice on the table next to her, helped her sit, and held the glass for her.

She downed half the glass, marveling in how good it felt sliding over her parched throat. Best juice ever. "What happened?" She asked when she felt like she could speak.

"At the risk of triggering something, what do you remember?" Gwydion asked.

The images and sensations that rushed back hurt, but it was a phantom throb. Nothing more. "Pain. So much fear and despair. Mine. Everyone else's. Every life I've lived before. All of it."

Min furrowed his brow. "I believe you ascended. I don't know a better word for it. Hold out our hand."

She did as requested without hesitation.

A dagger appeared in his hand. Neat trick. The blade was polished to a high shine, and the handle looked like intricately carved ivory, with a Pegasus. He jabbed her palm.

"Ow." She pulled away instinctively, before realizing that hadn't hurt. She wiped her thumb across the well of blood. The wound underneath vanished as she watched.

"You can still be hurt," Min said. "But it takes a great deal to make the wound permanent. You're becoming immortal."

She liked the sound of that. It meant not dying again, didn't it? Something else was in her head now too. Not just her past lives, but a pull. A need to be back where the battle was. To watch over the fallen, and bless the worthy.

And save the innocent? That wasn't why she'd been created, but she needed... "What else happened?"

"A stray Scud missile landed near you." Gwydion let out a noisy breath. "It stuck a heavily populated building. It should have killed everyone, including you."

Her gut soured. She didn't deserve to live, while they died, because she'd been cursed. That wasn't fair.

"It didn't kill anyone." Min settled on the bed next to her. "You prevented it from causing death. The building was destroyed. The people inside all survived. Because of you."

Because she had the gift to decide who lived in battle, and none of those people deserved that dark fate. They didn't choose this. Relief and righteousness filled her.

She glanced at the windows. The gray light that had been there when she woke up was now almost black. "What time is it?"

"It's Sunday night. About nine." Gwydion nodded at the clock.

She was disappointed. But it didn't make much impact on her heart, with everything else going on there. "We have to get back to base soon." They should already be there. "How long until they declare us AWOL?"

"Your CO knows we were near the blast." Gwydion didn't look as worried as she felt. In fact, he had fewer lines of stress on his face than he had since she met him. He looked more like the carefree man she remembered from the past. "It bought us some time. But we don't have to go back. You can do whatever you want. We can walk away from all of this right now and never look back."

She wanted to give him that. He was tired of fighting. He'd been front and center for every war that drew her back. It had devoured his heart over the years.

Her memories told her all of this, but even if they hadn't, it was written on his face.

"I can't. I belong here. Serving those who do battle." She wanted to give him what he asked for, but she couldn't.

His sad smile said he'd expected her answer. "Your doctor can declare you incapable of returning to the front lines."

"My doctor will respect my wishes."

Gwydion nodded. "Always."

"So how does this work? What do we do next?" She had to return to duty, but she couldn't give them up. She wasn't. An interrupted weekend of catching up wouldn't sate her.

Min lifted her with no effort, to move her into his lap. "The two of you will be discreet, and I'll go find Starkad."

She leaned into his chest, and reached for Gwydion's hand. "You despise Starkad."

"I tolerate him for you. And next time you have leave, I'll consume all of you and your time."

She loved the sound of that. "It's a date." And because she refused to die again, this life they'd all spend enough time together to learn what she saw in each of them. To not only recognize that she loved them all, but to understand why.

Odin's curse wouldn't steal her life again.

EPILOGUE

6 Months Later

Kirby and Gwydion sat on the plane, parked at the gate, waiting for the other passengers to disembark. Min was waiting inside, and nervous flitters danced in Kirby's gut at the thought of seeing him again. But the other passengers were anxious to see loved ones too. She had eternity with her men. There was no reason to shove anyone aside in a rush to get off the plane.

Besides, Gwydion was the same amazing company he had been for the last six months. He sat next to her, the arm between their seats moved out of the way so she could lean into him.

"I miss limitless ice cream," he murmured against her fingertips.

She had a whole list, but now that they'd landed, the desperate need to do everything all right now had faded. "Real hamburgers. Sleeping past five am. Air conditioning."

"Privacy." He brushed her hair from her neck, and traced his lips along the bare skin, sending pleasant tremors through her.

"Gods, yes. Privacy." They'd had more privacy than most—she had as close to her own tent as anyone got—but canvas was worse than thin apartment walls when it came to what people could hear through it. She and Gwydion hadn't managed to be as discreet as they wanted. They were one of those couples on base everyone knew about but no one talked about.

But Desert Storm was over, and lifetimes of possibility stretched out in front of her.

Gwydion trailed his fingers along the edge of her thigh. She shouldn't feel much through the dense fabric of her BDU's, but every touch was more intense when it came to him. Power and strength flowed between them, subtle but alluring.

"Showers," he said. "Needlessly long. Indulgent. In the kind of place where I can pin you to the wall and fun you until neither one of us can stand."

The silly smile she'd worn for most of their flight grew with the images he evoked. Ghosts of sensation danced through her with the fantasy. "I do like the way you think."

"Of course you. Because I'm brilliant and fucking amazing."

"You are amazing at fucking."

"Which is why you love me," he said.

"No, I love you because..." She grasped for the right words. He was smart, funny, incredible in bed—it was true—sympathetic, caring... He'd been there for her in half a dozen lives—

"Don't fall over yourself to list every reason all at once," Gwydion teased.

She laughed. "That's exactly what I'm trying not to do. I love you because of everything."

"If I were a less secure man, I'd make you spell it out anyway. Then again, if I were a less secure man, I wouldn't read your sexy love letters from your other boyfriend aloud while you got off to his poetry."

Min definitely had a way with words. She'd kept all of his hand written notes. They were tucked safely in watertight pouch at the bottom of her duffel bag. "See?"

Gwydion nudged her forward. "I love you too. Always and forever. Let's go see what's changed in the world over the last year."

A spike of anticipation coiled in her stomach as she stood, at the idea that Min was so close. They grabbed their bags from the overhead bin. Gwydion reached for hers.

She shrugged the strap over her shoulder instead. "I can carry one little piece of luggage."

"Fine. Take away my shot at chivalry." His smile peeked through his grumble.

As they strolled onto the hallway that connected to the airport, the March chill bit into her skin, reminding her she was in a tank top, not a jacket. It was delicious. Late winter in Virginia, where it would be months before it got even close to as warm as the coolest days in Kuwait.

Min's primary home was in L.A., but he was here working with his latest investment. Something called America Online. His letters insisted he was going to connect the world via computer.

Kirby didn't understand the appeal in that, but Min didn't have gaps in his centuries of experience, and he did have an eye for innovation, so she was willing to wait and see.

They stepped into the airport, and there was Min, waiting a few feet back from the gate. He looked incredible, and his heated gaze melted her insides in the best way.

She dropped her bag and fell into his arms. Into his kiss. Each hungry clash of their mouths zinged through her with desire, and she gripped his arms tight, needing something to cling to. He nipped her lips enough to sting, danced his tongue with hers, and devoured her groans.

When they broke apart, she struggled to find her breath. He drew a finger along her bottom lip. "I need to stop now, or I'll undress you and take you right here." His voice was a baritone rumble sliding down her spine.

"Wouldn't be the first time." She pressed her body into his, reacquainting herself with every hard line.

"True. But I don't make the laws in this place, and being arrested for public indecency is one more obstacle to keep me from you." He bent to grab her bag.

"Oh sure, let him be the gentleman." Gwydion's protest was playful.

She turned back to him, and brushed her still-tingling lips over his. "He's not already carrying one of his own."

Gwydion rolled his eyes, but his smirk disrupted the look. "I'm kind of surprised he didn't pick you up too."

"I considered it." Min rested a hand at the small of her back and pointed her toward the exit.

Their chatter was superficial as they located the luggage carousel and grabbed the rest of their things. Kirby had so much to say to both of them, but Gwydion was right about missing privacy. She wanted just them for the next several days, and anything important she had to say would wait until they weren't surrounded by crowds.

When they stepped outside, she shivered at the icy blast that washed over her. She loved it.

"We need to get you a real coat," Min said.

"Or, we could spend most of our time indoors between now and L.A. and not worry about." Kirby was only half-kidding. "More realistically, not yet. I need the novelty of frigid temps to wear off first."

It was a short stroll to a limo that waited at the curb. Min and Gwydion had never hidden their wealth, but this was a new level of ostentatious. "Do you live like this every day?" Kirby couldn't imagine someone else driving her around all the time.

"No. However, I needed someone else driving today." Min nodded at said driver as the man opened held the back door open for them. "I'm not waiting any longer to have you."

Heat spilled through her, making her forget her inappropriate clothing for the weather. She slid onto a leather seat, and Min joined her. The world vanished on the other side of privacy glass when Gwydion shut the door behind him. He took the seat across from them.

The car bounced faintly a few times, she assumed as their luggage was loaded up and the driver took his seat, and then they were pulling into traffic. A barrier separated them from the front of the car. It really was like being in their own world.

"Now I don't have to behave." Min grabbed her hips and lifted her.

She straddled his legs, letting warmth and desire overtake longing. When he kissed her, she knew there wouldn't be any interruptions this time. His mouth was firm and demanding as he devoured her moans.

Kirby had enjoyed every minute with Gwydion, but Min was a different flavor. Fortunately, Kirby sandwich with extra meat was on her list of things to do over and over.

"Knowing you were out there, so close but just out of reach, nearly drove me mad." Min growled against her lips, before biting the fleshy swell.

She couldn't grasp any response beyond a moan as he glided his hands under her top and slid his palms up her stomach. Sparks flowed between them. She'd loved the letters, but this was a billion times better.

A third hand snaked up her spine, Gwydion, and unsnapped her bra. The tension binding her breasts fell away, but it didn't relieve the tightness in her nipples.

Min broke the kiss to pull her tank top and bra over her head, and lowered his mouth to her chest. He lay wet, open kisses along her skin, down to her breasts, before wrapping a tongue around one pink nub and drawing it into his mouth.

She gasped and arched into his attention when he nibbled her nipple.

Gwydion sat next to Min, gripped Kirby's hair, and kissed her hard. She lost track of whose hands roamed where as teasing touches covered her bare skin. Desire thrummed between her thighs. It was easier to sink into the overwhelming attention than to focus on an individual act.

Kirby alternated between their demanding kisses, their mouths falling to other parts of her body in the empty space. Her hips gyrated, grinding her against Min's legs and looking for relief for the pulse in her core.

The car slowed as they merged with the other traffic leaving the airport, and Kirby glanced at the dark glass. "Can anyone see us in here?"

Min kissed the hollow behind her ear, and nipped her earlobe. "No. But if you'd prefer otherwise, I know places where I can take you in front of an entire room."

"I didn't say that." Fresh images flashed in her mind, of Min making her beg, making her come, while a crowd of hungry people looked on and got each other off.

"Is that a no?"

Her panties were going to be soaked by the time she got the rest of her clothes off. "I didn't say that either."

"Good. Because we have a lot of missed time to make up for, and I hear you have a list of desires." Min undid the button and zipper on her pants.

She half-stood, half-crouched to shove the rest of her clothing off, stumbling back with a giggle when everything got tangled in her boots. Her bare ass landed on the opposite seat.

"Let me help." Min lifted one foot into his lap, and loosened the laces.

"Me too." Gwydion knelt next to her, and glided his fingers between her legs.

She groaned and bucked against his light touch. He ghosted along her skin, never parting the folds. "How is that helping?" she managed between gasps.

"It's doing wonders for me."

She could play that game, too. She slid down his zipper, and grasped his cock. His skin was hot against her cool palm, and his low sigh was intoxicating. She stroked in time with his light touch, sliding closer to climax.

And then she was free of her boots and her clothing. Min grasped her wrist and tugged her back to him. "The two of you had months to play. It's my turn."

While she'd been distracted, he'd pushed his own trousers off. He sat sideways on the bench, leg stretched out and dick standing at attention. Her memories hadn't exaggerated how big he was.

She straddled his legs again, intending to tease and draw things out a little longer. He gripped her hips and slid inside her with a single thrust. She was slick from the playful anticipation, but he still stretched her out and sent delicious friction spilling through her. The penetration was almost enough to make her come.

Min didn't move in her once he was buried to the hilt. He glided his hands along her thighs, over her ass, and her back, to pull her into him, and kissed her again.

Two fingers slipped along her exposed slit, drawing her juices back to her rear entrance. She and Gwydion had managed a lot for two people with limited privacy, including easing her into anal sex. She thought she was ready when he nudged her second opening with his cock.

He slid inside slowly, giving her time to relax and adjust between each inch forward. Being penetrated this way was an experience all its own. Twin spots of friction rested in her, and just a hint of sting hummed over her skin.

When they both moved in time with each other, a cry of pleasure tore from her throat. Min raised his mouth to suck on her nipples again, lavishing one with intensity before moving to the other.

Gwydion slipped his fingers between her legs to stroke her clit.

The orgasm that had hovered just out of reach crashed over her, and she swore a light show exploded behind her eyelids. Her head was lighter than air, and every incredible touch flowed into the next.

She recognized the familiar grunts of Gwydion reaching climax. Sounds that had permanent residence in her fantasies and dreams. A wave of oneness spilled inside her. She felt him, everything about him, more intensely than ever, when they were like this.

Min's groans called to her memories, and she knew he was close as well. Another wave filled her, stealing her thoughts and sending her floating.

The world slowed, and she languished in the synchronicity of three heart beats. Right now, they were the only people in the world.

Kirby wasn't sure how long she lay there, but the reality of a leg cramp crept in. She reluctantly extracted herself from the pile. "I don't want to get dress," she said with an exaggerated pout.

"I don't want that either. But it won't be for long." Min brushed his thumb over her bottom lip. "I'm so glad I found you, Huntress. I love you dearly and completely, and my heart belongs to you for as long as you'll have it."

She opened her mouth to return the sentiment. She'd said it to Gwydion so many times, the words felt natural.

Min covered her lips with his finger, stopping her. "Don't." His voice was kind. "You know my condition. Not until you mean it completely. Until you don't feel you'll ever want to take it back. Until you're willing to give me all of that part of your heart."

Kirby smiled into his touch, and nodded. That day wasn't far off, but she was grateful he was flexible in his rigidity.

She grabbed her clothes as Min and Gwydion dressed themselves. Safety and security wrapped around her, despite the cold world outside. Life was about to become indescribably incredible, and she was looking forward to every single minute of it.

~*~

SEDUCTIVE SOUL

A UBIQUITY PREQUEL

CHAPTER ONE

Ronnie had been told life on earth, in a physical body, would be the height of sensory overload. In the best way possible.

Hearing it and experiencing it were two entirely different things.

She sat at a table against the bar wall, watching St. Patrick's Day festivities roaring around her.

The bright colors, the laughing and shouting people, the scents of hot wings and alcohol...

And the taste... *God*, the taste... She was as close to Heaven as most demons ever got.

To think she'd argued about having her Earth orientation today. Upper Hell management knew how demons reacted to having a physical form for the first time, so part of *orientation* was to live through a holiday. To go out and experience as much as a demon could.

Ronnie's book-knowledge of holidays told her this wasn't a big one. She'd been hoping for a celebration like Thanksgiving—eating everything in sight. Or Halloween—an excuse to wear her wings and party with humanity while their inhibitions were down.

The lessons implanted in demons' heads needed to be updated to say this holiday had it all. Okay, technically, no one else was wearing wings, but they did have funny hats on, and not a single person gave her a second glance for the feathery black extensions attached to her shoulder blades.

"Another drink, miss?" The bartender set a large glass mug with something green in it in front of her. He was nice. He'd been bringing her a variety of flavors all night.

She had an unlimited budget for the week, but free drinks were more fun. "What's this one?"

He laughed and shook his head. "Can't figure out if you're for real or yanking my chain. It's green beer." He was as attractive as he was generous—blond hair, bright-blue eyes, and an aura that crackled and sparkled like a kaleidoscope through a prism.

Which also meant he was walking chaos laced with deception, but Ronnie didn't have a problem with that. Every time he brought her something new, he brushed against her. Physical contact was at least as good as food. Even the light touches sent tingles racing along her skin.

She took a sip and cringed at the horrible taste. "It's vile." And she loved it. Every new sensation, good or bad, was something she could add to her list of things she'd experienced.

He chuckled again. "It's an acquired taste."

"So are demons." A voice came from the chair on the other side of Ronnie's table, and another person appeared in the previously-empty seat.

Unlike the mortal serving Ronnie one drink after another, the new arrival was definitely a demon. His aura lit up the room and sucked the light from it at the same time. And if bartender-guy was cute, this guy was drop-dead *Hubba Hubba*.

The thing was, when she tried to focus to see his features, she couldn't name what they were. She couldn't tell what about him made him sexy.

"Where did you come from?" Bartender-Guy stared at the new arrival with wide eyes.

"I was already here," Demon-Guy said.

He hadn't been, but a demon could appear in the middle of a room instantly, and convince most people they'd been there all along.

The bartender shook his head and wandered off.

The demon turned to Ronnie. "Don't focus too hard. You won't see what you're looking for."

"What?" She couldn't pull her gaze away. Watching him sent a whole new level of sparks, racing through her veins. It heated her skin and tingled on every sensitive part of her body and throbbed between her legs.

He shook his head, and the fuzzy edges of his look faded, then vanished. "If you don't have a perfect type, I'm harder to see."

His aura swam into focus—emerald on molten gold. Not as heart stopping as the influence he radiated to convince people of his beauty, but definitely gorgeous. Especially combined with the Kool-Aid-red hair, the barely-there scruff of beard on a square jaw, and amber eyes that seemed to peer into her soul. Demons and angels took on forms that resembled the way they saw themselves, so most were attractive. But this guy... *Hello, hottie.*

"You're an incubus," Ronnie said. Which explained why his voice pulsed through her core to the point where she wanted to throw caution to the wind and finger herself right here in the middle of the bar.

Yeah... masturbation was the first thing she'd discovered and fallen in love on Earth.

"Why do you say that? I might be a leprechaun." He winked.

She laughed, not caring that the lust spilling through her was at least a little magically induced. "Leprechauns aren't real."

"Says the newbie demon who's going to work next week for a company that not only monitors the world's web browsing, but is also run by Heaven and Hell."

"I'm not new." She wouldn't argue the rest. Most of them—agents of Heaven and Hell—didn't get bodies these days unless they worked for Ubiquity.

"You're so new, you don't realize Mr. Friendly buying you the drinks can't figure out why the fuck he hasn't gotten you drunk yet."

"Wait. People really do that?" Before arriving here, all of her knowledge had been crammed into her head via magical demon learning. And there was a lot. But everything she knew about meeting other people and plying them with booze seemed implausible to her. "Why doesn't he just ask me if I'm interested?"

The Incubus frowned. "Lucifer never taught you that? Hmm... Some people use deception to get what they want because they're terrified of rejection. I, on the other hand, prefer the more direct route."

"Which is...?"

He was seated next to her in a blink. He leaned in, mouth close enough to her ear that his hot breath caressed her cheek. "I'd love to help you find all the buttons on that physical form of yours."

Objectively, he was good. Her body didn't care about *objective*—it was pleading for another taste. Or more. "Does that usually work for you?" she asked.

"Only with the younger demons. Everyone else slaps me for it." He pinned her wrist to her leg.

With his tight grip, fingers pressed into her skin enough to leave a light ache, and an intense gaze that bored into her soul, she liked his nearness too much to consider slapping him. How was she supposed to respond?

Climbing into his lap, grinding against him, and seeing what kind of things an incubus could teach her seemed like a good idea.

"You two have already met, then," a new voice interrupted.

CHAPTER TWO

Ronnie suppressed a sigh. Lucifer had introduced her to Izzy when she arrived on earth a few days ago. She didn't mind the scenery—with Izzy's slight build, dark-blond hair, and pale blue eyes—but she also enjoyed his company. Tonight though, the fallen angel had the worst timing ever.

Despite the interruption, she was happy to give him a warm hug. Especially since she was supposed to be meeting him here.

His words sank in, and she broke away to look him in the eye. "Wait. You know each other?" she asked.

Izzy grasped her fingers and tugged until she was seated again, then gestured. "That's one way to put it. And in case Irdu hasn't warned you yet, you *really* want to steer clear of him. Unless you're looking for a serious night of no-strings sex." His smirk implied the warning was tongue-in-cheek.

"I'd say, *Guilty as charged*, but there's no guilt for what I do." Irdu smirked. "Also, I rarely do *serious*."

Pieces clicked in Ronnie's head. She had to make a few assumptions, to reach her conclusion, but it felt like a solid one. "You told him I would be here," she said to Izzy.

He shrugged. "I didn't. I recognized your name when he mentioned he was helping with your orientation, and Irdu invited me to join you."

"But"—Irdu rested a hand on Ronnie's thigh—"he didn't tell me you'd be so stunning."

She liked the warm weight of his palm pressing through her jeans. "Have you met a lot of demons who aren't?"

"Touché. But I've also met a lot who aren't nearly as fun." Irdu stroked his thumb in lazy circles along the inside of her leg.

The barely-there touch sent a new flavor of anticipation dancing along her tongue. It was like a hint of cinnamon in coffee—enough to tease the spice without being obvious. "Maybe I won't be fun for long. I'm just not jaded by life yet." She was enjoying this banter.

"Some demons are created uptight. But you..." Irdu danced his fingers up her arm, to trail along her bottom lip. "You look like a demon who knows how to appreciate the world. *Fun* screams from you. And when it comes to screams of fun, I'm an expert."

"Your lines are really bad." Ronnie flicked her tongue out, to lick his fingertip.

He pulled away with a wicked grin. "But they're working."

They really were.

Izzy watched them, amusement dancing in his eyes. "Fair warning—this is Irdu's job. Finding the new demons. Introducing them to the world."

"And you came along to enjoy the show?" Ronnie didn't have a problem with that.

Irdu scooted his chair closer, pressing his leg into hers. Nothing about this was subtle, and no bit of her minded. "It wasn't selfless on his part," he said. Even when he wasn't projecting, his voice was liquid seduction, drawing up her spine. "Izzy likes to help."

"Help you seduce fledging demons?" Ronnie leaned into him.

Izzy chuckled. "I was being more generic when I said *introduction to the world*. There's no way to replicate that high we get the very first time we step foot on Earth, but seeing it through someone else's eyes comes close."

Irdu leaned in, his mouth near her ear again. "Everyone experiences this world differently. Some of them want to hear it all— loud music. Beautiful sounds of nature. Others want to see stunning art or sunrises in Tibet. Or they're looking for incredible scents—cherry blossoms and roses and bakeries.

"Most want to taste or feel. Sweets. Spices. And yes, that frequently means seduction. And sex." He drew his nose up the side of her neck.

"I'm fond of all of the above." Her reply came out in a breathy whimper. If this was the introduction, she might not survive the foreplay.

Irdu nipped her earlobe. "Me too. And as much as I'd love to explore that here, I guarantee several of the things I'd like to show you would be frowned upon."

People tended to overlook what they didn't want to see. It was one thing that made it easy for demons to blink in and out of rooms. But Ronnie suspected her being naked in the middle of a bar might draw attention. "What do you propose?"

"That we all go back to my place and find out what you like most." He took her hand, then reached for Izzy's.

The bar vanished, and they were in a new room.

Ronnie was impressed. Again. It took a powerful demon, to phase from one place to another in the blink of an eye. A flawless blink was even more difficult when someone had passengers.

Irdu's place was so much grander than the shoebox she lived in. Plush, violet carpet that ended at polished hardwood. Furniture with no rips or stains. Bright artwork. And the faintest hint of cherry in the air.

He kept hold of her hand and led her toward the dining area and an oval table. There was a counter nearby, with several bowls sitting on it.

"I was thinking we'd start with my favorites." Irdu leaned close, mouth near her ear. His voice was smooth and low, rolling over like a feather-light caress. "Touch and taste." He dipped his finger in one of the bowls, then placed it in her mouth.

She licked the dark-chocolate syrup, tentatively at first, but then with more hunger when the shock of bitter and sweet hit her tongue. She sucked his finger clean, relishing his throaty groan. That was going on the *favorite sounds* list.

He pulled away with a *tsk*. "Do you want more?"

"That's the point, isn't it?"

Izzy's smile and Irdu's smirk said it most certainly was.

Irdu waved his fingers. "Take off your clothes."

CHAPTER THREE

Ronnie raised her brows. "Excuse me? No seduction? No finesse? Just *get naked?*"

Izzy was quiet, but she didn't miss the way he watched her with open lust and desire. It was different. And yummy.

"I don't really do drawn-out foreplay during orientation," Irdu said. "This is fun and games, sure, but not romance."

Did she have a problem with that? Desire flitted through her, lingering from the teasing in the bar and the hint of sweet on her tongue. "Do you do this with everyone?"

"If they're up for exploring *touch*, I do. You can tell me *no*, and we'll do something else."

"What if I tell you *yes*, and then change my mind once we get further into... whatever this is?" She didn't think a change of heart was likely, but she had to know.

"You can stop me whenever you want. But if you let me keep going, you have to trust me."

She was considering taking her clothes of for him. Damn straight, there needed to be trust.

Demons had a different perspective on *good* versus *bad*, but they were honest about it.

"All right," Ronnie said. She grabbed the bottom of her shirt and tugged it over her head. The way Irdu and Izzy watched her every move sent heat spilling through her. They didn't even need to touch her to turn her on. That was a neat trick.

"And the rest of it," Irdu prompted.

With each piece of clothing she shed, the air kissed another spot on her body. The cool, combined with the guys' heated gazes, made her pulse hammer in her ears.

And then she was standing naked in front of the men. She didn't have hang-ups about nudity—hers or anyone else's—but the appreciation with which they studied her filled her head with whispers of wicked impulses.

"Now lie down." Irdu gestured to the kitchen table.

She raised her brows. "There?"

"Was I unclear?" Challenge and command filled his question. He offered a hand, while she sat on the edge. The furniture didn't wobble under her weight. His table probably didn't come from a second hand shop, though.

She lay back on the polished wood. It was cold and hard against her back. Definitely the least comfortable thing she'd ever reclined on. So delicious. A thrill rushed through her at how vulnerable she was. Not really, since she could blink out of here at any time, but she preferred to sink into the surface appearance of the situation.

He slipped a blindfold over her eyes, and her heart jammed in her throat.

"This is supposed to be about exploring my senses." Her words came out with a squeak.

A barely-there caress brushed her collarbone and traveled down, stopping before he reached her breast. "And you'll appreciate the others more if you temporarily lose access to one."

Silence settled in, and her anticipation spiked. She squeezed her thighs together, to suppress the pulse between them.

Hands pulled her legs apart again. Something wrapped around each ankle. The texture was smooth, but the tension was tight. She could wiggle her feet an inch or so in any direction, and that was it.

She swallowed hard. A whimper slipped out when he secured her arms above her head, the same way he had restricted her legs.

Ronnie could leave. Vanish and reappear in her apartment or anywhere else. She could tell him to stop.

Those sounded like the worst possible options. He hadn't even touched anything intimate, and she was wet and eager for what came next. Something mingled with her anticipation. Fear? Whatever it was, she enjoyed it.

"You said you like taste." Irdu's voice was warm and low, rumbling through her. "You're obviously fond of chocolate."

A light weight pressed at her lips, and she parted to let it in.

He dipped a chocolate-covered finger into her mouth again.

She licked the digit clean, loving his groan as much as the flavor.

And then something drizzled onto her nipple, heavier than water and thick enough for her to feel it dribble down her breast. A new sensation followed. A mouth, hot and wet. A rough tongue, circling her nipple. Lips, sucking away the mess. She arched into the touch.

"You like that," Irdu said. But the sucking never stopped. Either he could throw his voice, or Izzy was lavishing her chest with attention.

Apparently this setup could get more intense.

"I like whipped cream better." Irdu fed her something sweet and cool this time.

She felt the cooler temperature on her other nipple, followed by more intense sucking. And then there were two mouths on her. The sensations alternated between chocolate and whipped cream being layered on her skin, and hungry tongues lapping it up. She writhed in pleasure, wanting to sate a need, but unable to reach.

"And then there's my favorite. Honey." Irdu dribbled the sticky sweetness along her lips, then crushed his mouth to hers, to devour her kiss and the honey.

Her hips thrust without her permission, trying to experience what the rest of her body was being lavished in.

All contact stopped, and for a moment, she swore her heart did as well. Then a warm, heavy drizzle hit her stomach and traveled lower. It pooled along her thighs and ran between her legs, mingling with her own juices.

A tongue licked along the inside of her leg, and she gasped. Was that Izzy or Irdu? She didn't care, as long as he didn't stop.

He licked higher. When he drew a path up her slit, she cried out. A pleasure she'd never felt when she masturbated filled her head and body.

Lips circled her clit, and a tongue flicked fast and hard. Climax sped through her, and she lost herself in the sensations when she came. She bucked and thrashed against whoever was sucking on her.

And he didn't stop. Fingers slid inside her, and another mouth was back on her nipples.

Her head threatened to float away.

The two men devoured her until she was spent and breathless, and her throat was sore.

The contact with her body stopped again, and she forced her heart to slow. Focused on taking deep breaths.

A new touch, softer and gentler, undid the bindings on her arms and legs, and then helped her sit.

When the blindfold fell away, she had to blink several times, to let her eyes adjust to the light.

Izzy watched her, a smirk on his face. He twisted to scoop her into his arms, and she didn't resist. She doubted her legs worked, anyway.

She leaned her head against his chest, as he carried her into the bedroom and laid her on the bed.

"Do you want to keep going?" Irdu asked.

"Yes." Ronnie's answer came without hesitation. Desire hummed over her, and every inch of her felt alive. Her body begged for more.

CHAPTER FOUR

Ronnie didn't have hang-ups or reservations about the naked human body. She understood most people preferred some level of modesty, and she could comply. But for her, the body was no different from any other container.

Or it never had been, before. With the anticipation of what came next, seeing Irdu and Izzy naked was extra-cherry-on-top yummy.

Irdu gripped the short strands of Izzy's light hair and crushed their mouths together. Twin groans danced along Ronnie's skin. Watching the passion was almost as tasty watching the passion as it was being in the middle of it.

Not every sensation racing over Ronnie's skin was natural. Since Izzy was mostly mortal, hints of his desire tickled her senses. Irdu was projecting something too. It was like an amplifier on the need that already filled the room.

They broke apart, and Izzy gave his attention to her. He crawled toward her on the bed and laid a series of soft pecks along her lips.

When she parted her mouth with a sigh, he deepened the kiss.

He tasted faintly of honey and sex. *God*, that was delicious. She pressed into him, wanting to devour every bit of what he offered.

"How is this supposed to help me avoid sensory addiction?" she asked breathlessly. "Because I can tell you right now, I'm not going to be satisfied with less in the future. You're setting a high bar."

Irdu knelt next to her, brushed her hair from her neck, and trailed his lips along the sensitive skin. "It's not a matter of avoiding anything. It's all about when and how you indulge. Right time. Right place. Right person... or people."

"I like the idea of *indulging properly*." Ronnie leaned into his touch. She gasped when he bit her shoulder. Traces of his magic wove through the playful mark, keeping the sting from evaporating right away. *Nice touch.*

"I don't care much for *proper*," he said, dragging a path with from her jaw to her mouth, "but I'm going to agree just this once." He captured her face between his palms and kissed her hard.

Each press of his lips was a new flavor of desire, racing through her veins. Spice and heat and tangy-sweet.

Izzy kissed down her arm, lingering when he reached the inside of her wrist. The light scuff of stubble was another texture for her to appreciate.

"You're uncharacteristically quiet," she said when she met his gaze.

Izzy gave her a playful grin. "I'm wrapped up in the hot demon sex. Not much to add beyond, *so glad I'm here.*"

A flush of heat spread through her, growing to white-hot when he wrapped his lips around her nipple. He flicked his tongue back and forth across the nub, making her groan into Irdu's kiss.

Irdu placed his palm against her windpipe with just enough pressure to shorten her breath. He used his weight to nudge her onto her back, and pinned her to the mattress. The follow-up kiss was intense and hungry, with him biting her lip and scraping his teeth along her chin.

He used his knee to wedge her legs apart and knelt between them. Her anticipation soared when he glided the head of his cock along her slit. Physically, she wasn't a virgin, but this was so different from pleasing herself.

Irdu thrust inside her, stretching her out and filling her up. *Way* better than fingers or a vibrator.

Izzy moved his mouth back to hers, while he kneaded her breasts and rolled her nipples between his fingers.

Irdu slid out of her almost completely, before gliding back in, letting her feel that first penetration again. He rolled onto his back, bringing her with him, so she was straddling him.

Ronnie was pretty sure a move like that didn't work when magic wasn't involved. Not that she was complaining.

He dragged his fingers up her back. Everywhere he touched left whispers of need to hum under her skin. He pulled her to him and drew one nipple into his mouth. He wasn't moving inside her, but feeling his cock resting inside her was tantalizing.

He glided his hands down her sides and over her ass, to spread her cheeks open.

She squealed in surprised delight when something cold touched her. The lube warmed quickly, as Izzy spread it over her skin. He nudged her asshole, then inched in slowly.

She hadn't considered that her first encounter would involve so much, like double penetration, but if she was going big... Irdu and Izzy were the way to do it.

When they were both buried inside her, Irdu started a slow rocking. There was a toe-curling friction, from being captured between them. Irdu raised his head again, to suck on her nipple, and she leaned into his mouth.

There were so many touches, she didn't know where to focus. The surge of desire filled her head until her brain felt like cotton candy.

Izzy slipped a hand into the mix and stroked her clit. The contact added another layer to the looming overload. Pleasure danced over her body even where they weren't making contact.

The non-stop attention drew her toward the edge of another orgasm. Izzy increased the pressure on her clit at the same time as the pace sped up.

Her world blurred and mingled into the desire that pulsed everywhere. She wasn't sure where one feeling stopped and the next started. She heard both men groaning, the spine-tingling sound mixing with her own shouts.

Ronnie lost track of time and her surroundings. Another new feeling overlapped the rest—multiple auras mingling and dancing and intertwining when the men came.

As the edge of her peak faded away, the world swam back into focus. The grinding and stroking had stopped, but the skin-on-skin contact was still there.

Izzy slipped out of Ronnie. The release of pressure drew a soft sigh from her. She rolled to the side, to lie next to Irdu, and Izzy collapsed on the bed with them. For a short while, the only sound in the room was their heavy breathing.

When Izzy extracted himself from the pile, Ronnie frowned.

He leaned in and kissed her lightly. "I have to go." His voice was soft. Soothing. Tempting. "Thank you for letting me join in."

A new thought occurred to her—one she should have had sooner. Demons and angels didn't place an emotional weight on sex, but he'd been mostly mortal for almost a century. Had he picked up that human habit?

"Will this make things awkward?" Ronnie hated to ask, but she needed to know.

He smiled and shook his head. "I wouldn't have done it if that were the case. Give me a call next time you want to hang out. I'm usually around."

She liked that. Then again, she was pretty fond of everything about this encounter.

Ronnie liked waking up here—the smooth, high-thread-count cotton on her skin, Irdu's warm body next to hers...

It was a shame this was only a one-time thing. And that Izzy had to leave last night. A demon could get used to a life like this.

"You want breakfast?" Irdu sat up and raked his fingers through his hair.

Ronnie trailed her gaze over him. Yup, still sexy this morning. "You're not going to kick me out and wish me the best of luck with life?"

"Tomorrow night. But this isn't much of an orientation if you only get a few hours of how incredible I am."

She laughed. "I thought the point was for me to figure out what I liked and learn how to control the impulse to indulge in everything. When did this become about you?"

"What? Oh yeah. It's totally about your self-discovery and that thing you said. Don't listen to me." His tone was playful.

She was torn between amusement and watching him walk across the bedroom. *Damn*, he had a nice ass. "Given all of that, I assume breakfast will be the ultimate in decadence," she said.

"It absolutely will be. You get to watch me cook." He yanked on a pair of sweat shorts and tossed her a T-shirt. "Put that on and follow me. And before you ask, too many clothes now means more to take off later."

She hadn't considered asking, but she liked his logic. The black cotton was worn and soft against her skin, and the print on the front looked like it read *Hendrix* at one time, but now it was more of a *niioi*. It hung a third of the way down her thighs, and smelled like fabric softener and the green of his aura.

She phased to semi-corporeal, long enough to reset her hair and solidify as clean. She padded into the other room and took a stool at the breakfast bar, while he moved around the kitchen.

He was a gorgeous sight to behold, as he pulled out mixing bowls, ingredients, and a skillet.

Ronnie knew how to cook. As in, the knowledge had been shoved in her head about how to follow recipes and what all the terminology meant. She'd discovered that, as with anything artistic, knowing and doing were two separate things. Most of her diet so far consisted of cold cereal, ice cream, and things other people prepared.

Irdu had the art down, though. There was no hesitation in his fluid movements, as he dumped dry ingredients into a bowl without measuring and cracked eggs with one hand. He pulled a white squeeze-bottle, like the ones some diners kept ketchup and mustard in, from the cupboard and slid it across the counter. "Heat that up, will you?"

That was something she could do. She held the plastic between her palms and pictured a flicker of heat passing through her hands. Enough to make the contents warm, without melting the container. The faint scent of chocolate greeted her.

When she set the bottle aside again, Irdu was watching her with an eyebrow raised.

"Did I do something wrong?" Ronnie asked.

"I meant in the microwave, but that works too. So you prefer fire?"

Ah. Lucifer had warned her about this. It took a lot of power to master manipulating one element, and most demons couldn't manage more than that, if they even got the one.

Ronnie dabbled in all of them. She didn't know how, but it came naturally. She wasn't supposed to make a big deal out of it. She also didn't want to lie about it. "I don't know that I prefer it. Fire heats things better than water does."

"Right." He grabbed another stack from the fridge, including a pint of strawberries. He handed her the fruit, a plastic cutting board, and a knife. "Unless you can summon blades, too."

"I'm not that good." Wielding magical weapons was strictly the realm of the three originals—Lucifer, Michael, and Gabriel. No one else had that kind of power.

She diced strawberries, while he worked whatever non-magical magic he was doing with food. Even if he didn't radiate sex appeal, she'd be drooling over the guy who could whip up crepes and filling with less effort than it took her to make canned soup.

He arranged the crepes on plates, including generous portions of the strawberries, and chocolate hazelnut spread from the bottle she'd warmed, then put a small scoop of fresh cream on top, before handing her a dish.

"I think I love you," she teased.

He took the stool next to hers, his own food in front of him. "I get that a lot."

She tried to get a little of everything on the fork—which was way too much—and crammed the first bite into her mouth. A rainbow of flavor flowed over her tongue. She groaned at the beauty of it and sank into each taste, on its own, and mixed together.

"Well?" he asked.

She paused, second forkful of food halfway to her mouth. "Whatever you do at Ubiquity, your talent is wasted." Oh right. He did this— showed new demons the time of their life before work started.

Why did that taste more sour than it had last night?

CHAPTER FIVE

Ronnie was being weird. She swallowed the strange feeling, to make room for more yummy food.

"Thanks." Irdu chuckled, and dug into his own meal.

They ate in silence for a few minutes.

"Besides eating and fucking, what are some of your favorite things about earth so far?" Irdu looked and sounded genuinely interested.

That was pretty attractive too. "Dancing. Music."

He wrinkled his nose and took a swig of coffee.

"What's the look for?" Ronnie asked, amused. She gestured to the shirt. "You obviously don't have too much of a problem with music."

"Hendrix. Zeppelin. Bowie. *Real* music. You say *dance*, and I think loud, obnoxious beat with more pounding than tune."

"I think you're overlooking the nuances of a hardcore dance remix."

He shook his head, but he was smiling. "To each their own, but you're totally wrong. It's too bad a weekend isn't enough time to correct that flaw in your education."

"Not with that attitude."

"Eat your crepe." Irdu hopped from his seat.

Ronnie wasn't going to argue with a command like that. When he returned, he held his phone. He swiped the screen a few times, then set it in a dock. Guitar screamed from invisible speakers, followed by Steven Tyler, doing the same.

She knew Aerosmith. Lucifer would never admit it in public, but he frequently had the band playing in his office. She tapped her toes against the rung of her stool in time to the music. The rhythm worked its way through her, until she was bobbing her head and then on her feet, swaying her hips. "You can dance to this."

"No. *You* can dance to this. I can watch." A deeper thread wove into his amusement.

Ronnie looked up to find him doing exactly that. As long as everyone was enjoying themselves... She lost herself in the song again, swaying and throwing herself into the guitars and drums and voices.

She didn't pause when Irdu stepped up to her. Instead of joining her, he knotted his fingers in her hair, at the base of her skull. He swallowed her startled squeak by kissing her hard. Sparks of green and gold raced over and around her.

Irdu steered her back to the stool, lifted her to sit, and slid between her legs. The lightweight fabric of his shorts scuffed along the inside of her thighs, and hints of the knit brushed against her bare pussy.

She was seeing the benefit of putting on fewer clothes for breakfast.

He grabbed a strawberry from the bowl and dipped it in whipped cream. He dotted the fruit lightly along her lips and licked away each dab of cream, before dropping the berry in her mouth and kissing her hard.

It was so easy to fall into his touches. Each one sparked in a slightly different way, humming through her.

"It's a good thing demons don't gain weight," she teased when they broke apart.

"It's a good thing demons don't suffer from a lot of human ailments. For instance, getting hung up on whether or not rough, hard, casual sex is appropriate."

"I'd definitely hate for that to be a road block."

Irdu dipped his finger in melted Nutella and dipped it into her mouth.

She drew her tongue along the pad, spending several seconds licking it clean.

"If I cover my cock in Nutella, will you suck that, too?" he asked.

Ronnie raised an eyebrow, grabbed the plastic squeeze bottle, and knelt at his feet.

His gaze never left her, and the sharp breath he sucked in between his teeth said she wasn't the only one enjoying the moment.

"I should warn you, in case it's not clear, I don't have any experience with this." She was willing to learn, though.

His smile grew devilish. "I'm a simple guy to please, and I don't have any problems with giving directions. First, you need to see my dick to suck it."

"Smart ass." She was laughing though as she tugged down the waistband of his shorts. She wrapped her hand around his shaft, and he shuddered against her touch. Need pulsed between her legs. This was making her wet, and she wasn't even touching herself.

She drizzled the cooling sauce along his length, then traced her tongue along the same path, licking up the sugary treat.

His groan was electrifying. She wanted more of that sound. She swirled her tongue around the head of his cock, earning an even deeper growl. *God*, the noises he made were as good as the food.

Irdu set the bottle aside and grabbed a fistful of her hair. "I want to see my cock in your mouth."

A whimper escaped her throat at the desperation that ran through his command. She wrapped her lips around him, holding his gaze, trying to judge his response. The flutter of his eyelids seemed positive.

She couldn't take his entire length, so she wrapped her hand around the base. The more she licked, sucked, and bobbed her head, the louder he got. His hips thrust in time with her attention, until he was fucking her face.

"Dip your fingers between your legs." His voice was gravel. "Tell me if you're as wet as you were last night."

She gasped when her fingers slipped along her mons. She couldn't talk, but she managed a nod.

"Play with my balls," he said.

She glided slippery fingers along his sac. His grunts grew louder, and his thrusts more punctuated.

She fell into the rhythm, squeezing her legs together as best she could, to suppress the throbbing need. It didn't work.

"Stop." It sounded like he had to force the word out. He pulled back from her touch, breaking all contact between them.

"Did I do something wrong?"

He grasped her fingers and pulled her to her feet. "You did everything right. And while I love a good facial, this weekend is about your pleasure first." He gripped her hips and set her on the stool again.

Irdu spread her legs with his knee and moved his hand between them. He stroked along her slit while he kissed her. The slow build was torturous and incredible, pushing her toward climax. He teased his fingers inside her, then pulled out to move to her clit.

Each time her breathing grew shallower and she was certain she was going to come, he'd change his position.

When he finally lingered his attention on her clit, orgasm ripped through her. She squeezed her eyes shut, letting the stars dance inside her eyelids and the clouds take her head.

She barely noticed when his touch fell away, but a heartbeat later, he thrust inside her in a single movement.

He hit the right spot to draw out her orgasm, and she cried out at the deep penetration. He moved his slick hand to her thigh and gripped hard enough to leave a mark, digging his nails into her skin.

Ronnie was hoarse when he spilled in her and that wonderful feeling of their auras mingling wrapped around them. She was going to have trouble, going back to her vibrator after a weekend like this, and it was only Saturday morning.

CHAPTER SIX

Irdu leaned his weight against the counter, not breaking away from Ronnie. She kept her head rested against his chest and her legs wrapped around his waist.

"I'm really not supposed to keep you *here* all weekend. Not stuck in this apartment, anyway." His voice vibrated through her. "I have to show you the wonders of the world."

"*Have* to? You make it sound like work."

"It is my job. But it's definitely not work." He stepped back to look her in the eye. "Especially today."

A new flavor of heat spread through her, sweeter than the whipped cream from breakfast. It was still just a weekend of orientation, but at least it was a fun one.

"Where do you want to go? Anywhere." Irdu made a sweeping gesture with his arm.

She didn't have to think. "Everywhere. I want to see it all."

"You'll get there. I promise. Pick a starting point."

That was harder. She ticked through the images she had in her head of all the beautiful places in the world. She might be better off rolling the dice to decide. Then she landed on the perfect spot. "Six Flags."

"You're one incredible surprise after another." He brushed a thumb across her cheek. "We can go *anywhere*."

"I figured you meant it the first time." And she'd considered Scotland, Japan, France, even Russia. "But if this is about exploring my senses, I want to ride some of the tallest roller coasters, hear people laughing, and see the results of brilliant imaginations. I want to smell cotton candy and booze and sweaty crowds, and I want to eat and drink and absorb it all."

"It's hard to argue with logic like that."

After a quick stop at Ronnie's apartment for fresh clothes, and a shower that was cut short when they ran out of hot water, they stood at the gates to Six Flags over Georgia.

She tried not to gape at everything, but even standing in line, waiting to buy their admission, was amazing. There was so much to take in—scents, sounds, sights. And the emotion...

Demons could feel the stronger human emotions, and here those were as potent as baking brownies. Most of the feelings were joy. Ronnie could get high on the second-hand euphoria.

They bought their tickets and stepped into the park. "Where to, first?" Irdu asked.

"A roller coaster." Ronnie's answer came without hesitation. She had a huge to-see list, but that was at the top. "The inverted one, and then the one that plummets us straight toward the ground."

"Ah..." Irdu looked hesitant for the first time since she'd met him, all of twelve hours ago. "If you want a roller coaster, you can ride me."

She leaned into him enough to push him in the direction of the first coaster. "It's not like you can get hurt on one of these things."

"No, but they can evict my breakfast."

Ronnie shrugged and stepped into the line. "I can go alone."

He gave an exaggerated sigh. "No. I guess I can keep you company." He didn't sound disappointed. But he did fidget more than normal in line.

She had images of roller coasters in her mind, from her preprogrammed knowledge. She'd seen a few videos. They looked like fun.

She and Irdu slid into their seats, legs dangling loose, and the operator checked their harnesses. She didn't know if the tension rolling over her was her own or from everyone else on the ride, but she loved it.

The ride jerked, then glided forward smoothly. It crept up a ramp, one painful inch at a time, cranking her anticipation along with it. They hit the peak, and the world seemed to pause.

Then the world dropped out from underneath her, as the coaster and passengers screamed down the first slope and into a turn. She spent the next minute and a half screaming and laughing, frequently both at the same time, while the machine introduced her to the kind of rapid shifts in gravity she could never get from magical flying.

When they slid to a stop back at the station, it was over too soon.

"Again," Ronnie said, as they stepped back onto the platform.

Irdu laughed. Any apprehension he'd had before seemed to be gone. "You mentioned the falling-to-our-death ride."

"Not the way I phrased it." She couldn't wipe the grin off her face

"It's all good. I'm still in." He grabbed her hand and kept her close while they wove through the crowds and back into the park.

When they reached the ride in question, the sign said there was a two-hour wait.

"We can stand in the ever-popular line ride, or we can come back later," Irdu said.

Ronnie had already experienced having her guts rearranged, and she wanted to see as much else as was possible. "Let's come back."

"As you wish." He wrapped an arm around her waist pointed her toward another part of the park.

It felt natural to lean into him. Her joy, plus his aura, felt like floating on a cloud. Best. High. Ever. They headed away from the rides, toward a series of small shacks. One boasted ice cream, and another pizza and pretzels. He passed all the food, and led her toward flashing lights and clanging bells instead.

People were shooting plastic guns at plastic targets. And for the most part, missing. She wasn't sure what the point was.

Irdu handed over his money and grabbed a gun. "Watch and be amazed." He winked.

"You set a high bar. I'm waiting."

He aimed and fired three times in rapid succession. He hit the target with each shot. It was possible he was controlling the elements, using a puff of air, to make the target *ping*. She didn't feel any shift in the magic around them, though.

He kept going, and a small crowd grew around them. Some cheered each time he hit, and others tried to distract him.

He never missed.

"You can keep going, but you're maxed out on the prize," the guy behind the counter said apathetically.

Irdu set the toy weapon aside. "I'm done."

A round of cheers went up behind him, but he was looking at Ronnie. "Which do you want?"

"What?" She was missing a point of reference.

He nodded at the giant toys on the back wall. "Pick."

The purple panda caught her eye, and she pointed. The employee grabbed it and handed it to her. The toy was two-thirds as big as she was. It was perfect.

She squeezed it tight. "I love it. I have no idea where to put it while we're here, but I love it."

"Good." He rested a hand on the small of her back and steered her away. The crowd disbursed.

"How did you get so good at that?" Ronnie asked.

Irdu shrugged. "In a past life, I was a competition shooter."

She laughed. Hardly applicable to their line of work. Maybe some day he'd give her the full story. If they ever spoke again after this weekend. The idea that they might not made her a little sad.

"Do you want lunch?" he asked.

She wanted to try all the food in the park. That was probably a bit over the top, though. "Yes. As long as the experience is something I can't get anywhere else."

He screwed his face up, then relaxed. "I have the perfect idea."

They rented a storage locker for the bear and headed back to the stand boasting *Pizza and Pretzels.*

"I'm pretty sure I can get either one from other places." She wasn't complaining. Simply making an observation.

"You said *the experience.* And I guarantee you've never had pizza like this." Irdu ordered two slices of pepperoni and a large soda. It only took a few seconds for Ronnie to be handed a paper plate with a massive orange triangle on it.

He led her to a white table. The paint was chipped in a few places, and the chairs looked like they'd seen better days.

As far as Ronnie was concerned, it was perfect, because it was real. She had no idea how to eat her food, though.

Irdu folded his in half, to take a bite. It looked effective. She mimicked him. A wash of flavor hit her tongue, tomato and spice and meat and cheese in a muddled blend.

"It's so greasy," she said between mouthfuls.

"Is that bad?"

It was overpriced, had a higher fat content than it did nutritional value, and the people around them consumed it like it was the most perfect substance ever created. "Absolutely not. I love it."

Ronnie was halfway through her slice, when she realized he was studying her instead of eating. She set her pizza down and reached for a napkin. "Do I have food on my face?"

He rested his thumb at the corner of her mouth and dragged it across her cheek, then leaned in and pressed his lips to hers. The kiss was greasy and messy. And of course, fantastic.

He pulled back, still looking her. "I love watching you have fun. It's contagious."

"*Contagious* sounds serious," she teased. "Maybe you should get that checked out."

"Only if you're the doctor."

She liked the playfulness in his voice. "I'll have to do a thorough examination, to make sure you're all right. Check everything."

"I wouldn't have it any other way."

They stayed until the sun set, doing as much as possible, while drawing each moment out as long as they could.

"My feet are killing me." So where her calves. Her voice was raw, and her cheeks were sore from all the laughter.

He stroked his finger along the back of her knuckles. "The ache will vanish when we phase back to my apartment."

She frowned. "I know." She couldn't hide her disappointment.

"What's wrong?"

"I like the ache. It's a reminder of the day." Probably a silly thing to think, but that didn't stop her from feeling that way.

Irdu nudged her from the dwindling crowds and backed her against a wall, molding his body to hers. He kissed her hard, stealing her breath and swallowing her groan of surprise. He dragged his palm up her stomach, to tease her breast, and wedged his knee between her legs.

She ground into his touch, memorizing every sensation.

He pulled back to rest his forehead against hers. "I can give you all sorts of new aches that will linger the entire night."

"You say the naughtiest things."

"This isn't naughty. This is barely foreplay."

She sighed happily. "You have so much to teach me."

It was Sunday night. They'd done so much in the past two days, yet it wasn't nearly enough. Technically, she had eternity ahead of her—as long as she didn't fuck up, have her physical-body privileges revoked, and get sent back to Hell. Not that she planned on it.

But none of what lay in front of her would be the same as this weekend.

"What are you thinking about?" Irdu asked.

That she had to extract herself from him soon. "You're awfully good at this." But of course he was. It was his job to teach newbie demons how to love life without going off the deep end of sensory overload.

A shadow passed over his face and vanished under an impassive mask. "Yeah. I'm a real professional." He worked his jaw, then snapped it shut.

She was going to push for more but didn't want to hear what he was holding back. This was attraction. A lingering aftereffect of spending a weekend wrapped up in him. She wasn't feeling anything beyond that, because this was just sex. The ache of having to leave Irdu was because they clicked, but she'd click with other people. Getting along didn't mean anything beyond that.

CHAPTER SEVEN

Ronnie took a seat at the conference-room table on the main floor of the Ubiquity building. She was one of six demons and angels starting work as Reapers.

When Irdu strode into the room, her stomach flipped.

"Morning, all." His gaze flicked over each face, lingering on hers for an extra second. "I'm Irdu. Your new manager. This morning we're doing a refresher about the job, and then you'll can have at it."

New manager? Her gut plummeted into her shoes, and irritation flared inside. He could have told her. It wasn't kind of an important piece of information to have. Keeping the information from her wasn't technically a lie, but it was deceptive.

They didn't have to hide what they'd done. Even if it hadn't been company sanctioned, Ubiquity didn't have an anti-fraternization policy, specifically because all of their employees liked to fuck.

"Any questions?" Irdu asked.

She'd missed most of what he said. She raised her hand anyway.

"Uriel." He nodded at her.

"*Ronnie.*" She didn't hide her irritation that he was pretending not to know what name she preferred. "Did you know before today who your new employees were going to be?"

He winced. "Yes."

Lying fucker. Why did it matter? Because it was a breach of trust. And that hurt more than a lot of things, even from someone she'd only given her body to.

She didn't have a follow-up question. She was content to simmer with her irritation for the next couple of hours, until he let them take a break.

"Ronnie. Give me two minutes?" he asked as she brushed past with the group.

She spared him the briefest glance. "No need."

She should feel some sort of satisfaction at shrugging him off, but her anger grew through more orientation. Through lunch. And through her being introduced to the demon she would sit with through training.

She tried to focus on how the computer system worked. How it found potential cherubs. How she was supposed to know which flags were legit and which were meaningless.

But she couldn't get her mind off Irdu. She pushed her chair away from the computer. "Can we take a break?"

"Sure." Her trainer shrugged.

Great.

She stalked directly to Irdu's office, pushed inside without knocking, and shut the door behind her.

"Ronnie?" He looked up, the question on his face matching his tone.

"You know what? I do want to talk." Not the most brilliant line she could have led with, but it was an opener. "Why didn't you tell me? *Orientation* is one thing. *Oh hey, I'm also your boss.* How hard would that have been?"

"I should have said something. You're right. I just didn't expect..." He raked his fingers through his hair. A gesture that had been so sexy sweet twenty-four hours ago, and now it pissed her off.

"Didn't expect what?"

He sighed. "I've done this so many times, acting as a gateway to this world. As an introduction. It gets repetitive."

She'd bored him? A lump grew in her throat, and she couldn't swallow past it. "I'm sorry to be such an inconvenience."

"But you aren't. You weren't. That's my point. I had a blast over the last couple of days. If I'd know things would go the way they did, that you'd be so much fun, I would have said something up front."

She pursed her lips. "And if things had gone the way they usually did?" She wasn't comforted by his words. "You would have had a newbie to poke fun at on Monday morning. Someone whose secrets you'd pried into. Someone who worked for you, that you could lord something over."

"No. I don't do that. I haven't done that. There's just a little fun in catching a new demons off guard. No harm."

"I'm so glad that the brand-new demons—me, others—can entertain you. During and after orientation." She let the sarcasm drip from her words. "You're a fucking asshole."

"I'm also your boss." His voice turned hard. *Now* he wanted to repeat it.

"Then I want a different boss."

"It doesn't work that way."

It could. She could demand it from Lucifer. She didn't think it would go over well, if people knew she had a direct link to the ruler of Hell. But she was so furious, she was willing to call in that favor. "Make it work that way."

"Fine." Irdu sank back into his chair. "Get back to work. Go be like every other spoiled new demon on the floor. Prove to me you're no different from anyone else."

She had no idea what her standing up for herself had to do with not being unique, but she was done giving him the satisfaction of her biting back. If he liked the tension that came the day after, this was probably almost as good as her stunned expression when she realized who he was this morning. She spun on her toe and returned to her trainer.

The conversation, the lies, and Irdu's excuse for all of it, rolled over in her head for the rest of the day. She tried to shove then aside, but the thoughts wouldn't be ignored.

When she got a break, she called Izzy. A sourness in her throat made her hesitant to dial, but she had to find out how much he'd known.

"Hey, angel." His happy greeting would have made her smile on any other day. He called her that because he recognized that demons and angels were the same at their core. They just called different places *home*.

Was his cheerful attitude today because he was waiting to see if he had someone to poke fun at?

"Did you know?" She winced at her abrupt reply.

"Know what? Are you all right?"

Ronnie leaned against a nearby wall with a sigh and scanned the hallway. She didn't need anyone overhearing this until she figured out what was at the root of this conversation. "No. Yes. I'm fine. Nothing life threatening. Did you know Irdu was my boss?"

The silence that greeted her churned up a storm in her stomach.

"No." Izzy sounded sincere when he finally replied. "Really? No. I had no idea. I would have said something if I'd known."

She felt a twinge of gratitude she wasn't the only one who thought her expectation was reasonable. "Promise?" She believed him, but she needed the reassurance. She'd believed a lot of things Irdu said, too.

"Cross my heart, angel. I'm sorry he did that to you. I have plans tonight, but if you want to stop by after work later this week, I'll commiserate with you."

"*Commiserate.* Is that a euphemism?" Ronnie tried to keep her tone light. She also needed to know that he meant what he'd said the other night, about the sex not disrupting their growing friendship.

He chuckled. A good sign. "Not unless you want it to be. I was thinking more like brownies and chick flicks."

"That does sound like fun." She was smiling now. "Thank you."

They chatted a little longer, which helped calm her mood. But as soon as she disconnected, she remembered why she'd been irritated in the first place. *Irdu.*

She was still fuming when she got home. She grabbed a pint of ice cream from the freezer.

Damn it, it was only half-full. Besides, she didn't want this pre-packaged, it'll-do-in-a-pinch stuff.

She wanted chocolate syrup, fed to her on strong, skilled fingers. She wanted warm honey, drizzled over her lips and breasts and pussy, and licked away by a hungry tongue.

Desire and memories flowed over her, turning anger to frustration, and then into need. Was she really upset with Irdu *just* because he'd lied? Demons twisted the truth all the time. Angels did too, as much as they didn't like to admit it.

No. It was because she had fun. If she closed her eyes, she could feel his hands gliding over her skin. She drew her palms along a similar path, kneading her breasts as she remembered him sucking her nipples warm, after the shock of ice over her skin.

Need pulsed between her legs, and she dropped one hand lower. Ghosted sensations lingered there. His lips closing around her clit. She undid her slacks and dipped under her panties, following the same trail with her hand that he'd taken with his mouth.

This wasn't going to be enough. Her body craved a touch besides hers.

She could go out. Find a random hookup.

Her body didn't want that either. A specific sensation was burned in her mind and on her skin. *Hell help her*, she was craving Irdu's touch.

CHAPTER EIGHT

Why did it have to be Irdu? She wasn't missing *him* specifically. Just the things he could do with his hands. And his mouth. And how he hadn't hesitated to go to all the silly places she wanted to go. Plus, he seemed to have as much fun as he did.

The next morning, as she got ready for work, her irritation had diminished, though it wasn't gone. In the empty spaces, loneliness flitted in. After a weekend of fucking around— literally and otherwise—not having plans at night was disappointing.

But she had Izzy, and now that she'd started work, she'd make new friends.

When she got to the office, the demon who was supposed to be her trainer directed her to one of the managers' offices.

Raphael. His name was stashed amongst her vast array of preprogrammed knowledge. He wasn't an original, but he'd been with Heaven for a long time.

She knocked on his open door, and he looked up from his computer.

"Uriel." He managed to sneer her name. "I understand you didn't like your first boss."

At least Irdu worked quickly. "We had a conflict of interest. And it's *Ronnie*."

"Great. Wonderful." He didn't sound like he was feeling either. "Was it the conflict that had Lucifer making demands of me first thing, or was his insistence because of you?"

Lucifer personally made the request? She probably shouldn't like the bubble of warmth that came with the knowledge. She definitely shouldn't be smug about it. "I don't know."

Raphael gestured to the chair in front of his desk. "Close the door. Have a seat."

Ronnie didn't like the saccharine that filtered into his request.

"I *do* know," Raphael said before her butt hit the chair, "because most of management knows about you. You jumped to the front of a significant waiting list, to get your job. You were here for less than a day before you wanted a change of scenery. Understand this—I don't care what makes you Lucifer's pet or what issues you have with anyone. You work for me now, and you follow the same rules as everyone else."

That sounded fair. She was going to argue that she wasn't Lucifer's pet, but she could reach a less contentious point in her relationship with Raphael before she tried to change his world views. "All right."

He narrowed his gaze. "Good. It's been *recommended* I have you train with my best. Ariel will be your mentor. Don't fuck with her stats."

"I'll do my best." Ronnie could be polite for a short period of time, but if he kept throwing shade, she'd lose the sweet demeanor real fast.

The contempt in his voice diminished a hint, as he gave her the rapid-fire version of what Irdu told everyone yesterday. He introduced her to Ari, who was sunshine, compared to Raphael's grumpy dark cloud.

Ronnie got the same run-down of the software and systems she'd had yesterday. The difference was, when it came time for a break, Ari didn't send her off on her own.

"Follow me." Ari grabbed her hand and tugged her toward the part of the floor where Irdu's office sat. "The vending machines in the east breakroom have way better chocolate."

Ronnie liked that kind of company knowledge. "Do you know all the good secrets?"

"I know all the best gossip." Ari bumped Ronnie playfully with her shoulder. She nodded at Irdu's office as they passed. "So he's an incubus, so demon..." Disdain trickled into her voice. She glanced at Ronnie. "No offense."

Sure. Ronnie twisted her mouth.

Ari grinned. "You're not all bad. And he's sexy." She lowered her voice. "He's been with Ubiquity forever, like Raph. But rumor is he pissed a few people off yesterday, like the higher ups, because some little newbie didn't like his policies and went over his head." She stopped in front of the vending machine. "Peanut butter, caramel, or peanuts?"

"Uh... I'm a fan of all of them." Ronnie's stomach was churning too much, for her to think about what kind of candy she wanted. Had Irdu ruined chocolate for her? "And I didn't go over his head."

The thunk of a candy bar hitting the tray acted as the perfect sound effect for Ari turning to Ronnie, jaw dropped. "Holy shit. You?"

Apparently Ari didn't know *all* the gossip. "And I didn't manipulate the system." Ronnie reached around her to grab the candy, and stalked from the room without looking to see if Ari followed. She wanted to get back to their desks and hide. No wonder Raph had been rude.

"Hang on." Ari fell into step beside her. "Dish. What really happened?"

We fucked. It was incredible. He took me on a roller coaster and bought me cotton candy. And if it hadn't been fun, he planned to make fun of me the next day at work. "He asked Lucifer to move me to another manager." *After I threw a fit because I got caught up in the status quo.*

"After one day? Harsh." Ari plucked the package from Ronnie. "On the other hand, you found me because of it, and I'm awesome."

"True." Ronnie's smile was genuine. She wouldn't fuck Ari, but she would go out for coffee with her, so that was a solution to some of the loneliness.

The rest of the day was uneventful, aside from Ronnie's replaying everything with Irdu in her head. Did she overreact? She couldn't get past the lie. That he'd held back who he was in case he wanted to make fun of her.

That obliterated so much of his attractiveness. But if he hadn't done that, or if he could actually figure out why she was pissed, she might forgive him.

That seemed highly unlikely.

By the time work was over, Ronnie had thoroughly bummed herself out, chasing the Irdu thought in circles. Was she that poor a judge of character? Why did she care? It was only sex.

Because not only did he make her body sing, but the rest of her time with him was fun too. They clicked.

When work was over, she blinked home. Normally she'd walk, but she was tired of hearing herself think.

Irdu was waiting in her living room.

Her heart jammed in her throat and fury raced through her. "What are you doing inside my apartment? How did you even get in?" Locks didn't keep their kind out, but she had alternatives. Wards, meant to distract any would-be intruders. A visitor would be distracted by the endless puzzle of the magic woven around her apartment, and forget they were here to break in.

"You mean how did I get past the wards? I'm focused on something else right now."

"What?" she asked.

"You."

Oh. The single word lifted her spirits more than was reasonable. She wasn't going to get sucked into whatever game he was playing, though. "Why? I'm no big deal. You'll have a new assignment on... Easter? That's got to be a big one. And until then, something tells me you can fuck whatever you want."

"I could. I can. I will."

Lovely. "Then why are you here?"

"I already told you." His tone was plain, but his intense, burning gaze sent fire skittering through her veins.

"You're focused on me. Right. Why?"

He sighed heavily. "You're not like... I'm an incubus. All it takes from me is the slightest nudge, for anyone who's attracted to me, and they drop their inhibitions and self-doubt. I could walk out your front door right now, and pick from half a dozen people on the street. With a wink and a smile from me, any one of them would let me push them up against the wall, rip their clothes off, and fuck them."

"And then, if it's boring, make fun of them after?" She needed to remember why she was bothered by his behavior, rather than focusing on his words. Because, *damn*, he painted some vivid images, and there was a part of her begging to be the person he chose.

Irdu pinched the bridge of his nose. "That's not how I meant what I said yesterday. Or, actually, it is. But not in a cruel way."

"Are there other ways to mean it?"

"I've been doing this for years. Not just the management, but the orientation. I've met so many demons. We're like people or angels or anyone. Some of us are stuffy, and some are fun, and some are... You work for Raphael now?"

Ronnie didn't want to understand what he meant, as far as Raphael's painfully abrasive personality, but she did. "Yes."

"I don't keep my management position from them so I can be cruel come Monday morning. It doesn't hurt anyone. It's always been the equivalent of a jump-scare, but with sex instead of horror." He raked his fingers through his hair. "I don't think I'm explaining this well."

"I guess I kind of get it." But she was reserving final judgment about his character until she spent some more time with him. "If you're bored with your job, who did you piss off, to get stuck up at Ubiquity?" She sat on the couch.

"What makes you think I'm not doing it because I love the job?" He took the seat next to her.

She wanted to scoot away, but the heat of his arm pressed into hers was a compelling reason to stay. "Because you just told me you're bored with the management aspect of things."

"I owe Lucifer."

That made two of them, though for Ronnie, it was probably for entirely different reasons. Lucifer was looking out for her. Acting as a mentor. Tempting her in ways an original angel really shouldn't. She wouldn't have minded having Lucifer conduct her orientation.

Though now that she'd had Irdu, she wasn't willing to surrender that experience. Being this close, with the words flowing easily between them, made her skin hum and her pulse skip.

"To answer your original question"—Irdu turned in his seat so he was facing her, and rested a hand on her thigh—"I'm here because there's more with you. It's not just a physical compulsion, though, *hell*, I like fucking you. I had more fun with you this weekend than I have... possibly my entire time as a demon."

That sounded like a teensy bit of an exaggeration, but Ronnie shared the sentiment. "What's going on between us?"

"I don't know. Lust. Friendship. Too much cotton candy. No way to know for certain, unless we spend more time together." He traced tiny circles along her inner thigh with his thumb.

She liked the idea of spending more time with him. However, despite the insistence thrumming between her legs, she didn't want it all to be in bed. "What did you have in mind?"

CHAPTER NINE

"Let's go see more of the world," Irdu said.

Ronnie grinned. "The cherry blossoms are blooming in Tokyo."

He leaned in, mouth near her ear, but never touching her. "You can play with my chopsticks. I can eat your sushi."

"Oh so bad. That doesn't even make sense when you think about it." She couldn't help but laugh.

"So don't think about it." He stood and pulled her to her feet. "Tell me you want to do this."

"On one condition."

He raised an eyebrow.

"You tell me you understand why I was upset. And you mean it," Ronnie said.

Irdu stepped closer, and his aura sparked and danced up her arm. "I understand." He kissed the backs of her knuckles. "And I'm hoping you never get as jaded as I am and that your enthusiasm rubs off on me."

She waited for his next words.

"And I'm hoping you rub all over me at the same time."

There it was. She shook her head. Not that she minded at all. "Let's go to Tokyo."

Their environment shifted, and a heartbeat later, they stood in the middle of a grove of cherry trees. The sun was still creeping up in the sky, casting bright morning light over the landscape. The rich scent of sweet flowers and fresh dirt flooded her senses. Petals lined the ground and occasionally fluttered down around them, like warm falling snow.

The noise of traffic was in the background. Chirping birds tickled Ronnie's eardrums. She couldn't wipe the smile from her face as she absorbed each and every sensation.

"You picked the perfect time to enjoy this uninterrupted." Irdu's voice blended with the chorus of nature, rather than disrupting it. He squeezed her hand, and gently tugged her along the path.

They walked for several minutes, and Ronnie cast her gaze everywhere. She plucked a few loose flower petals from Irdu's hair, then held out her hand, hoping to catch a couple like she might with snow. "I can't wait to see snow." She hadn't meant to say that aloud.

He pulled her closer and leaned his head to hers. "I know you're not innocent or naive, but the way you watch the world around you..."

"What?" She couldn't decipher where the thought was going.

"It's pure. Genuine. Real."

A flush of heat spread through her cheeks at the awe in his voice. "I don't know what to say to that."

He wrapped his arm around her waist and spun to face her. "You don't have to." He stepped closer, and her body molded to his. "But if you'd like to change the subject, I can move from telling you how sweet you are, to reminding you what you do to me." He grabbed her hand and brought it down to cup his semi-hard shaft.

She was getting a feel for how he liked to detract from serious conversations with sex. That was fine. Their relationship was more sex than it was serious. "You're so crude. What if people are watching?"

"They'll be jealous. I could let them all join us, if you'd like. Playing with you. With us. With each other. Not force them, but rather free them to understand there's nothing wrong with the desire."

"No." Ronnie was content with the way things were. "Though, I'll keep it in mind in the future."

He kissed her lightly. "I could take you for afternoon tea in England, and feed you scones with cream and jam?"

"It's the middle of the night in England." Time zones were part of her built-in training. Knowing when and where it was dark or light was helpful in her line of work.

Irdu seemed to think for a moment. "Australia?"

She had to give him points for trying. "How about we skip the scones until later, and you take me home, and feed me strawberries and cream instead?"

"We've already done that."

"Are you bored with it?" A sliver of hurt tried to creep in.

"No." He kissed her forehead, her nose, and her lips. "As long as you're having fun, I'll do it over and over, because I'm enjoying all of this, and I'm enjoying you enjoy it."

He cupped her face and nipped her bottom lip several times, before kissing away the sting. "But before the strawberries, I want to taste you."

Desire and anticipation cranked through her. She liked the way her body reacted each time he touched her. He made her heart skip and her mind happy.

It was good she didn't have to define what was happening between them, because she couldn't. For now, she was going to live the fuck out of it.

CHAPTER TEN

The instant they appeared in Irdu's apartment, hungry kisses turned to frantic groping. Hands, caressing and squeezing. Nails, scraping along flesh. Clothing, tearing in Ronnie and Irdu's desperation to feel more skin on skin.

Was she spoiling herself, by getting used to sex on such a regular basis?

Who cared? She was going to enjoy it for all she was worth.

After the clothing fell away, Irdu stepped back and trailed his gaze over her. "I adore looking at you. Spending time with you. Your gorgeous face." He trailed a finger along her cheek. "Your amazing smile and laugh." He brushed a feather-light touch over her lips. "This stunning body." He traced a path down the center of her chest and over her stomach, then stepped to her side. "And a sexy fucking ass." He slapped one cheek hard enough to send a *crack* through the room.

She yelped in surprise at the gesture and the sting. That was *good*. "Again?"

"No." He shook his head.

She liked how he pulled off sexy and imposing even naked. He was chiseled, hung, and fierce. She jutted out her lower lip and glanced over her shoulder with wide eyes. "Please?"

"Hmm..." He glided his hand over the fading sting, and then along her other ass cheek. "It *would* be fair if they matched." He slapped her again.

Ronnie gasped at the hint of pain. A tingle spread between her thighs and traveled along her nerve endings, to light up her entire body.

Irdu caressed each cheek. "*God*, I'm glad we get to spend more time together." He spanked her again. The sting was sharper this time and lingered longer.

"Why's that?" Her question was breathy.

He kneaded one buttock. When he pulled his hand away, she expected another slap.

The lack of one cranked her anticipation higher.

"Because I want to find every one of your buttons." He spanked her again, startling her.

Adrenaline spilled in her veins, and her desire was cranked to full-blast. "That might take a while." She hoped, anyway.

"I hope so." That his words echoed her thoughts was another reason to appreciate whatever this was between them. He slapped her ass one more time, then glided his hand between her legs, to nudge her pussy. He teased her opening without entering her.

Irdu moved in front of her again, gripping her ass tightly and drawing out the lingering heat from the spanking. He pulled her body into his, and his cock dug into her stomach when she molded to him.

He kissed down her chest, to kneel at her feet. "I told you I wanted to taste you again." He nipped the inside of her thighs with his teeth and traveled higher.

She gasped and pressed into his mouth when he licked along her slit. He wrapped his lips around her clit. A low hum reverberated from the back of his throat and vibrated against her swollen button.

Ronnie knotted her fingers in his hair, needing something to hold onto. He pushed his fingers inside her, and she arched into his touch. With each new lick and suck and tickle, her pulse hammered harder.

She rocked her hips in time with his attention. Orgasm sped up on her without warning. She pulled his hair when she came, and he didn't let up on the licking.

When she shuddered away from his touch, he eased up.

He helped her drop to the floor, to sit next to him. He crushed his mouth to hers, and she dove into the taste of herself on his lips. His chin. His cheeks.

Slowly, her world stopped wobbling, and she loosened her grip on his hair.

"How are your legs?" he murmured against her lips.

"Stable. Recovering."

"Enough to kneel?"

Her anticipation swelled again, as his intent sank in. "Probably," she said.

"Good. On your knees."

She smirked at the command and did as she was told, while he stood.

The way he gripped her hair sent a sharp sting through her scalp. Had he felt the same when she did that? She hoped so. It was an incredible sensation.

"This time I'm not holding back." He fisted his cock.

Another new experience to add to her list. "Okay." She took him in her mouth.

He hit the back of her throat, and reflex kicked in. She willed the gag away. She licked while she stroked him, watching the expressions of pleasure dance across his face.

"Play with yourself," he said. "Make yourself come." He held her head in place, thrusting into her mouth.

She glided her hand between her legs. Her clit was tender. Tingles raced through her, magically enhanced by Irdu. Sparks teased her nipples. Prickles glided up her spine. Invisible fingers touched every bit of her simultaneously.

Climax built more slowly this time, but when it plummeted in, she lost herself in it.

His tug on her scalp drew her back to the now. She pulled her touch away from her tender body and stroked him with slick fingers. Each time he pumped his hips, he struck the back of her throat.

She recognized the grunts. The surge in his energy. He was close. A warm, salty spurt hit her mouth. She tasted him, memorizing the flavor of him on her tongue.

He slowed to a stop and slipped from between her lips. And then he was kneeling next to her again. Kissing her. Pulling her into his lap. Caressing her face and devouring her sighs.

Ronnie lost track of how long they sat there for.

Irdu eventually stood, lifting her, and carried her to the couch. They curled up around each other. The leather was cool against her heated skin, and his body was hot to the touch.

He watched her with an expression that stole her breath. A pleased smile danced on his lips.

"I don't like arguing with you. Everything else we do together is so much more enjoyable," Irdu said.

Ronnie agreed. But logic twinged with a light protest. "You've only known me for... four days? How old are you?"

"Older than you."

While she didn't need to define their relationship yet, she had a hard time believing he could be so infatuated with her. "This can't be the first time you've met someone like me. And I'm not willing to say this is love."

"Whoa." Irdu held up his hands. "You can throw around the world *lust*, but be careful with the other *L* word."

"I agree. But why me?"

He brushed his lips over her forehead. "Because you're different. I mean it. Yeah, I've met other demons who know how to enjoy life, and who know how to have a good time, but you're you. The way you do everything is distinctly Ronnie. I like it."

She could see this becoming more, the longer they spent together, but for now, she didn't feel a need to define it beyond *friends with incredible benefits*. A new thought entered her mind, and she frowned.

He kissed the tip of her nose. "Don't do that. What's wrong?"

"Nothing. Something I need to deal with." She wanted to tell him, because she hated the idea of keeping things from him. But she didn't want her issues to be his burden. "I just need to reconcile with the idea that in a month, you'll be doing orientation with someone else."

"I will be. That's my job. I'll probably even enjoy it. Not the way I do with you, though."

She got it. "I don't have a problem with you sleeping with other people." She'd expected the words to taste foul, but they felt right. She didn't own him, and she believed him when he said their connection was unique. It was to her, as well.

"But you don't want me to do the orientations anymore," he said.

She shrugged. "I don't like knowing that sex is your job. But I'm a bottom-tier demon. I don't get a say in whether you do your job or how."

"I don't want to do it anymore."

Ronnie was surprised and relieved and all sorts of other thing she didn't have a right to be. "Why not? You get to fuck someone, on the company dollar, at least once a month. You can play your little blindfold game with them. Introduce them to their physical body in full-surround sensation experience.

Irdu rolled his body, catching her off guard, and straddled her. His weight against her was possessive and intimate. He locked his knees at her hips and rested his hands on either side of her head. "If you tell me right now to fuck off, I'll be a little sad. But if you say you want me taken off orientation detail, I'll go back to Lucifer."

She measured her words. This was the kind of request that felt big, as far as any sort of relationship was concerned. This was Irdu's career. "I won't ask you not to sleep with anyone else. I can't bind myself to a promise like that either. In some ways, I'm only a week old."

"That's not what this is." He dipped his head to brush his lips over hers. "Hooking up with someone because you want to is different than doing it for work."

Yeah. It was. "What does that mean for you? Job-wise?"

"I'll worry about that. I wouldn't offer if I wasn't willing to face the consequences. Is this what you want?"

"Yes."

He bit her bottom lip hard enough to make her groan, then kissed the sting away. "So it's official."

"What is?"

"I'm your on-call fuck buddy, and you'll be the same for me."

"You expect me to drop everything when you want to get laid?"

He scrunched up his face. "Not *everything*. But yes."

She liked—loved—this arrangement. "All right."

She stayed with Irdu that night. It was an easy thing to blink back to her apartment before work, and get ready.

When she got to the Ubiquity building, she made a quick detour by the *good* breakroom, for candy and as an excuse to pass by Irdu's office.

Her gut sank when she saw him packing his belongings into a box. Fuck. Did she get him fired?

CHAPTER ELEVEN

"What happened?" Ronnie tried to keep the panic from sliding into her voice.

"Nothing bad." Irdu stepped past her and closed the door behind her. He returned to rest his weight on the edge of his desk, facing her. "Lucifer likes me way too much as a toy, to let me walk away from this place."

She gestured to his half-packed belongings. "Then what's all of this?"

"I told him I wouldn't do the orientation anymore."

"Did you tell him why?" She should have covered this last night. At the time, she was just happy Irdu was willing to give up the newbie slog. Now reality was sinking in. Did Lucifer know this was her fault?"

"Yes," Irdu said.

Her breath caught. She hoped it didn't make Lucifer think she wasn't cut out for this.

"He demoted me." Irdu didn't sound upset. "Kicked me back to Development Manager. Away from the reapers."

"I'm sorry."

He stalked toward her, pressing into her until she collided with the door. He framed her head with his hands. "Don't be."

"Why not?"

"I'm a big boy; I'm responsible for my own actions. Besides, this is what you and I discussed."

"But..."

"Take the apology back," he growled.

She searched his face. He was right. She wasn't responsible for him or anyone but herself. She could nudge or prod someone, point them toward their potential, but at the end of the day, she hadn't made up Irdu's mind. He had. "I take it back."

"Good." He knotted his fingers in her hair and jerked her head back. The sharp tug made her gasp. The way he claimed her mouth tingled across her entire body. "Now that we have that out of the way, take off your pants," he said.

His arrogant assumption flooded her with desire. She quirked an eyebrow. "What? No finesse? No seduction?"

"How furious will Raph be if you're in here for too long?" Irdu paused. "On second thought..."

It was tempting, to piss off the cranky angel. But she'd only been at Ubiquity a few days. She could wait a *little* longer before making more waves. She kicked off her sandals.

Irdu sucked along her neck. "I think this entire arrangement is going to work out great."

Ronnie had to agree. Fuck-buddies... Friends...

Whatever else life at Ubiquity had in store for her, she was glad to have Irdu in her corner. And on his desk. And in either one of their apartments...

This was the beginning of something wickedly fantastic.

~*~

COURTING MORTALITY

BROTHERS OF FATE
BOOK ONE

CHAPTER ONE

As you are, for all of time
To taste neither love nor death
When you find the one worth more than life
She'll draw her last mortal breath

Eli dropped his phone back into its cradle, and rubbed his face in exhaustion. He could call the shipping company all day long, and still get nowhere. It wouldn't matter how many people he reamed for the critical-but-delayed, package. He'd still wouldn't get it today.

His brother's voice drifted in from the outer office, and he growled. Loki was the last thing Eli needed. Especially Loki's jokes, with sexual harassment written all over them. Sometimes Eli wondered how that man actually owned his own company.

"And she says '...isn't *choking hazard* the warning label they put on tiny objects?'" Loki's laughter floated through the office.

The laugh that joined in—pleasant but sarcastic—made Eli pinch the bridge of his nose.

It was the best way he'd found to suppress any other reaction. For instance, the way his imagination careened out of control and his cock sprung to life when he heard Marley's voice.

"I bet that ruined your plans for the night." She must be back at her desk.

"Not really. I have other talents." The confidence in Loki's voice never wavered.

Eli stood and made his way into the main office. He needed to talk to her anyway. Kicking Loki out of the office was just an added benefit.

The bad jokes and innuendo continued as Eli crossed the short distance to Marley's desk. With the four-foot high cubicles, it was easy to see what most of the people in the room were up to. Or at least, if they had their attention on their computers. Most of his people had their heads down, headsets on, to take support calls. Marley didn't work the help desk, though. She fixed the issues that couldn't be resolved with a simple phone call.

For instance, it looked like her current task was to keep Loki busy. Or maybe it was the other way around. Marley leaned back with her hands on the arms of the chair. The posture accentuated the way her T-shirt hugged her breasts. She shook her head, attention still focused on the man standing next to her.

Loki looked up. The corner of his mouth pulled into a smirk when he saw Eli. His gaze shifted back to Marley in an instant, and he leaned on the cubicle wall, closing the distance between her and himself.

Her full lips twisted in disbelief. Her voice didn't carry as far, but the subtle sarcasm was enough to reach Eli's ears. "Lucky her. I guess that's why they say, 'Those who can, do. Those who can't, make up euphemisms about why size doesn't matter.'"

Eli should tell her to get back to work. Over the centuries, he'd watched his brother destroy countless lives, both literally and figuratively. Loki had never hesitated to kill, maim, or render someone psychologically crippled, if it suited his purposes.

Eli definitely saw the appeal in Marley. With full breasts, round hips, and a narrow waist, she haunted plenty of his fantasies. The way her plump lips pursed when she was annoyed and curved when she smiled short-circuited his thoughts. Her sense of humor and intelligence, though—the sharp wit and ability to think through anything—were what drew her to him the most. And made her far too independent, compared to the women his brother usually preferred.

Eli had gotten used to a lot of things in his long life. That people actually knew who Loki was, where very few even realized he had brothers. That Eli had needed to shorten his name—Byleist—to something easier for modern tongues to wrap their brains around.

But Loki's repeated attempts to hit on Marley still set Eli on edge. Eli didn't seen himself getting over that any time soon.

Loki didn't flinch at her slight. "You're good. I almost bought that. Have dinner with me."

Marley's, "Seriously. Again?" echoed Eli's thoughts perfectly.

Loki moved around the cubicle wall, and his leg brushed hers when he sat on the edge of her desk. "The odds are, the more times I ask, the better my chances you'll say yes."

Eli had stepped in on Marley's behalf the first dozen or so times this had happened, but she'd asked him to stop, and said she could handle it herself. Even now, he had to force himself not to say *something*.

He'd tried to tell himself it wasn't jealousy. He knew it was, though. Even if he couldn't have Marley, everything about her called to him, and most of the time, it took all of his restraint not to step in on her behalf when some unworthy dickhole hit on her.

"Game theory doesn't work that way." She sat up, and moved her chair back a few inches. "The odds are the same, every time you roll the dice. Besides, no-chance-in-hell multiplied by not-in-this-lifetime-or-the-next will always equal zero."

Eli couldn't completely hide his smirk, and had no desire to hold back his pointed reminder. "Don't you ever work?"

Loki winked at him, before turning back to Marley. "I'll be back another day."

There were lots of things Eli was grateful for, and at the top of the list was that his brother owned his own antique store, instead of working for the family business.

Some days Eli questioned why a family of gods—his family—did something as banal as running an insurance underwriting firm. Logically, he got it. Over the centuries, as their followers had dwindled and life had become more structured, Eli and his family had to do something to stay busy. The demand for miracles, and the destruction of entire sects of opposing tribes, had really sloped off. Since Eli's father, and really most of his family, were gifted with the ability to control the elements, they knew more about acts of God than almost anyone, so they'd just gravitated toward insurance.

Marley spun in her chair the moment Loki was gone. She tucked a strand of black hair behind her ear. "I don't suppose you're in such a splendid mood because my cable came in?"

Her teasing pulled him back into the conversation, and reminded him of why he was actually at her desk. "About that."

Her brows knit together, and she studied him for a minute. "Good thing I don't have a hot date tonight."

He agreed, though his reasons didn't have anything to do with work. He beat back the emotional response to her retort. Even if she wasn't vehemently opposed to getting involved with people from work, hell, even if he wasn't her boss, his fate wouldn't let him do more than relegate her to daydreams. "The hubs came in. The cable and connectors weren't with them. Tomorrow morning."

Her shoulders slumped. "We've got less than a week before the move."

He knew. Everyone knew. The countdown reminders went out every morning via email. Their branch of the company was moving into a new building over the Christmas break, which meant all the network wiring had to be in place before a single workstation was set up. As IT director, it was his job to make sure it got done, and he knew Marley could handle the work fine on her own. Or, she would've been able to, if she'd had the time they'd been promised months ago. No one could wire the entire place by themselves in just a few days. Sure, he could summon lightning, fly, and even heal people and sometimes bring them back from the brink of death. However, even as a god, he didn't have the kind of power it would take to pull off a miracle like wiring and testing an entire building in a single day. He couldn't make the cables appear out of thin air. He didn't have the power to materialize them into the places they needed to be.

"I'll help." He knew she wouldn't let him do the work. It would be a blow to her pride. He wasn't sticking her on the job alone, though. Not this late in the game. "We'll probably have to pull an all-weekend shift, but I promise I'll comp you for it."

She shook her head, but a smile had crept in, erasing some of the frown-creases in her forehead. "I guess I'll have to make sure I'm not out too late tonight."

"I hope not." He couldn't keep some of his relief from leaking into his voice. He should want her to find a nice guy and settle down. At least her life wasn't at risk, with someone else. Not the way it was with him. That fact still didn't console him. Fortunately, they had work to do, and it was a nice distraction. "Planning meeting, my office?"

She didn't protest, and moments later she was perched on one of the chairs while he thought aloud, and made notes on the white board. "Supposedly, the missing bits will be in by eight tomorrow." Since they'd been scheduled to arrive today, and nobody had been able to explain to his satisfaction why the shipment was delayed, he'd demand blood if he didn't have the waylaid packages first thing in the morning. "So I figured we could start at ten."

"We want to get it done this weekend, right? Why wouldn't we start at eight? Or seven, with prep. We're already looking at living there all weekend. Might as well pick up those spare hours at the end of Sunday," Marley said.

He hated the idea of making her give up her weekend for work, but didn't mind spending some uninterrupted time enjoying her company. "Seven it is. I'll bring the coffee."

"You do know how to treat a girl." She leaned on the desk, arms crossed, enhancing the seductive curve of her breasts.

She had no idea. He'd jump at the chance to show her exactly how he wanted to treat her.

Marley watched Eli sketch a rough outline of the new building floor plan. When he'd come out of his office, he'd looked like a spring ready to snap from the tension. He was slowly relaxing. His arms were loosening up, and his movement becoming more fluid, which was nice. With short, platinum hair, striking blue eyes, and a slender form that looked as if it could wind its way through anything, she always enjoyed watching him work. He was even more attractive, when he was in his zone. The way he sank into the explanation, and passion drove his every movement.

When she'd started the job, she'd felt guilty about staring. After all, mixing business with pleasure had cost her last job—hell, almost her entire career, and it hadn't even been *her* pleasure. When she'd interviewed with Eli a couple of years ago, she'd been broke, frustrated, and at her breaking point. Her former boss made sure she didn't get any good references, so she'd started telling potential employers they couldn't contact her last manager. That had just made things worse.

When Eli had asked why someone with her qualifications was looking for work after so long, she'd told him the truth, unfiltered. Flat out. She'd been fired for refusing her manager's advances, and if that was going to be a problem, they could cut the review short and not waste the next hour of their lives. He'd hired her on the spot.

Since then, she'd recognized the fact that there was no harm in appreciating how good he looked. About six inches taller than her meant he was the perfect height. His button down shirts didn't hide his defined arms, and heaven knew she fantasized about him binding her arms back with his tie. Besides, they hung out on weekends a lot—as friends of course—and he was even sexier in a T-shirt and a pair of jeans.

On top of all that, he was smart. She didn't have an issue with the occasional intensely graphic dream, as long as that was all it was. She'd do the same if he were a random stranger on the street.

"And no, I promise this isn't the Death Star." His casual joke dragged her back to the work-half of the conversation. With some guys, she'd think it was self-effacing. With him, she knew to step back, and look for the hidden humor instead.

"Are you sure?" The retort slid from her tongue with little thought. "Because I'm thinking, if we fired at that exhaust port there"—she nodded toward a random spot on the rough map—"we could blow up the whole ship. No more wiring to do. Problem solved."

His deep rumble of a laugh sank into her skin, tempting her. "If we're going that route," he said, "we'll just have the rebels take out the entire thing for us, and spend our weekend marathoning some real movies instead."

"I'm in. Unless you have a hot date." Sometimes she wondered why he didn't date more. Why a guy like him was still single. For the most part, though, she took it for granted that he could frequently make room outside of work for the way their bouts of geekiness played so well off each other.

He shrugged and made random marks on the white board, instead of looking at her. "Last woman someone tried to set me up with had the ability to wipe out an entire city block with the wave of her hand, and no idea who Admiral Ackbar is."

She laughed at the exaggeration of what he called a cursed love life, appreciative he'd built on the Death Star joke. "You poor thing. Don't worry. Somewhere out there is a woman who gets your references. You'll find her."

He met her gaze for the briefest moment, before looking away. "I hope not."

Super weird. She shook off the questions his comment raised, and hopped to her feet. The joking was fun, but she had to get things back on track. As much because of time constraints, as because she needed a distraction from the part of her wishing they had plans together tonight, that might take them into tomorrow.

She grabbed the dry-erase marker from him. As her fingers brushed his, she tried not to linger on the warmth that raced between them. It didn't matter how many times she joked about his only having the one marker, he'd never gotten more, which made her wonder if he appreciated the excuse to share as much as she did. His heat brushed her bare arm, as she sketched in a series of outlet spots. She nudged her rambling thoughts back, and stepped away again.

"If we drop near these spots, it should keep the signals strong, and minimize the boosters we'll need."

He cocked his head, studying it for a moment. "And this is why I'm glad I hired you. Let's do it."

They spent the next several hours tossing ideas back and forth, peppered with jokes and obvious as well as vague references. Marley's cheeks ached from laughing.

Eli's phone vibrated on his desk, as it had so many times while they talked, and he glanced at it. His mood flipped from happy to sour in an instant. "Fucking asshole." His quiet curse filled the room.

"What's wrong?" Her question was sincere. She didn't want to see him upset.

"Nothing." He sank into his chair, and raked his fingers through his hair. "Just fucking asshole is all. I should let you get home. Let you enjoy your night, before you surrender your freedom."

She took note of the time. *How did it get to be so late?* The light banter with Eli, the way they joked and slid from one topic to the next, was just so easy.

She should at least try to remember why it was a bad idea to have a crush on her boss. She summoned a pleasant expression, and stood. "I *should* probably get home. See you tomorrow?"

"Bright and early." Anticipation mingled with his teasing.

Or maybe she just wished that was what she heard. Not that she needed to be hoping their attraction went both ways. The last thing she wanted was to lose another job over a little flirting. Except unlike last time, she'd be the one to blame.

CHAPTER TWO

Eli wasn't surprised to see Marley's car already in the parking lot of the new building. He was five minutes early, and she'd still beaten him. He balanced the coffee cups on top of each other, while he flipped through his key-ring for the right key. Normally he'd nod in the right direction, and command the keys to float over and take care of the rest. But he didn't know who was watching. At least the electronic locks would be in by mid-week. Unless his brother decided to play another *prank*.

The reminder of the text from Loki yesterday sent a rush of irritation through him. The cock-up had actually visited a warehouse halfway across the country, just to distract the person shipping Eli's cable long enough to cause another day's delay.

Eli paused inside the front entrance, and inhaled deeply. The entire place had the lingering scent of sawdust and paint, and it was nice, just this once, to smell it overlaid with the familiar zing he associated with Marley.

"Hello?" His greeting echoed through the empty halls.

"Conference room." There was way too much cheer in her voice, given the hour. Unless she'd found that hot hookup the night before after all.

He swallowed the surge of envy, and followed her voice. When he rounded the corner at the end of the hall, he paused in the doorway. She was sitting on the row of cabinets against the back wall, legs swinging, arms on the counter top, every inch of her gorgeous body extended and accentuated. Even with a hoodie hiding some of her curves, it was a struggle for him to force his gaze to her face. The cold from outside still dotted her cheeks with pink, and her lips curved into a smile when she saw him.

"Morning, sleepyhead." Her cheer was contagious. A part of his mind asked what it would take for him to bring a bigger smile to her face. Pulling off her sweatshirt. Sliding his hands up her stomach. Stroking and caressing every inch of her, until she wore a giant grin the rest of the day, and then some.

Which he wasn't going to do. He banished the thoughts, crossed the room, and handed her drink over.

A soft sigh escaped her parted lips, when their fingers met. "Your hands are warm."

His hands were always warm. A side effect of being the son of Fárbauti. His father was named after the lightning that struck dry brush and caused forest fires, and while Eli hadn't inherited all of his family's gifts, he still had that heat flowing through him. Not that he was going to tell her that. "Or yours are cold."

He covered her hands, sandwiching them between his palms and her coffee cup. A new type of heat seared through him at the contact. It was accompanied by the desire to pin her to the counter, and let his fingers roam over every inch of her until they were both hot and spent.

He tried to be subtle about pulling away, needing to get some space between them, before his imagination drove out of control. "I'll put the hubs in the server room." Strain tinged his voice. With any luck, she hadn't noticed.

"All right." Creases lined her forehead, and he saw the corners of her mouth tug down, before she hid her lips behind her coffee cup.

It didn't take as long as he'd hoped to relocate the boxes, but he still couldn't rein in his rambling thoughts. He couldn't shake the questions about whether or not she'd actually gone out the night before. Normally he didn't care whom his employees dated, or how they spent their free time. Marley was different. She occupied his thoughts when she shouldn't.

There were more important things in the universe than the fleeting nature of lust. Except in his case. Where any feeling that became more—love for instance—had the potential to kill that one woman…

A sickening creak filled the room, and he winced at the now crushed rack component in his hands. He had to have squeezed too hard while he was lost in his thoughts. Fortunately, they had extras.

"Tell me that arrived broken." Concern tinged Marley's joke. "There's no way you just crushed a solid steel shelf component, right?"

Shit. He hadn't meant for her to see that. Could he just laugh it off? He set the metal cage aside, and turned to face her. "I didn't like the way it was looking at me."

Her uncertain laugh filled the room, and summoned more of his regret and frustration. "Seriously, are you all right? I mean, I don't know, you seem…off this morning." She leaned against the door frame, gaze raking his face, and concern clouding her expression.

"Everything's fine." It took more willpower than it should've to force his tone to stay even. "We need to get to work."

She didn't step aside. "Soon. First tell me what's up today? Don't give me this 'nothing' bullshit. Is this more serious than you're telling me? Shit, they're not going fire us, if we don't get this done. Are they?"

No. He knew for certain no one was letting him go. Not that he wanted to explain the ins and outs of that to her. He could just picture the conversation now. *No, we're not getting fired, because my father is an ancient god, who didn't know what to do with his life besides start a property and casualty underwriting company, and no one else in the family knows how to make the computers sing the way I do.*

Then she'd want to know why he was making shit up instead of giving her straight answers. No, he wasn't having that conversation. "No one's getting fired."

She uncrossed her arms, and some of the tension drained from her face. "So what is it?"

Nothing he was comfortable telling her. And yet, the words slipped out before he could think them through. "Not that it's any of my business—"

"Let me stop you right there." She held up a hand, palm toward him. "If you start a sentence that way, you know it means you shouldn't even be thinking whatever you're about to say, right?"

He probably knew it better than she could imagine. "Exactly." He brushed past her, a surge of want flowing through him when his shoulder met hers.

She grabbed his sleeve. "But it also means I'm not letting you walk away without finishing your statement."

Damn it. Maybe if he got this off his chest, he could admit to himself he was being jealous and irrational, and then they could get back to work. "There's no inappropriate thought. I promise. You seem like you had fun last night."

"I guess you could call it that." She relaxed further, teasing sliding into her response. "And what's all this 'it's none of my business,' crap? First, since when do we pull punches with each other?"

His thoughts ground and clicked on her words, as he searched for hidden meaning but didn't dare find any. "I don't—"

"I'm not finished. Second, I went out to try and unwind, some painfully-persistent guy hit on me with some of the cheesiest lines ever, and I'd rather put it behind me."

Relief flowed through him, tempered by his need to keep his reactions under control. "I'm sorry it wasn't a great experience."

She tightened her grip on his arm. "I'm not."

He shouldn't ask, but lust-driven possessiveness pushed the question out anyway. "What happened?"

"Nothing specific. Nothing horrible. I just would've rather..." A flush spread over her cheeks and she ducked her head. "Nothing. You're right. We should get on this whole work thing."

Marley had almost verbally slipped in the server room. She was still trying to wrap her brain around the fact she'd seen Eli crush a quarter-inch thick piece of metal like it was paper. There had to have been a week point in the rack, but the sight still had her distracted.

On top of that, after her abysmal encounter at the bar the night before, the coffee, and the spark she swore was tangible flowing between her and Eli that morning, she'd almost confessed she would have rather have spent the evening with him than cruising any bar. But she wasn't crossing that line. Toeing it, maybe. She wouldn't deny that. Smudging it? On occasion. Jumping completely over it? Not today. No, wait. Not ever. Right. She had to remember that.

Fortunately, once they started working, things went back to normal. She crimped connectors on the cables he measured out. With no eye contact, it was easier to pretend she wasn't attracted to him, and just talk.

"At least tell me Mister Last-night didn't do what the previous guy did." His teasing laugh fell short, and he snapped his mouth shut when her head shot up.

Please don't let him be talking about... "Which last guy?"

He glanced in her direction before turning back to his cable. "The one who wanted pictures."

She never should've given him so much detail after that date. She'd done it because she liked the idea of him making a similar request, and had been trying to judge his reaction, but that didn't mean it was a good idea. "It wasn't like that."

He put down what he was doing, and gave her his full attention. "Is something wrong?"

"No." She turned back to the cable, crimping as furiously as possible while still being accurate. She wouldn't look at him from her spot on the counter, pretending it wasn't a big deal.

Eli extracted himself from the spindle and snakes of wires, and crossed the room. He took the crimpers from her hand, and set all of her work aside too. "Except you just crimped an RJ45 onto that cable instead of an RJ12. What's up?"

Oops. She never made mistakes like putting a network connector on a phone cable. Her pulse raced through her veins at his light touch, making it hard to think. She needed to look away, but his gaze held her captive. If she'd been drawing a blank before, it was nothing compared to now.

He'd put the thought in her head. The reminder one of her dates had asked for pictures when he'd dropped her off. Told her if she wasn't going home with him, she at least owed him a topless shot to keep him warm that night. And part of her had never shaken the fantasy of doing that for Eli.

The temptation of turning him on, without ever touching him. "You're telling me you can't guess?"

The corner of his mouth pulled into a lazy smile. "I'm telling you I don't want to guess."

She couldn't ignore the mental images of what it would feel like if he leaned in and kissed her. "I just... It's not as though I had a problem with the request from Mister Send-me-pictures. Just with the requester."

There, that hadn't been so bad. They could gloss over it, laugh about it, and go back to work. Except she'd rather they took a break and got down to other things instead.

"Really?" His thumb stroked the inside of her wrist. Did he know he was doing that? She sure as hell did. The feather-light sensation spilled through her, desire growing between her legs. He stepped closer. "Who would it take, then? Just out of curiosity."

They needed to get this project done. To step away from this line before it was too late. Who was she kidding? It had been too late months ago. At least for her. "Well, I'd have to like the guy first. Actually being attracted to him helps." Would Eli have any idea she was talking about him? What the hell was wrong with her? And why couldn't she stop?

His voice dropped an octave. "And I would assume you can't dive straight into things. You'd want seduction. Teasing. The right words to set the mood..."

Even as she told herself to back away now, images raced through her thoughts, of stripping in front of the camera, one piece of clothing at a time, knowing Eli was her audience. A hands-off, private show where she'd caress herself, pinch her nipples, slide her fingers between her legs, and get off on the idea that she could turn him on that way.

The vivid image wouldn't leave. Her sex whimpered for attention, and her breasts ached to press into his palms.

CHAPTER THREE

Eli had two choices. Back away—and there was no way he could hide how hard he was if he did—or go with the flow until Marley told him to stop. As long as he remembered this was only a physical response, nothing more than lust, and let her call the shots, it would be fine.

His cock strained against his jeans when she licked her lips. Well, not completely fine. He needed to do something about his body's response, even if he was ignoring his reservations. Screwing her was a bad idea for more reasons than he could list. But things would be mostly fine.

He stepped closer, holding her gaze. "In other words, in order for you to text a guy sexy pictures, you'd want a genuine lead in. For example, 'if I were there right now, I'd slide up behind you, and trace the back of your neck with my lips.'"

A tiny mewl, so soft he wasn't sure he heard it, tore from her throat. "That's a good start." Her voice was low and husky.

He raked his gaze over her, pausing on her chest before looking her in the eye again. "Say this unnamed guy followed up with more. For instance, 'next I'd slide my hands up your stomach...'"

Her breathing sped up, but she didn't pull her hands out of his grip. "From the right guy, especially if I was imagining him there, that would do something for me."

His dick throbbed at the thought of being on the receiving end of those pictures. Or better, pushing between her legs and making the hypothetical conversation a reality. Which sounded like the most incredible idea ever, but he was pretty sure it was because all the blood had rushed from his head. He needed to decide now. Could he risk this with her? Could he keep her on staff, keep her friendship, keep her alive...if he let things get physical?

Her frown contradicted the fact her chest was still heaving. She pulled her hands from his, and disappointment welled inside him. She scooted sideways on the counter, and hopped to her feet, not making any more contact between them.

He forced his voice to remain steady. "So really, all you're asking for is a gentleman who isn't afraid to pin you down in the bedroom, but still has more consideration for those around him than for himself."

"Exactly." The word was flat, and she wouldn't look at him. The flush on her lips and the pink in her cheeks proved she was as turned on as he was. All he had to do was tug her back into the conversation. Push things a little further.

The decision over whether to nudge things further or back away now warred in his skull, until he shook his head. "Too bad for Mister Last-night he wasn't that guy."

"Yeah. Too bad."

He turned away, and took a deep breath to clear his head. It didn't help. He yanked the last of his restraint up past arousal and desire, and forced his voice to stay steady. "If you have enough of those crimped, we should drop them before we make more, or we'll get a big tangled mess."

"Sure. Good idea."

He couldn't ignore how the disappointment and confusion in her tone matched his thoughts. He'd heard it enough times, relating to failed projects, that it tore away another chunk of his resolve. This was the right way to go, though. They didn't need to do something she'd regret. He'd be worried about the other consequences, those related to his curse, but he knew better than to call lust anything other than what it was.

He still couldn't look at her. It would take at least a couple of minutes to subdue his cock's raging want. He nodded toward the cubes they had agreed to start wiring in. "I'll drag everything over."

He knew the busy work he was doing, fiddling with nothing in particular, wasn't fooling her. What had he been thinking? Just a couple minutes of harmless flirting, and he'd almost blown a fantastic working relationship. Behind him, he heard the shuffle of her doing what he'd asked, but silence filled the remaining space between them. This was going to be awkward, unless he brought it under control now.

"Marley, listen." He turned to face her. "I didn't—"

"Don't." The single word was clipped. "Whatever that was, whatever it is you're thinking, whatever you're about to say, don't make it worse. It's done. It's over. It was what it was. And now this is a different time and place."

"I didn't—"

"Please?" She finally met his gaze.

The desperation in her request devoured him. He didn't want to leave things unresolved, but since he wasn't sure what to say anyway, and he didn't want to refuse her request... "Done."

"Thank you." Her sad smile left a gaping wound in his chest. Seconds later, her emotion vanished behind a mask of business. "I'm going to run line for the first block of cubes. Feed me the right cables?"

The builders had wired the walls, but it was up to Marley and him to do the external work. Along each section of wall in the office, there was a single panel with multiple outlets. A latch allowed them to open it up and add more if they needed, as well as get to any wires to troubleshoot.

She sat on the ground, legs crossed, and held out her hand. He passed her a cable, cut the right length to run under and reach the first cubicle in that block.

He knew the conversation was over. She wasn't going to mention it again, and probably preferred to forget it had happened. But he couldn't stop it from replaying in his mind, the fantasy ending in a different way each time, but always with clothes coming off. She fed the cable through the bottom section of cubicle, and pushed it until it hit its next exit point—a built-in spot in the metal trim, for electrical and network wires.

Even now, quiet, composed, engrossed in her work, she was gorgeous. Each movement enhanced the way her waist slid into grabbable hips, and her tendency toward biting her lip when she was focused threatened to make him hard again.

Her fingers brushed the electrical outline on the cube trim, and a sickening crack filled the room. She fell back, head slamming against the floor, and the lights blinked out.

"Marley?" Panic crept into his voice, as she lay there. Unmoving.

Shit. He dropped to his knees, ignoring the jolt that reverberated through him, and pressed his fingers to her throat. No pulse. "Marley." He scooted closer, fear gripping his insides.

Her chest wasn't moving. He leaned his head down, ear next to her face. She wasn't breathing. Her heart wasn't beating. Damn it. Had he done this? Was it the curse?

No. He took a deep breath, and forced the irrational thoughts aside. It had been seconds at best. And it wasn't his fault. It wasn't as if he'd fallen for her. Faulty wiring had caused this— and for some odd reason the breakers hadn't flipped until it was too late—and he needed to save her now.

He cradled the back of her neck in both hands, and rested his thumbs in the hollow of her throat, directly below her jaw where her pulse should be. He turned his attention inward. There was the spark he needed. Not too much. Nothing to jolt her. Just enough to massage her system back. It wasn't all science. He had just enough power in him to draw her soul back from the edge of death, on top of kick-starting her heart.

His heart rested in his throat. Even though he knew bringing her back should be easy, fear stole his confidence. A chill swept his entire body. Ancestors, don't let her be gone. His chest clenched, as the idea that he might not be able to revive her took shape in his mind.

He had to, though. He closed his eyes, and let tiny pulses of electricity flow from him to her. Seconds ticked away, and...nothing. Frustration crept in. He could heal any injury she'd sustained, and keep her from suffering brain damage.

Unless she didn't want to come back. No. Marley was too full of life for something so fatalistic.

She still wasn't responding. Anger surged. She couldn't be dead. Please. Ancestors help me. He'd never forgive himself or the fates, if she didn't wake up.

Marley gasped for breath, and her eyes flew open. She struggled to drag in more oxygen. Why the hell didn't she feel like she couldn't breathe? She drew in deep swallows of air. Something pounded inside her skull, hammering and splintering already fractured thoughts.

"Marley!" Eli's frantic voice sliced through her confusion. Gentle palms rested against her cheeks, drawing her further out of her own head. "Breathe. Slowly. Just relax."

She couldn't. Nothing made sense. What had she been doing? Why was there a giant, gaping black hole in her memory? Snippets rushed back to her, snapping into place.

Eli pressed close. How desperately she wanted to toss decency to the wind, and just let him have his way with her. Oh, God. Had they...? Had they what? Why couldn't she remember?

"Look at me. You need to calm down." Eli moved her head, forcing her gaze onto his face. "Breathe in, just once."

She focused on his voice. His gorgeous blue eyes. Because it was easier than falling into the pit in her head. She did as he said.

The corner of his mouth tugged up. The cobwebs cleared some more, but not enough. It felt like a million ants were dancing under her skin.

"Now let it out slowly."

She obeyed again, repeating the action several times, until she could form words. "What happened?"

He chuckled, and offered her a hand. Why had she been lying down? As she sat, she did a quick check. She was fully clothed. Her head hurt like hell. And it was dark in the room. "And why are the lights off?"

He shifted from his kneeling position to sit on his ass, across from her. "Something wasn't grounded. You were electrocuted. It..." He closed his eyes and swallowed. "It knocked you out. Blew a fuse. I'm just glad it wasn't worse."

She rubbed her arms through her sweater. Something about his words made ice run through her veins. She should go to the emergency room, but that would mean admitting something severe had just happened. The idea made her as uneasy as the missing last few minutes in her memory. A tiny nag tickled the back of her thoughts. Electrocuted, blank memory. Was it even more serious than Eli was saying? But he wouldn't hide something like that from her. Right?

She tried to stand, and her equilibrium made the room tilt and spin in protest. She sank back to her knees, and pressed a palm to her forehead.

"We need to take you to the hospital." He rested a palm against her cheek. "You're done working for the day."

His concern warmed her as much as his touch did. But her headache was already evaporating. It was almost as if his fingers were sapping away the pain. Not that such a thing was possible. It would be as ridiculous as wondering if he'd just done something like bring her back to life.

Sure, there was enough electricity running through those wires to stop a heart—that was safety one-oh-one when working with live wires. But it wasn't like Eli, or anyone, had the power to bring people back from the dead. She'd just gotten a little dizzy. "I'll be fine. We have too much to get done."

"Marley, no. Rest here for a couple more minutes, and then when you feel well enough, we're going to the hospital."

"No." She resisted the urge to lean into his touch. The longer his hand lingered, the more her pain evaporated. She almost felt back to normal. "I'm not leaving this half-finished mess."

"I'll take care of it." His thumb trailed along her cheekbone, stroking softly.

His concern warmed her further. Pride surged inside. She wasn't going to let a little tiny shock keep her down. Besides, she felt a lot better. He was overreacting; she just needed to sit for a minute. "I'm fine." She kept her voice firm. "And I'm not going anywhere."

He opened his mouth, and she held up her index finger. "No," she said. "I know you're the boss, but this is my project, and I intend to see it through."

"I don't—"

She narrowed her eyes.

He shook his head, still caressing her cheek. "All right. But the moment you wobble again, the workday is over."

She stood slowly, hoping she wouldn't falter, and even more concerned he'd decide she couldn't handle work after all. The room wasn't spinning anymore. Good. "But I will let you leave the circuits off until we're finished. We can get LED lanterns or something in here, right?"

CHAPTER FOUR

Marley scooted on the carpet, until her back connected with the wall. Every inch of her ached from bending, crawling, and feeding cable through small tubes for the last however-many hours. It was dark outside, and a couple of LED lanterns around them provided the only light in the building. The rush she'd felt after her post-electrocution dizziness passed had evaporated hours ago. But at least Eli finally stopped hovering and treating her as if she were made of porcelain.

While she'd really enjoyed the attention, she knew she shouldn't have.

He sat across from her, the lamplight casting his features in shadows, making the scruff of his unshaven face look even more rugged. Damn it, why did he have to be handsome and considerate? Why couldn't he just be an asshole boss like most of them?

The reminder that he was her supervisor snapped her back to reality. "We're more than half done. That bodes well for our schedule."

He glanced at his phone before dropping it back into his pocket. "And it's not even ten. Wow. I owe you dinner. And then we'll get back to it?"

She nodded. They'd made headway, but not nearly enough that they'd be done before tomorrow, if they called it a night. "Anything but pizza."

"You love pizza."

Just the word turned her stomach. "Yeah, but last night...cold pizza, warm beer, and a live band that was louder than they were talented—I'd just rather walk away from that memory for now."

"All that on top of the asshole. No wonder your night was a bust." He stood and offered her a hand up. "Note to self and all that."

At least if she was blushing, the dim light would hide it. She tried to be subtle about pulling away, before they could do an encore of the awkward moment from that morning. She might not be able to say no this time. "I want to get the west section prepped while I'm still thinking about it, and then we can break."

His gaze raked over her, lingering on her face for a moment. "All right. Tell you what. I'll order dinner and finish up in the executive office, and we should be done about the time the delivery guy arrives."

"Who are you going to get to deliver out here so late?"

He winked. "I know people. Trust me."

They hashed out a few more details, and he walked away to finish his tasks. The silence sank in around her for the first time that day, and gave her thoughts a chance to ramble. Combined with exhaustion, her brain did something she never let it do. It wandered into thoughts of what it would be like to spend time with Eli outside of work. Not as friends, but more along the lines of how different the night before would have been if he'd been her date.

She let her mind trip lazily over the delicious thought, while she worked. It was easier to lose herself, when she didn't have to worry about her attraction to him being written all over her face. With no one to see her gaze drifting off to nowhere, it didn't matter.

She would've invited him in at the end of the night. There was no question there. Offered him a drink. Maybe slid up next to him on the couch. Before today, she'd wondered if he'd be the one to make a move, but after the incident on the counter, there was no doubt he'd take charge if the situation was different.

"You okay?" His concerned voice broke into her rambling thoughts. She scrambled to her feet, and whirled to face him, pulse kicking up another notch. "I've been calling you."

She stashed the images in a mental side-drawer, and gave him what she hoped was a neutral smile. "I'm fine. Just engrossed."

"I see that." Was that awe? "You did all this in twenty minutes?"

She looked around the room, surprised herself. She'd been so lost in thought, she hadn't realized she'd finished prepping the quadrant, and then some. "I guess."

He stepped aside, and gestured toward the other end of the building. "Food's here."

She fell into step beside him. The familiar scents of lemongrass pork and curry wafted over her, and her stomach growled in response. He'd ordered from one of her favorite places. "I didn't know they delivered."

He shrugged. "The owner owed me a favor."

They reached the office that would be the CEO's after the move, and she paused in the doorway, any response evaporating. He'd lined the walls with a handful of flashlights—she had no idea where he'd gotten the extras—all pointing straight up like electric candles. A blanket sat in the middle of the room, with a neat arrangement of takeout and two place-settings. A wine bottle even sat in the middle, adding an elegant feel despite the paper cups.

Had he brought all that with him? Bribed the take out boy to pick it up? She didn't care. She wouldn't be able to drink more than a cup, since they still had work to do, but the gesture still warmed her.

"I figured we might as well pick the nicest room in the building for dinner since there's no furniture anywhere, including the kitchen. Sitting on the floor in here should be a lot more comfortable than the cold tile in there." He waved a hand, and it seemed to grow brighter in the room, as if all the lights cranked up a notch. "Take a seat." He rested a hand at the small of her back, and nudged her forward.

She burned the memory of his touch into her thoughts, along with the entire setup. It was an incredible feeling, and a lot better than focusing on whether he'd really just made the flashlights intensify. She desperately needed to find a guy who got her on this level, and wasn't her boss.

Eli leaned against the wall, watching Marley talk. They'd cleaned up dinner at least an hour ago, and he knew they needed to get back to work, but he couldn't bring himself to interrupt. They both sat on the blanket, less than a foot between them, and she was as animated as he'd ever seen her. Arms moving and eyes bright, even in the dim light.

"No. I'm serious." Her smile was gorgeous and genuine. "My grandfather would tell these bedtime stories, every time he visited. Bible stories. But only the ones with dismemberment or beheading. Who needs Grimm, when you've got gentiles and worshippers alike getting their heads chopped off?"

He'd always been a fan of the brothers Grimm. Their version of the stories was more accurate than anyone else's up to that point in history, and no one had told the tales quite the same since. Still, she had a point. "I can't argue with that. It definitely sounds like a way to scare someone straight."

She laughed—that was an amazing sound. "It didn't work on me, but I'm odd."

"In the best way possible." He couldn't tear his gaze from her face.

She met his eyes, and pink flooded her cheeks. She ducked her head. Her voice dropped in volume, but her enthusiasm didn't vanish. "What kind of stories did you grow up on?"

The single question brought his entire universe crashing back into focus. There'd been hundreds of tales over the centuries. He'd watched people write down the original history, and then witnessed as it warped and mutated over time, as each story was retold, and the occasional new one was created.

But one stood out over all the others. A reminder of why it didn't matter how much he adored Marley. Even if she weren't off limits for professional reasons, there could never be anything more than a physical relationship between them. "There was one..."

She looked up again, eyes soft and curious. She scooted closer on the blanket. "Tell me?"

He shouldn't. He should put everything away now. They had a deadline to meet. They had... Every excuse evaporated from his thoughts, when she leaned forward, arms resting on her crossed legs and attention focused intently on him.

Maybe repeating the curse would help him get his thoughts back in order. "All right," he said. "But there's no beheading, or other body parts being cut off." At least he hoped not. The sudden thought terrified him, and he squashed it. He'd never forgive himself.

"I'm sure I'll live."

He hoped so. He dredged up the thousands of years' old memories. "My grandmother used to tell me this when I was very young. We'd sit around the fire every year at holidays, and beg her to relate the story."

"You and Loki?"

"And our other brother Helblindi."

"I didn't know you had a third brother."

Most people didn't. Hell, most people didn't know Loki had any brothers at all. They thought Eli's brother was the son of Odin.

Stepbrother to Thor. As if. Sometimes Eli hated that no one knew his history, but at least he hadn't been written into comic books and films with an entirely different bloodline.

"Blake manages affairs overseas. Maybe someday you'll meet him. Anyway." Eli breathed deeply, and let his memories drift back. "She'd always start off by reminding us we were the stuff of legends. That brothers born in threes—it never happened in our family. The oldest was always meant to take the reins of the household, and the youngest to explore the world. But when there was a middle brother, balance was disrupted."

Her brow furrowed. "That's a little harsh."

He'd never thought of it that way. "I guess. I'm the youngest, so I didn't mind." At least, he'd never minded until just a couple of years ago, when a frustrated brunette sat across from him in a job interview and told him outright that she'd be one of the best employees he ever had, but there was some shit she wouldn't tolerate.

"It's just a fairy tale anyway, right?" She almost sounded like she was trying to convince herself.

It was so much more than that, but he didn't correct her. "There was a poem she'd recite. I can't remember all the words, but she'd chant it in front of the fire, the words mingling with flame. Sometimes I swore, if I stared at the flames long enough, I could see them becoming real. The words." He shook his head to clear away the vivid memory. He hated to lie to her. He remembered each verse as if it were in front of him. But speaking the words always felt like giving them power. At least speaking all of them. There was one verse she had to hear.

She stared at him, mouth barely open, eyes wide. "What was the general idea then?"

He swallowed. "No one would be suited to take over family affairs, unless he proved himself. Instead of assuming his birthright, the first brother would hop from wife to lover to wife, traveling the world, drifting for ages, until he finally found the woman who could calm his heart."

"Helblindi." She repeated the name flawlessly, even though she'd only just heard it.

He nodded. "The second brother would know fame. Celebrity like none of us had ever imagined. And it would change him into something none of us recognized."

She looked like she wanted to speak, but she snapped her mouth shut again. Silence hung between them, until she finally asked, "And what about the youngest?"

The words flowed to his lips without thought. After centuries of pondering them, he knew them better than his own name. "As you are, for all of time, to taste neither love nor death. When you find the one worth more than life, she'll draw her last mortal breath."

"Wow." Her single word was shaky. "Harsh. But it's just a fairy tale, right? Meant to scare you as a kid, by being vague and threatening?"

He forced something genuine into his smile. "Sure. Absolutely."

She caught her bottom lip between her teeth. "Still, it's not a very nice thing to tell a kid."

Or to burden an immortal soul with. "It is what it is."

He wished to everything ever it wasn't. Now more than ever, he wished it wasn't real. But the scare that morning... The rest of the curse was true. And he wasn't willing to take that chance with her. He didn't dare fall for Marley and risk her life.

CHAPTER FIVE

Cold flushed Marley's cheeks, and jarred her back toward consciousness. She and Eli had worked for a few more hours the night before, including testing every last connection in the executive offices twice. When exhaustion had become impossible to ignore, they agreed to nap for a couple of hours. But she was certain they'd fallen asleep several feet apart.

The familiar scents of new paint and recently unwrapped everything filled her head, but she wasn't ready to open her eyes yet. Every moment of the night before was seared into her thoughts. And even though it was cold in the building—no heat plus an overnight snowstorm meant it was probably almost freezing—her back and arms, and everywhere Eli touched was warm.

She wasn't sure when she'd curled up against him, or who had pulled the blanket from dinner over them, but she wasn't complaining. She let sleepiness have control, and stretched back against him with a sigh. His arm snaked tighter over her hips, fingers brushing the bare skin above her jeans, where her hoodie had tugged up during the night.

Floating in that wonderful haze between wakefulness and sleep, every touch lit her thoughts on fire as much as it warmed her skin. He moaned and pulled her closer. This was incredible. His palm glided up to her stomach, and his warm breath caressed the back of her neck. Was he awake, or was this all just a reaction for him?

His forehead rested against the back of her skull. "You're freezing." His soft words barely reached her ears. "I know a cure for that."

The innuendo sent need and a wash of images surging through her—letting him warm her up. His skin pressed against hers. Those skilled hands searching out her buttons.

Her every nerve ending pleaded for more. She pressed tighter against him, and the hard length digging into her butt. "I'm listening." She wouldn't open her eyes. Wouldn't destroy this moment by letting reality seep in completely.

Desire surged between her legs, and her head swam with images of their clothes coming off, his mouth roaming her body, and his thick cock—currently pressed against the small of her back and tempting her—as it dove inside her.

His hand brushed the bottom of her breast, and she arched her back with a moan. When he glided higher and caressed her nipples through the fabric of her bra, the dampness in her panties grew. Her hips rocked, her ass grinding against his erection.

Something whispered at the back of her mind. A reminder that she shouldn't do this. Fuck it. She wanted him, and she knew the attraction went both ways. She was tired of hiding behind the past. Eli wouldn't threaten her job, and she needed to stop using her fear as an excuse. Even if there was nothing between them beyond the physical, she was going to enjoy every minute of it.

She reached a hand behind her, seeking him out by touch alone. His groan echoed through every inch of her, and sent pleasant chills over her skin when she grasped his cock and stroked through his jeans.

"Stop." His arm fell away, and seconds later cool air flooded in around her, chilling everything he no longer touched.

"What?" Confusion flooded her, and she rolled into a sitting position so she could look him in the eye. "Did I misunderstand?" Keeping her tone clinical and cool was the only way she could keep the hurt from leaking into her voice.

"No." He turned away. "I shouldn't have done that, though. I'm sorry."

What did that mean? "So we were both good with it, and nothing's wrong, but it's not right?" Uncertainty and doubt twisted her gut in on itself. It took every ounce of her control to keep her tone steady. Even then, she wasn't sure she managed.

"You should get home." He folded the blanket. "I can finish up here."

The ache of rejection grew in her chest. None of this made sense. "No." She stood in front of him, forcing him to look at her. "We don't operate this way. Talk to me."

His gaze bored into hers. "We do this time. The conversation is over. I've got this. Go home."

His cold command destroyed the wall of composure she was building around herself. She narrowed her eyes, and tried to obliterate any feelings using anger. "You're the boss."

Eli wanted nothing more than to call out, apologize, and spend the rest of the day with Marley. The only thing that kept him from stopping her, from pinning her to the wall and stripping her down, and doing everything to her they both wanted, was his fear of what it would cost her.

Seeing her hurt, betrayed expression was better than seeing her dead.

He tried to lose himself in his work. The hours ticked away, as he finished his wiring and cleaned up the traces of their presence in the building. But he never managed to banish the images of Marley from his thoughts.

The entire drive home, fantasy taunted him. Of christening one of those executive offices. Stripping her clothes off a piece at a time. Kissing along her bare breasts. Hearing her gasp, as he tasted her nipples. Tasting every inch of her skin. Sliding his cock inside her. Watching her ride him. Drinking every gorgeous curve, and making her moan until she was spent from pleasure.

He pulled up in front of his house, unable to shake the images. It was true there was nothing he wanted more... Except for her to live.

What he needed was a cold shower, and something to distract him.

He stepped through the front door, and a growl slipped out before he could stop it.

"Late night?" Loki lounged on the living room couch, ankle crossed over the other knee, and arms stretched across the back.

Eli tossed his keys on the stand by the entrance way. He was rarely in the mood for his brother anyway, but knowing he'd been responsible for the delayed cable... For Marley losing her weekend. For— "Get out."

Loki didn't move. "How's your top worker? A little extra tingly after yesterday?"

A denial rushed to Eli's lips, and he cut it off. He rolled the words over in his head, looking for the angle. It was easy enough to assume Loki thought they'd slept together, but denying it meant admitting he'd at least had the thought. Not that he could deny it at this point, but he was going to try. "I don't know what you're talking about."

"Charged. Lit up. Electric?"

Rage roared through Eli. He should've known the accident yesterday morning was more than just shitty wiring. He crossed the room in a few short steps, grabbed Loki by the front of his shirt, and hauled him to his feet. "You asshole. Stay the fuck away from her."

Loki laughed, and held up his hands. "I don't know what you're talking about."

But he did. Eli knew it. An entire family of people who held the gift of elements—specifically electricity. It wouldn't have taken anything for Loki to shock Marley. It would've been a passing thought. Eli had no idea about the why, but the verbal taunting was too much to ignore. Except it didn't make sense. "Why Marley? I thought you liked her."

"She's fine, I guess. It's you I don't like. This will make you miserable. She's just a casualty."

Right. The drawback of having a brother who was not only immortal, but had zero regard for human life. Every couple of decades, Eli managed to forget about that. Fury poured through him. "Don't go near her, or her environment, again."

Loki wrenched out of his grip, straightened his clothes, and stared back, eyes cold. "Or what?"

"Or I'll find a way to make your eternity a living hell." Energy crackled over Eli's skin. Sparking and flickering. His clothes might not survive. He didn't care. He wasn't going to rein the fury in.

Loki patted him on the shoulder, and stepped around him. "Like yours is? At least I know you've got practice."

Eli snarled. Keep this verbal or make it physical?

"I'll make you a deal." Loki cut him off, before Eli could swing.

Eli turned to face him, rage gnawing at his senses, roaring to be let out.

"I'll stay away from her. I'll even resist the urge to off her just to see how you react, if you keep your distance from her as well." Loki smirked.

No. Not in a million— Eli cut off his own rampaging defiance. "Deal." The single word sounded foul as it struck his ears. He'd intended to anyway. Besides, as reason clawed its way back into his skull, he remembered the best way to win an argument with his brother and piss him off at the same time was to concede.

"Wait, what?"

"I'll stay away from her, if you will. It's a deal."

Loki's mouth worked up and down, but no sound came out. He held up his index finger, and then dropped it. Finally he shook his head and turned away. "Good. Enjoy the rest of your weekend."

As Loki walked out the front door, Eli collapsed onto the couch. None of it made any sense. Why had Loki tried to hurt Marley? All that, just for a bargain he knew Loki wouldn't uphold?

He had no intention of keeping his promise to Loki, either. Even if he needed to keep some distance between himself and Marley, he needed to also make sure she was safe.

He needed to find a way to keep her from the harm of his curse, and everything else associated with his family. Maybe it was time for him to move on. Leave the family business behind. Make up his mind about whether Marley was safer with him keeping an eye on her or just leaving her to her own life.

CHAPTER SIX

Marley had never been a fan of company Christmas parties. The first time she'd gone to one, she'd been nineteen and working the help desk for her college. All those years ago, it had sounded like a good idea. That had been the day she realized a lot of her coworkers were different people when they were off the clock. And drunk. And had nothing in common with her outside of knowing the people at the core of the gossip about who'd tapped whom in the copy room. No office party she'd attended since had been any different.

The reminders of why she hated these events raced through her mind, as she leaned against the bar in the Brazilian grill. She watched her colleagues filter in, and gather in packs of two or three. She twirled her straw in her Diet Coke. She'd been tempted to ask for a shot of rum in it, but these weren't the people she enjoyed drinking with.

Except the one person she couldn't locate. The only reason she hadn't ditched the party and just gone home. She hadn't seen Eli for the last three days; he'd only corresponded with her via email, and hadn't come out of his office while she was in, because he was *busy*.

She knew it was bullshit, and she intended to call him on it. If this was the only place she could track him down—short of going to his home, which was next if it came to it—then she was waiting here until he showed up. Confronting him over email didn't feel appropriate. It was too easy for him to brush her off. To avoid looking her in the eye.

She figured this was her best chance. Lots of people, no room for a scene, and nobody really paying attention to them anyway. And it was his father's company. He wasn't going to flake out on a holiday party for his own family's business.

An hour became two. She told about five million people—or ten, she lost count—that yes, it was cold, and yes, she thought it might snow and give them a white Christmas, and of course she was excited their work week ended today, because movers were relocating everything to the new office starting tomorrow.

Thinking about the new building dredged up memories she wasn't sure she wanted, but couldn't help sliding into. As people gathered for dinner, she still hadn't seen Eli. Had she missed him? If he was working to avoid her, it would be easy to do in this crowd.

She grabbed a table with some of the people on her team, unable to keep her gaze from roaming over every face in the room, over and over again. Dinner came and went.

The room grew quiet, heads and chairs all swiveling in the same direction, when Finlay Ugagnkin, the company CEO and Eli's father, stepped to the front of the room. Most people just called him Mr. U. Marley had wondered since the first time she met the older man, if Eli would age that gracefully. Finlay—he insisted people call him by his first name—had the same platinum hair and strikingly pale eyes as Eli, and as far as Marley could tell, not a single wrinkle on his face. He might as well have been in his mid-thirties. Lucky guy.

Finley rambled through his standard spiel. She liked that he thanked everyone for their hard work, and let the entire company know what their year-end profit sharing would look like. It wasn't a bad speech. She just had other things on her mind.

"And before I let you all get back to your conversations"—Finlay's voice took on a serious tone.

Marley snapped back to attention at the shift in mood. If the room had been quiet before, it was deathly silent now. At least she hadn't been the only one who'd heard the change in his voice.

—"I have an announcement to make. I have to admit, I've known this day was coming for a long time, but I still hoped it never would."

Her brows rose, and her gaze locked on Finlay. That sounded serious. He'd just told them they'd had a record year with revenue, so it couldn't be about the company. But knowing what it *wasn't* about didn't alleviate the tension suddenly crawling under her skin.

"Eli." Finlay gestured toward the back of the room. "You're not making me do this alone."

Marley turned with everyone else, as the familiar figure pushed away from a wall and wove his way through tables. Her stomach flipped in on itself. Maybe she shouldn't have eaten that...well, any of it. He looked amazing. Button-down shirt with no tie, untucked from his jeans, and all of it hugging that incredible form she hadn't been able to get out of her head since waking next to him.

She swallowed her desire, and kept her gaze fixed on the center of attention.

Finlay gave Eli a quick handshake and shoulder clap, before turning back to the room and speaking. "I couldn't be more proud of my son. And not just because he's done things with this company's technology no normal person could accomplish. He's excelled in so many ways most fathers only hope for."

Eli's smile was casual, but never shifted. If the compliments embarrassed him, it didn't show. Marley tried to convince herself it was coincidence his wandering gaze never landed on her.

Finlay continued. "So I admit, I begged and pleaded and bribed him when he handed in his resignation, earlier this week. Today was his last day with us."

Marley's stomach dropped into her shoes. A loud hum echoed in her ears, drowning out the sudden rush of whispers. Last day? No warning? Her mind whirled with confusion. It couldn't be because of her. Could it?

She'd thought they were friends. Talked about everything. And she hadn't had any clue this was coming. Had she read their entire relationship wrong? A tiny voice in the back of her head asked if this opened the door for things to happen between them. Her doubt shoved the hope aside. He hadn't warned her at all.

The room erupted in confusion. People congratulating Eli. Others giving him their goodbyes. Dragging him further from her with every moment that ticked by. Her brain worked on overdrive. She was stunned and hurt at what had just happened, but she still just wanted a few moments alone with him. When she saw him break away, she managed to excuse herself and do the same.

"Eli." She caught up to him as he stepped outside. The snow had just started. Even though the sun had set already, the streetlights reflected the clouds in the sky. Flakes drifted through the air, melting before they touched him. That was an illusion, right? She was just imagining he didn't have a single spec of snow on him?

"I have to go." He wouldn't look at her.

"Bullshit." She grabbed his arm. "You can give me two minutes. You owe me that at least."

He finally met her gaze, and her chest felt like it might shatter. There was so much sadness and regret in his eyes. "You're right. I'm sorry I couldn't tell you."

"Not even a hint?" That wasn't what she wanted to say. She needed to ask what this meant for him and her. If she was never going to see him again, she might as well find out if there had even been a chance of *them*.

He shook his head. "I'm sorry. There wasn't time."

The apology wasn't what she wanted to hear. "About this past weekend."

He pulled out of her grip, and stepped back. "It was nothing. A slip is all. I need to go."

She stood in the falling snow, watching him walk away, struggling for any words to bring him back. But the finality in his voice... She didn't know what to do with that. She didn't know how long she stood there, before someone joined her outside. And then a couple more people. Apparently, the party was over. She shook more hands, walked to the parking lot with a group of people, and dropped into her car, mind still a blank.

The lot emptied as she stared at the snow building up on her windshield. A whisper of resolution wormed its way into her thoughts. No. This wasn't the way it was going to happen. She'd hidden from a lot of things in her life, but she couldn't ignore this connection with Eli. If he wasn't interested, he'd have to tell her. This quiet brush off wasn't going to cut it.

She took a deep breath, and pulled onto the road. Several inches of snow were already packed into the asphalt, so going was slow. She didn't care. She was heading to his house, and she was going to say what she needed to.

CHAPTER SEVEN

Eli paced the length of his living room. The hurt on Marley's face was etched into his thoughts, taunting him with every step. He hadn't turned the lights on yet. The falling snow and clouds reflected the glow through the large windows framing his living room enough to keep him from tripping on something.

He should've broken ties with her sooner. Months ago. He knew the consequences, and he'd still let himself get lost so deeply in how much he wanted her, he was second-guessing his decision to never see her again. It wasn't as though he had to confess his undying love to her. Or dying love. Whatever. Maybe just a night together would have been enough to sate his curiosity. Probably.

Not that she was a one-night-stand kind of woman, but he also knew the idea wasn't completely foreign to her.

He shook his head to banish the thoughts. No. It was done. It was over. He'd made the right choice. He could build his own start-up. He had the connections, the ideas, the funding. And he'd always wanted to...

Something disrupted the peace outside, and he paused. The crunch of tires on snow. He wouldn't look. Whoever it was, it wasn't for him. Seconds later, a knock filled the empty room. After countless weekends of having her over for weekend movie marathons, he only knew one person who knocked instead of using the bell. He didn't know if he should groan, or praise his ancestors.

He yanked the door open. Marley stood on his front porch. Snowflakes dotted her hair and eyelashes. She looked at him, jaw clenched and eyes hard. "You have to hear me out."

He could've argued, but the desire wasn't there. Stepping aside, he gestured her in.

She hovered in the entryway, chewing on her bottom lip, her eyes searching his face.

"I'm listening." It was the best he could manage. Even in her winter clothes, she was gorgeous. Cheeks flushed, a rainbow of emotions on her face, accentuated by that stubborn streak she only showed when she really wanted something.

She took a step closer, and then another, until she stood toe to toe with him. His breath caught, and he clenched his hands, forcing them to stay by his side.

Her fingers interlocked at the back of his neck, frigid against his hot skin. She rose on her toes and pressed her lips to his.

He wouldn't kiss her back. He wouldn't give into this, or admit she tasted incredibly, and made his pulse race and his cock beg for relief. He wouldn't—

Fuck it all. He tangled his fingers in her hair, and yanked her head back for a better angle. She whimpered, and ground closer. He dove into the kiss, tongue finding hers, exploring her mouth.

He nudged her back against the wall, and then pressed into her. Her body yielded and molded to his. His body begged to be closer to her. Pleaded with him to rip away irritations like clothes, so he could feel her skin against his.

He wasn't sure where he found the will, but he managed to grasp the sanity he needed to step away.

She looked up at him, eyes wide, and drew a finger along his cheek, "I knew I wasn't the only one who felt it."

Was he going to have to hold an intelligent conversation? The blood had rushed from his head and into his lower extremities, and he wasn't sure that was an option. "You're not the only one."

She licked her bottom lip, holding his attention captive. "And now you've eliminated the one thing that was holding me back. I want to know why you resigned, but by hell I want you more."

Not the only thing keeping them apart. The thought nudged the back of his mind. The cruel, horrible reminder. "Marley, it's not that—" His words vanished in a groan when she slid against him, hip grinding against his arousal.

Some of the playfulness slid from her face. "Tell me you want me to leave. Say it, instead of dancing around it. Tell me you're not interested, and I've read us completely wrong. Do that, and I'll go."

"I can't." No, that was the wrong answer. He needed to do exactly what she'd just told him to. Except, instead he said, "Tell me what *you* want."

"You."

"Me too. You have no idea how much." That wasn't right. What was he doing? And why couldn't he take it back?

She traced a line down his chest, until her finger stopped at his waistband. "So what's stopping you from taking advantage of me?"

Death. Misery. A thousands of years old curse. "Not nearly as much as should be. I'm seconds away from stripping you naked, one piece of clothing at a time. I want to run my hands over every inch of your bare skin, caressing and pinching, and drinking in every moan. And I desperately want to explore every switch you have, until you scream so loudly, the neighbors know how much you're enjoying yourself."

She tugged at the button on his jeans, but didn't undo it. The bravado had vanished from her voice, replaced with breathlessness. "I like the sound of that."

He couldn't stop this. His desire was too strong. But he could at least set some boundaries. "You have to promise me something first."

"I'd probably promise you my soul right now, if that's what it took."

That was exactly what he was hoping to avoid. "Nothing that severe." He nipped at her bottom lip, and his senses flared to life again. "Promise me, whatever happens here tonight is just physical." He trailed his lips along her jaw and up to her ear, whispering, "Everything else, work, emotion, who we are outside of this moment, gets checked at the door."

She hesitated, and he swore his pulse ground to a halt.

"I promise." Her quiet voice barely reached his ears.

The promise was harder to force out than Marley thought it would be. She shoved her doubt aside. It wasn't like she expected—or wanted—more. Sure, the attraction was there, and three years of flirting and getting to know each other both mentally and emotionally had amped up the tension between them, but they'd never been more than friends. Her staring, lusting, all of it, had never been more than physical.

When Eli kissed her again, every inch of her whimpered with need. His mouth glided along her jaw. Each light sensation traveled along her skin, making her nipples ache, and dampness grow between her legs.

He shoved her coat to the floor. Disappointment flooded her when he stepped back, but the heat in his gaze deepened her desire. "Ancestors, you're gorgeous." His voice had dropped an octave. "I want to see more of you."

Was she blushing? How could she not be? Or was that just the pulse of want flowing through her? "Turn on the lights." She tried to keep her tone playful.

He shook his head, and then intertwined his fingers with hers. "I have a better idea." He tugged her toward the living room, and the large wall of windows, where the moonlight, reflected off the snow, spilled across the carpet. His breath was hot against her skin, when he stepped in and traced a line along her ear with his lips. "Strip for me. A single piece at a time."

Her pulse ratcheted up at the idea. "What if someone sees me?" Not that there were any houses nearby, and the road was blocked by trees. Besides, did she really care? The throb below her waist, the slickness the idea caused... She liked the thrill and the risk of doing something so indecent.

He let go of her and put a couple feet between them. "You don't have to."

She really might do anything, if he kept his hungry gaze trained on her like that. She kicked aside her shoes and socks first. He raised an eyebrow when she slid her hands down her sides, and then to the middle of her sweater, and undid the buttons one at a time. The knit caressed her hyper sensitive skin, when she slid the top down her arms. She'd never realized something like this could make her so wet. So strung out with need.

"Jeans next." There was no room for argument in his demand.

She bit her bottom lip, and pushed her pants to the floor. She tossed the discarded clothing aside, hyper aware of how exposed she was in just a bra and panties.

"So sexy." His words were almost a growl. "Now your bra."

Seconds later, the lacy lingerie joined the growing pile of clothes. The cool air in the room was a sharp contrast to the flush over every inch of her body, and her already hard nipples stiffened more at the light caress. She wanted his hands on her. Flowing over her bare skin. But this attention was incredible too. "What now?" she managed.

The corner of his mouth tugged up. "Play with your breasts for me. Show me how you like to be touched."

She glided her hands up her stomach, ignoring the plea from her aching clit that she pay attention to it instead. She cupped her breasts, and pinched the twin nubs. Rolled, caressed, and tugged.

His moan sent tingles rushing over her. "Are you wet?"

She nodded, not sure she could find her voice.

"Check for me," he said. "Slide your fingers between your folds. Slowly."

She kept one hand on her breast, while the other moved down. A whimper tore from her, when she brushed her swollen clit. Her fingers were coated the minute they dipped under her panties. She closed her eyes and focused on her surroundings. His voice, her own touch, the attention.

"Keep going." His voice was closer this time, his breath hot against her neck, but no other part of him touched her.

Her already racing heart spun into turbo mode, when his fingers brushed her hips, and seconds later elastic scraped down her legs. She continued to stroke her aching button. Resisting the urge to go faster. When his lips brushed her thigh, she cried out. His tongue flicked over her wet fingers and sex, and her legs almost gave out from the sensation.

He pulled her hand aside, and wrapped his lips around her clit. Orgasm climbed through her, and she rocked against his face. Her head felt like it was full of helium, and she didn't have the voice or enough presence of mind to make any sound beyond groans of pleasure. He shoved two fingers inside her, hard and rough. She cried out in response, as the climax crashed over her body.

Her pussy clenched around his fingers, and she shuddered with pleasure, as he continued to lick and suck her, pumping in and out. She tried to pull away when his touch became too much. He grabbed her hip with his free hand, drawing the orgasm out, until she didn't know if she could stay upright on her own.

He finally drew away, and stood. "Look at me."

She realized she'd had her eyes clenched shut the entire time, and forced them open. He stared back, his gaze intense and holding her captive. She heard the distinct sound of a belt buckle, and realized he was undoing his pants.

"I want you riding my cock. I want to fuck you until you scream. And I want to hear you come again."

She managed to find her voice. "That's a big list."

"I'm sure we'll manage."

The confidence in his voice glided over her bare skin. "Do you have a condom?"

He shook his head. "We don't need one. I promise."

She'd heard that before. "Because you're some kind of magical god, and can't get me pregnant or give me anything?"

He smirked. "Exactly."

She didn't know if it was the heat of the moment, or something deeper, that told her he was being far more serious than she was. She was on the pill, so pregnancy wasn't a concern. He didn't date enough for her to worry about STD's, so she would be safe. "You're lucky I trust you."

His hands rested on her hips. He spun her away from him, and then pulled her back to his front. The rough cotton of his shirt bit into her skin, and his cock dug into her ass, hard and demanding. "You have no idea how lucky I am."

He rested his hands on her stomach, and worked them upward. A new wave of lust increased her ebbing arousal, when he cupped her breasts. His rough fingers found her nubs, and sparks of pleasure and pain rolled through her with each squeeze. She rocked against him in time with his ministrations.

She didn't have time to be disappointed when the attention stopped. He tangled one hand in her hair, and yanked her head back. He kissed and bit along the soft flesh where her shoulder met her neck. With his other palm, he found her spine, then moved it over her ass, and between her legs. "You're still so wet." As he spoke, he nudged her forward. Her breasts flattened against the glass. When had they moved so close? The cold glass was another layer of exquisite agony against her tender nipples.

His fingers slid inside her easily. He pumped slowly, cock digging into her ass cheek, teasing.

"I thought you wanted to fuck me." She liked the way the crude language tasted.

"Hmm... I like the way you say that." His lips vibrated against her shoulder. "I want to hear it again. Beg me."

"Fuck me, please?" She wiggled against him, and felt his shaft pulse in return. "Fuck me hard and fast, Eli. I want you inside me. Please?"

Hands on her hips, he guided her back a few steps, and then pushed her forward. Her palms flattened against the window.

The head of his cock nudged her, and then he thrust forward without further warning. Her moan mingled with his, as he stretched her out. The slow teasing was gone. His pounding was fast and frantic. Her breath came in short gasps, as he hit her at just the right angle. "Come again for me Marley. I want to hear you scream."

She was so close. Her head swam, and every inch of her hovered on the brink. He dug his fingers into her hips, slamming her hard. When he found her still tender clit and massaged it, a scream of pleasure tore from her throat. Somewhere in the midst of it, she heard his grunts grow frantic and fast, and then melt into a long groan as he peaked as well.

The pace slowed, and she knew she couldn't stand this time. He slid out of her, and seconds later, wrapped his arms around her, keeping her from collapsing. He sank to the floor, helping her down, and pulled her into his lap.

She curled up, and rested her head against his shoulder

He brushed a loose strand of hair off her forehead, and kissed her lightly. His thumb traced tiny circles over her spine. "I'm so glad you came over tonight." The hunger was gone from his voice, but the commanding power remained.

She smiled, and rested more of her weight against him. "Me too."

CHAPTER EIGHT

The storm had cleared up at some point during the night, leaving the sky black except for the shock of white moon, and the snow untouched in Eli's back yard. Like the front of his house, two entire walls of the bedroom were floor-to-ceiling windows. All he could see beyond the glass was a blanket of white over the trees that spanned most of his back yard.

Moonlight splashed across the form next to him. She was still wrapped in sheets, but she'd kicked off the blankets sometime during the night.

He'd have to say goodbye soon. He studied the way the cotton draped her naked form, hugging every seductive curve. He wouldn't let himself admit he was going to miss her. That thought led to others, with more dangerous consequences.

His hand hovered less than an inch from her face, as he followed the line of her cheek without ever touching her. Her dark hair spilled out over the white pillow cases.

"Some people think that's creepy." Her mouth curled into a smile, but she didn't open her eyes.

"Waking up at this unholy hour?" He couldn't help his smile at the teasing note in her voice. But he wouldn't lean in and kiss her. He'd gotten that out of his system.

"Watching someone sleep." She finally looked at him, grin in place.

They'd spent half the night exploring each other. She made the most incredible noises when she was turned on. They were even better when she came. But it should have been enough to get her out of his system. The only reason he hadn't already sent her home was the roads were dangerous. Or at least, that's what he tried to tell himself. "I was going to wake you up."

"Mhm..." She sat up, and the sheets fell away, exposing her bare breasts and perfect skin.

He struggled to keep his attention on her face. "But I know you don't have work, so I thought I'd let you sleep."

She ducked her head. "I haven't slept that well in a long time."

He wanted to ask her to join him in the shower. To make one last memory. But he'd already pushed the limits of their relationship too far. He needed to stick to the same promises he'd coerced from her. "Can I make you breakfast?"

She shook her head, and scooted to the edge of the bed. "I'm good. Thanks. I should let you have your privacy back." If she noticed her clothes were folded on the chair next to her instead of still strewn across the living room, she didn't say anything. He hadn't been able to sleep, and the few times he'd managed to extract himself from her, he'd paced with no purpose, before crawling back into bed and wrapping himself around her again.

She dressed in silence, not looking at him. Every inch of his instinct begged him to say something. To make the situation better. But he knew this was how it had to be. He had to let her go. He hated to be that asshole. But at least she'd still be alive at the end of the day.

She stood, and impulse snaked through him. He shot his hand out and grabbed her wrist. "Wait." When she didn't struggle to break away, he tugged her back to the mattress.

He knelt in front of her and rested his hands on her cheeks, forcing her to look at him. He let the sincerity fall into his voice. "I'm so glad you came over last night. That we have this memory. I will never, ever, forget it. Or you." He kissed her hard, searing the moment into his thoughts, where he knew it would stay. "I'm sorry that's all there is. That I can't give you more."

She pulled away, and gave him a weak smile. "Yeah. I get it." She didn't look back, as she made her way to the front door. The latch clicked. Seconds later, her tires crunched on the frozen snow.

He flopped back against the pillows. Only a selfish fucking prick would have taken that from Marley last night knowing it could never be more. Ancestors, he was an asshole. Then again, so was whoever had cursed him, so at least it ran in the family. He lay there, until the light started to creep over the trees and the clouds drifted back in. With any luck, Marley was home by now. He hoped the plows had cleared away enough snow, she'd make it safely before the next storm started.

And he needed her to hate him as much as he hated himself. Then at least she wouldn't be back. She'd be safe.

Lightning cracked across the sky, drawing his attention to the windows. He frowned at the electrical activity. That wasn't normal this time of year. Especially as a lead-in to a blizzard.

His phone buzzed, and he reached for it on the nightstand, out of habit. He rolled his eyes when he saw the text message was from Loki.

And then he read it.

You broke your promise.

Eli's chest almost caved in on itself in fear. Another slash of lightning split the sky, followed by ear shattering thunder. *Marley.*

He didn't have time for a car. He pulled on whatever clothes were within reach, and flew out the front door. His feet left the ground as he picked up speed, and he soared at low altitude toward her apartment. At least she liked to take the back roads. He wouldn't have to worry about anyone seeing him. Not that he cared right now. Maybe the message was just meant to tease him. To see how he'd react. But knowing his brother, Eli couldn't take that chance.

The snowdrops melted and evaporated before they reached him. He cut a horizontal path through the storm, three thoughts looping in his head.

Please let it be nothing. Let me be overreacting. Let her be all right.

Stupid, myopic, narrow-minded, moronic, melodramatic... Marley's list of insults faded into a mental roar. She wasn't sure if she was talking about herself or Eli. Elusive, vague, possibly stuck in a fairytale from his childhood. That was Eli.

It had all clicked for her in the last twelve hours. The odd comments he'd make about hoping he never found the woman of his dreams, his insistence there was nothing between them, and the haunted look he'd had when he told her the story on Saturday night. He thought that stupid curse was real. The last thing she needed was that kind of baggage in her life. Especially if it belonged to someone else.

Snow fluttered onto her windshield, and she turned on the wipers. Large, fluffy, white flakes seemed to appear out of nowhere, blanketing the road within minutes.

A pushover. A coward. Indecisive, and too quiet for her own good—that was her. She hadn't even tried to argue. Just sat back, and let him make the rules. Not that she wanted to be with a guy who wasn't interested, but everything he did, all of his actions said he was. She'd just accepted his brush off without questioning it, though.

And she was nobody's booty call. Fury and hurt rushed through her. She wasn't going to let this eat at her. She was going back.

Except, the roads had gone from clear to covered in several inches of snow, almost faster than she could blink. She slowed, eyes focused on the road. Maybe she'd go back after the storm let up.

Lightning reflected off the clouds hiding the sky, adding an eerie glow to the dawn, for the briefest second. Something cracked nearby, louder than a gunshot, and Marley's heart hammered in her chest. She didn't like this weather. She gripped the wheel until her fingers ached, squinting through the falling white. Maybe she'd be better off without her headlights. There was no one else on the road, and with the sudden storm making it so dark, all they were doing was reflecting back at her.

Another crack lit the sky enough to blind her further. Her eyes grew wide, and she slammed on the brakes when she saw the tree just a few feet in front of her. The car slid toward the fallen trunk, not listening to her attempts to avoid the obstacle. She spun the steering wheel with the skid, the way she'd been taught, and the car listened. It drifted away from the tree at the last second. It tumbled over the drop-off, and her world tilted as the vehicle rolled.

Marley's world went black.

"Marley." The voice clawed at the edges of nothing fogging her brain.

She knew that voice, so why couldn't she remember?

"Marley!" He was persistent.

Eli. Right. He sounded worried. Snippets of memory floated back to her. He should be. He'd been an asshole.

"Open your eyes. Talk to me. Something."

It sounded like a reasonable request. Her skull screamed in protest, as she forced her eyelids open. More of her world crawled into focus. She was cold. All of her. Except the warm bits on her neck and cheeks where his hands rested.

"Thank you." Relief shone through his concern. A smile cracked his solemn expression.

She shifted to sit up. It didn't hurt the way it should. Wait, why should it hurt? She looked around her. She was sitting in the snow, several feet from her car, which lay on its roof. Was she thrown clear? Red splattered the ground. So much red. She raised her hand to her head, and brought it away sticky and covered with... Was that blood? It couldn't be her blood. She felt fine. "What are you doing here?" she asked Eli. "What am I doing here?"

He opened his mouth. A giant white ball of light slammed into his gut, tearing him away from her, and tossing him back several feet until he collided with a tree.

"Fuck, you're persistent." Loki floated to the ground next to her, feet never touching the snow.

Wait, floated? Ball of lightning? She had to be hallucinating. She remembered the tree in the road. Was she unconscious?

Loki's gaze raked over her, chilling her more than the snow she sat in. "I was worried about you. I wasn't ready for this to be over quite yet."

What? Out the corner of her eye, she saw Eli pick himself up. His posture shifted, every muscle tense, eyes tight.

Loki held up a hand. "Time out."

She had to be dreaming. That was the only explanation for this bizarre scene. She was really lying unconscious in her car. She hoped someone would find her soon.

Eli didn't relax, but disbelief marred his expression. "Are you serious? I don't care what the fates say; I told you what I'd do to you, if you touched her."

At least in her dreams, Eli was still sweet. Overzealous maybe, but sweet.

"Ditto." Loki smirked. "And we should get to that. But someone wants an explanation. I'll give you a minute to tell our lovely guest what's going on, and then we can resume seeing if one of us can die."

Wow, she was screwed up in the head. She looked between the two of them. Eli tense, fury etched in his icy expression. Loki calm, still floating—possibly chuckling? Terror slid into her veins. If this wasn't a dream, she was fucked. If this was real, she didn't want an answer from Loki. Something about his demeanor terrified her.

Then again, if she wasn't dreaming, Eli had been holding back some pretty significant things too.

CHAPTER NINE

Marley looked back and forth between the two brothers again. Even if this was some sick, twisted dream, she wasn't going to cave to the creeping fear inside. She locked her gaze on Eli. "Tell me what's going on." Her voice cracked, and she hid a wince. "All of it."

Eli's fingers twitched by his side, and he bounced on his toes. He took a step closer, and she narrowed her eyes to keep him at arm's length. Part of her wanted the comfort he could provide. But she wasn't going to sink into it. Even if they'd had that kind of relationship—the kind where he wrapped her up and kept her safe, instead of just listening to her vent on a bad day—she wouldn't let that happen right now. She needed answers.

His entire frame shook when he exhaled, but he never relaxed. "The story I told you the other night? The curse about the three brothers? It's actually about me. About all three of us. The first time I heard it was thousands of years ago, when I was just a kid."

Loki laughed. "You actually told her the story already? And neither of you has..." His chuckle echoed over snow and trees. He looked at Marley, something icy hiding in his eyes. "You know a curse isn't meant to be straightforward, right? You're familiar with Grimm. Aesop. Disney? You never take that crap at face value, especially if you've only heard part of it."

She struggled to wrap her thoughts around the information. Thousands of years ago? Aesop—like the fables? The answers should be right there, but all she could think was these men were trying to tell her they were actually immortal. Or at least really, really old. The last twenty-four hours had to be getting to her. Unless this was all a joke.

The new idea gnawed at her thoughts. They'd said his name was Loki. As in the trickster god. What if this was all some sort of elaborate hoax? Because that's more logical? She ignored her own, nagging question.

"We're gods." Eli interrupted her spiraling thoughts. "All of us. Loki wasn't inconveniently named by parents with a sense of humor. He's *the* Loki."

"No." She shook her head. A tiny voice in the back of her mind insisted she listen. That she take him seriously. But it was insane. There was no way this was real. Was it all just a joke? The resignation at the Christmas party. The night before, with Eli. Was it all some sort of cruel prank she didn't understand? Were there wires holding Loki up? She glanced at him out of the corner of her eye, not wanting to study him too hard and prove her theories wrong.

Terror snaked in to join her doubt. No. People didn't float. Gods didn't walk the earth working tech jobs, and she was afraid of a shadow. It was nothing. So why was the fear under her skin more convinced by their stories than her rationalizations?

"Marley?" Eli took another step forward. At least the concern in his voice was familiar.

And maybe part of the same sick joke that landed her here. She boxed her cowering nerves in the back of her mind, and stood. She wouldn't look at Loki. Whatever he had to do with this, it was all incidental. Eli had been at the heart of it the entire time. Playing...some kind of sick game with her. "I'm calling the auto club," she said. There. That at least sounded like a rational thing to do. She should have done it to start with.

Her feet sank into the snow, as she trudged in Eli's direction. She tried to ignore that hers were the only footprints in the clearing. That her car was the only vehicle. She didn't look at Eli, as she brushed past him and headed for the slope leading to the main road.

"You even brought her back to life. Twice." Loki's taunt hit her back. "And she still doesn't believe you. How incredible is that?"

He was just spewing words. It didn't mean anything. She repeated the mantra over and over again, as she made her way toward the highway. The fact his words made her gut clench, and her head ache, and her logic wonder if he was telling the truth, didn't mean anything.

And she definitely wasn't the tiniest bit disappointed Eli wasn't coming after her. No. That didn't hurt most of all. She didn't care what he did with his life. He'd made it clear she wasn't a part of it.

Eli watched Marley climb back toward the street. Every inch of him pleaded to go after her. To wrap her up. To comfort her until she was calm, and then talk her through the truth of who he was, slowly and rationally. To run her a bath. Rinse away the tension and the grime. Make lo—

He cut the thought off, before it could manifest completely. That was a dangerous path to go down. In fact—he turned his attention to Loki—he had other priorities. Like keeping her alive. His desires weren't as important as her survival

He sneered, and balled his hands into fists again. Even if it wasn't the curse, the accidents all hinged on Loki. And that meant, because of his own interaction with her, Eli had put her in danger. He wasn't going to let her suffer again, but he could turn his frustration on Loki. "Seriously, what's your issue with her?"

Loki rolled his eyes. "I already told you. I hate seeing you happy."

Eli roared and lunged. He had to make sure she was safe. That this wouldn't happen again.

Loki shook his head. "Not today. Probably not for several centuries." He vanished before Eli reached him.

CHAPTER TEN

Marley pulled on her favorite bathrobe, and tried to sink into the fluffy terry cloth. She toweled her hair dry, scowled at the fog on the mirror, and left her bathroom behind. The shower hadn't helped chase away her confusion. Was ten am too early to drink?

She made her way to her living room. When she'd climbed back to the road, leaving Eli and Loki in the clearing, she realized she didn't have her phone on her. She normally kept it mounted on her dashboard when she drove, because she liked listening to music in the car but hated morning radio programs.

There was no way she was walking back into that clearing. Her logic circuits couldn't handle that sight again. Especially as other pieces of her memory started to click into place. Odd things she'd seen Eli do in the past. Accepting she'd watched him crush steel plates, and make flashlights glow, and get knocked into a tree by a ball of lightning and not die, meant admitting to concepts she wasn't ready to deal with.

So instead of calling the auto club, she'd walked until someone picked her up. She'd been covered in blood, so that had taken a while.

It was nice to finally be home. She just wished she understood what had happened. She still couldn't wrap her brain around what took place in the clearing. And she couldn't get rid of the pit in her gut, either. Couldn't ignore how incredible the night before had been. And how it was apparently a lie. Or a joke. Or something. She didn't even know anymore.

Part of her brain asked why someone would set up such an elaborate prank just for her. Or for anyone, really. Unless she was on hidden camera. She resisted the urge to look around her.

That same part of her insisted she couldn't rationalize this away. The pieces didn't click into any explanation other than the one Eli had given her. But gods? No. It wasn't true. She was remembering things wrong. She'd rolled her car. Even if she had walked away unscathed, she had to have hit her head, for there to be so much blood. Never mind that she hadn't found a wound. Her memory couldn't be trusted.

A knock on the door jerked her from the rationalizations. Eli? No. She shoved the hope aside. She didn't want to see him. Not ever again. Even though just thinking something so final pricked her eyelids. It was probably a...

She didn't even know. Her gut flipped in on itself and she pulled her robe tighter around her, when she opened the door and saw who was on the other side.

"I had to make sure you were all right." Loki's cold tone didn't match the sympathetic statement.

Ice snaked down her spine, erasing the warm comfort of the shower she'd just left behind. "I'm fine. Thank you. But I think you need to leave." She swung the door shut as she talked.

He didn't say anything else, and the door latched shut between them. She snapped the deadbolt into place, and an irrational fear pulsed inside. Why didn't she have more locks?

"I'm not a vampire." Loki's voice startled her, and she whirled. He stood in the middle of her living room. "You don't have to invite me in. Knocking was only a courtesy."

Her pulse screamed into overdrive, carrying a whisper of terror with it. She swallowed it all. How had he done that? A magician's trick or something. There was no way Eli's story was true. Was there? "How did you know where I live?"

He held up her phone. "You left this in the clearing. Who actually keeps their own address in their contact list?"

"What do you want?" It was the most she could manage without her voice shaking.

Phone still in his hand, he sank onto her sofa, and leaned back. "You're a really rude hostess. Aren't you going to offer me a drink?"

She forced steel into her voice. Whoever this asshole thought he was, she wouldn't be intimidated. "You're not a guest. Answer my question or leave. Both, preferably."

"Smart, mouthy, obnoxious... No wonder Eli loves you."

Love. The word slid past her entire jumble of thoughts, and tugged at her heart. She pushed the reaction aside. "Eli doesn't love me. Eli is terrified of commitment."

Loki shrugged. "Believe what you want. You're right about the second one..." He trailed off. "Anyway. All that matters is you believe it, and so does he. It means I succeeded."

He was being cryptic, right? There was no way she was just being dim. His words didn't make any sense. Was he insane? Normal, rational people didn't break into their brother's employee's apartments. Right? Especially not to make vague small talk? She needed to get him out of here. He'd tossed her phone on the coffee table less than a foot away. If she called the cops, would they get here before he could do something?

Call Eli.

She banished the thought immediately. Trusting Eli hadn't done her a lot of good to date. Not if he was keeping things from her like being a god who had a psychotic brother.

Loki stood, and was directly in front of her in a few short strides.

Panic joined her mounting fear, and she stepped back. Or she tried. Her feet wouldn't move. Her panic grew. She tried to put her arms up, to twist, to turn, but it was like something invisible had bound her.

He traced a finger down the side of her face, over her jaw, and along her collarbone. His touch made her skin crawl. An odd tone lined his voice. "I only ever wanted one date. Just to give you a test-drive. But no, you had to fall hard and fast for my brother from day one."

She hadn't fallen for anyone. Well, maybe she had, but not that quickly. She struggled harder, but nothing moved. His tone terrified her. What was going on?

"Don't misunderstand." He dipped his head toward hers, and trailed his nose along her neck, breath hot as he spoke. "This isn't some misplaced crush. I just wanted to know if you were any good in bed." He tugged the edge of her bathrobe. It wasn't enough to pull it open, but it left more of her chest exposed. "Not that it matters now. The game is almost over. Or at least, your part in it is."

"What game?" She could still talk. Every inch of her itched to recoil from his touch. What was he going to do with her? Helplessness made her pull harder at her invisible bonds, but it didn't do any good. Shit, he really was a god. Or something equally terrifying, and he had her bound and helpless.

"Life. Yours, anyway." He smiled, and she swore he was part wolf at that moment. Looking to play with his food before he killed it. "Everyone's life is a game." He traced a finger over her lips. "Here's the thing about the *curse*. Eli is a bit narcissistic." He chuckled. "I guess it runs in the family. But he hides it better than the rest of us. He's only ever focused on that one verse. The one bit he thought related to him."

Reality sank deeper the harder she tried and failed to break free of whatever held her prisoner. Every moment spent with Loki stole more of her hope, and she was pretty sure snapped another thread of her sanity. But at least while he was monologuing, he wasn't doing anything else. "What are you talking about?"

"He always ignored the part about ruling our father's kingdom. Dad can't stay in charge forever. Eli always glosses over the bit that says the first son to discover his happiness will rule the kingdom, with his partner by his side. He ignores it, because he's already decided he's destined to lose his true love, if he ever finds her."

Loki tangled his fingers in her hair and kissed her hard. He pressed close, every inch of his hard frame rubbing against her. His tongue forced its way into her mouth, as he held her captive. Her skin threatened to crawl away from both his touch and the power in it.

He broke away and stepped back. "Meh. Not sure what the big deal is about you." His gaze raked over her. "But Eli's not as bright as he thinks he is, so to each his own. The thing is, he thinks confessing his love to you is going to kill you. That whole, 'She'll draw her last mortal breath' thing. It doesn't mean death. It means your immortality. I'm not guessing this. Not the way he did. I know. It's happened before.

"But this works in my favor—his belief of your impending doom. As long as you don't believe he loves you, and he won't admit it to himself, you'll just die when I kill you. BAM!"

The shouted word made her jump. Tears of fear pricked her eyelids. He was insane. A mad god held her captive in her own living room. Her heart threatened to hammer out of her chest. "If he doesn't believe it, you don't have to kill me."

Loki smirked and winked at her. "Nice try. Thing is, even if he won't admit it, it's true. He almost burst a blood vessel just watching me flirt with you, and sweetheart, you're not close to worth my time. Watching you die...that's going to devastate him. It'll be centuries before

273

he even looks at another woman the way he looks at you. And that's plenty of time to make sure he's not the heir."

She licked her lips. It was the only thing she could do, besides talk. "But he doesn't love me. I promise." It hurt to say, but she was certain. "And I'm never going to see him again."

"You're right again about that second point." He rested a palm on her bare chest, directly over her hammering heart. "But this time, he won't be able to bring you back. I know how to stop that from happening."

Eli sank back against his door, frustration pumping through him. He needed to keep his thoughts busy. He needed to not think about Marley. And he needed to find Loki. He could fly, but he didn't have his brother's ability to teleport. So he'd spent the last several hours calling everyone he knew—every place Loki might be—trying to track the fucker down.

Nothing.

He had to find him. Had to make sure Marley was safe. His phone buzzed in his hand, and he looked at it in an instant. The text from a blocked number made his heart sink and every inch of him ache in frustration and fury.

You should have stayed away.

No. Bile rose in his throat. It wasn't real. The message was a joke.

His toes twitched in his shoes. Except he couldn't take that chance. He burst through the front door, flying toward Marley's apartment for the second time that day. He reached her apartment within ten minutes, the longest of his existence. His heart sank when she didn't answer his knocks. He tried the doorknob. It was unlocked.

He rushed into the apartment, and froze just a few steps in. Marley sat in an easy chair, bathrobe spilling open, empty prescription and vodka bottles on the table in front of her. No.

He closed the distance between them without another thought, and pressed his fingers to her throat for a pulse.

Her skin was cold. She wasn't breathing. She didn't have a heartbeat. He closed his eyes, and repeated the gesture that was all too familiar after the last week. Hands at the back of her neck to hold her head steady. Thumbs against her throat, near the veins.

He reached inside her, looking for the spark he needed to pull her back. She can't be gone. This isn't real.

He couldn't find what he needed. That tiny warmth that would indicate she was still connected to her life, however tentatively.

He dove deeper. It had to be there. He had to pull her out. He rested his forehead against hers, despair sinking into him. "Please wake up, Marley." The words spilled out without him processing them. "Please. I love you so much. You can't do this. I'm not worth it." He pressed his lips to hers. But there was nothing there. She was gone.

"Wow. You're a real romantic, aren't you? Too little too late, eh bro?" Loki's taunt shoved Eli's grief aside, and replaced it with rage.

Of course his brother was here. Eli knew surrender wasn't Marley. That she'd never have done something like this to herself.

Something inside Eli snapped. Eons of fury, frustration, and putting up with Loki's shit tore through him. He lunged at Loki, unfiltered rage driving him. He wrapped a hand around Loki's throat, pouring all of his power into the grip, and slammed him in into the nearest wall. He wanted to threaten his brother, but was too furious to find his voice.

For the first time in their existence, he swore he saw fear in Loki's eyes. Good. Loki needed to pay. Marley's was the last life he would destroy.

"Eli." Marley's familiar voice speared through his haze, and he swore his heart stopped. Some of his fury evaporated in confusion. His grip loosened, but he didn't let go of Loki.

Loki's fear vanished, and was replaced with irritation. "Ancestors damn it." His body flickered into the ethereal, and then re-solidified under Eli's touch.

"You're not leaving. Not yet." Marley's voice was cold.

Eli didn't know what was happening, but he knew Loki wasn't going to live through it. He tightened his grip again.

"Stop." Marley's hand rested on his arm, her skin soft against his, calling to his heart. A familiar, but foreign electricity seeped into him. Why did she feel powerful? Marley didn't have that kind of touch. "Eli. You and I need to talk." To Loki, she said, "And I really should let him kill you. Not that I could stop him."

Loki shrugged. "It doesn't really work that way."

"I didn't think immortality was an actual thing until today," Marley said. "I was wrong. Maybe you are, too."

Was this confusion what Marley had felt like in the clearing? Except the pieces were clicking in Eli's head. The things Loki had said about the curse being more than it seemed, the specificity of the words last *mortal* breath, it was all starting to make sense. He'd revel in Marley not only being alive, but possibly being immortal in a moment. First he had to get rid of the immediate threat. "Explain after I destroy him."

Her attention never left Loki. "If you come near me again. Or my family. Or anyone I've ever said hello to on the street. You'll regret it." Her voice was low and threatening when she spoke. Emanating a kind of confidence Eli had never heard from her. He was used to self-assurance, but not like this.

Loki didn't even flinch. "You're not that kind of powerful, hon. You're just a baby in the grand scheme of things."

Eli squeezed his neck again. Loki's taunt ended in a strangled, choking gag.

Marley frowned. "Try me and find out. Or I can let you two fight it out now."

Eli smirked at the implication she wouldn't ask him to stop.

"You'd kill your own brother?" Loki asked him.

He still wasn't sure he believed it, but Eli had the upper hand—the woman he wanted was by his side. Smiling at Loki, Eli dropped his grip on his brother's neck. He balled his hand into a fist, pulled back, and let the punch fly.

Loki's head bounced off the wall with a satisfying *thunk*. He raised his fingers to his split lip, and brought them away covered in blood. Shock and disbelief marred his expression. "How did you...?"

Eli didn't know. He shouldn't have been able to draw blood so easily. When they were younger, Helblindi had been able to keep Loki from vanishing, and that had was the only way Eli had ever been able to hurt Loki. Helblindi wasn't stronger; it was just a different gift.

Did this instance have to do with Marley? Eli would ask for answers later. Right now, he knew she was safe. He growled, and Loki vanished.

Eli spun to face Marley, not sure what to say. He couldn't lose her again. Especially now that he'd figured things out. She was here. Safe. And in his arms. He tunneled his hands in her hair.

She pressed a single finger to his lips, before he could kiss her. "You're an ass. You never stopped to think falling in love might not mean death and eternal misery?"

Loki had known. Apparently for a long time. That's why he'd worked so hard to drive Eli and Marley together, to make sure Eli fell but didn't admit it before trying to take Marley out of the picture. It was an idea intricate and twisted enough it had to belong to Loki.

But that also meant Marley really was Eli's for eternity. "I'm a little slow sometimes."

"As long as it's only sometimes." She brushed her lips over his. "And I love you too."

Relief coursed through him, rapidly joined by lust when she shifted her weight against him. "You heard that?"

"Only kind of. I think whatever this magic, voodoo...whatever it is, was still sinking in. I wasn't completely back from the dead yet."

He didn't need to hear anymore. He crushed his mouth to hers, memorizing every taste and sensation. His cock hardened, straining to get closer to her. This was incredible. He still wasn't sure what to do with the knowledge Marley might be like him now—immortal, destined to be by his side.

CHAPTER ELEVEN

The new sensations coursing through Marley were incredible. She'd actually been able to stop Loki from leaving the room. Had the power to take that kind of control. Electricity filled her veins, whispering promises of what she was capable of. Showing her new layers of color she'd never seen in the world.

And none of it compared to Eli's hungry, demanding kiss. She dove into the attention, and returned his intensity. Her skin hummed to be closer to him. A giggle slipped out when he shifted to abruptly sweep her off her feet. He pressed his lips to hers again, as he cradled her. His eyes were soft, but that same domination she remembered from the night before hid behind his compassion.

"This time, you're not leaving in the morning." In a few short strides, he'd crossed her apartment to the bedroom, and sat her gently at the edge of the mattress.

She snaked a hand up the front of his jeans. "I wouldn't give you a choice."

His entire body jerked, when she caressed his bulge. She teased through fabric, arousal growing with his every response.

"Ancestors, Marley, you're killing me."

She took the hint, and slid down his zipper. When she wrapped her fingers around his shaft, he sighed and swayed closer. Her gaze met his, as she glided her tongue over the head of his cock, light and teasing. He shuddered when she took his length in her mouth. She wanted to fuck him again. To feel him inside her. But she wanted to taste him first. Eternity meant they had time.

She moaned, letting the vibrations run along his cock. He rocked against her. When she caressed his sack, he inhaled sharply. She sucked and licked, slowly letting him increase the rhythm.

He pulled out abruptly, and dropped to his knees, so he was eye level with her. "Your mouth is amazing." He kissed her hard, tongue diving in and owning her. He pushed her bathrobe off her shoulders without interrupting the kiss. One palm cupped her breast, kneading and sending daggers of want through her.

Going down on him had already made her wet, and the new attention amplified it.

He broke away, breathless, and rested his forehead against hers. "But I need to be inside you again. I want to watch you as you come. See that incredible expression of pleasure, when you reach the brink and I push you over the edge."

"You have too many clothes in the way for that."

He gave her a wicked grin, and shed everything. He nudged her back on the bed, knee between her legs and brushing her swollen sex. "Problem solved."

She wasn't sure how he managed it, but seconds later, he was on his back with her straddling him. His hands rested on her hips, and his cock poised at her opening.

She grabbed his shaft and stroked, letting his head bump her clit. His grunts matched her heavy breathing, letting her know he enjoyed this as much as she did.

He covered her hand with his. "I was serious." He glided his dick over her slit and thrust inside her hard and fast.

She sank into the pleasure, rocking against him. He set the frantic pace. His groans grew shallower, and she could tell he was close. She cried out in surprise when his thumb found her clit. He pressed tiny, hard circles around the engorged nub. Orgasm washed over her suddenly, stealing her breath. She clenched around his cock, milking him.

He pounded inside her, not letting up on her button until he came, filling her and thrusting, until he was spent.

She rested against his chest, memorizing every sensation. His heartbeat. The warmth of his skin against hers. His cock softening but not sliding out yet. His hands on the small of her back, holding her close and wrapping her in a familiar and incredible safety.

"You're amazing." His soft words melted into the peaceful aura around them.

She smiled against his chest. "I'm pretty fond of you, too."

They both lay there for a while, not talking. Marley wrapped herself in the soothing rhythm of his chest rising and falling. She could get used to this. Who was she kidding? She already was. It felt like she'd been missing this for ages.

"Are you asleep?" Eli's question rumbled through her ear.

She rolled off him, and rested her head on his shoulder. "No. Just enjoying the moment. I'm not really...like you now. Am I?"

"Hard to say. I've found you electrifying since I met you."

She laughed and draped a hand over his chest. "That's corny, and I'm serious."

"I thought it was clever." He rested a hand on her cheek, thumb stroking her skin.

A current raced between them, like a pulsing wave of static electricity. It only lasted a few seconds, but she knew she hadn't imagined it. "What was that?"

"You're definitely not mortal anymore." He tilted his head up enough to kiss her on the forehead.

She should be more surprised. In the last few hours, she'd discovered gods were real, one wanted to kill her, and one had been keeping his distance to keep her alive. Oh, and then there was the one who signed her paycheck.

It all still sounded ludicrous. But knowing she was one of them now somehow felt right. She snuggled closer to Eli. Or at least, knowing it was because he was her eternity felt right.

She'd adjust to the rest as time went on. Apparently she had a lot of that in her future.

~*~

SEDUCING DESTINY

BROTHERS OF FATE
BOOK 2

CHAPTER ONE

The world is yours, as you search for her soul
No lover shall bind you to the land
The one you discover, who quiets your might,
Will bring your journey to an end

Blake stepped into the local coffee shop the hotel concierge had recommended, and breathed in the heady scent of espresso roast. Thank the ancestors he wasn't one of those gods who didn't get to experience the effects of caffeine and alcohol.

The landscape inside was familiar, even though he'd never been in the place. A glass case, only half full of pastries; eclectic furniture; a gaggle of people in suits, waiting for their drinks and more concerned about their phones then their surroundings—

Hello, there. His gaze lingered on the woman at the front of the line. Her slacks and matching jacket hugged generous curves, the clothes not too snug but not so loose her figure was obliterated. Styles and fashions changed as the decades and centuries passed. Some for the better, while he wasn't so fond of others.

However, a sensual woman with a Renaissance body always made his blood roar.

The way she worried her bottom lip, chewing on the plump swell, erased his dread about the looming interviews and sent desire rolling over his skin. No glow surrounded her, so she was mortal. Not that it mattered; he only wanted a distraction for the next night or two, while he was in town. She'd be a pleasant contrast to the dragging nation-wide tour that had been his last two weeks.

He stepped up next to her. The faint scent of plum and mint greeted him, carrying mental images of her joining him in the bathroom. Him lifting her onto the sink. Cupping that full ass. Finding out what her mouth felt like. He stowed the fantasy and flashed her a winning smile. "May I buy you a drink?"

In heels, she was only a few inches shorter than his six-two. She looked up, eyes wide, and his breath caught at the hazel pools staring back at him. Déjà vu scurried through his veins, overlapping the present with a memory he couldn't quite grasp. Flickers of sensation danced over his body. Lips pressed together. Bare skin gliding against his. Heat, and heavy breathing, and passion. He mentally shook aside the sensation.

She looked over her shoulder, and then back at him. "You're talking to me?"

Amusement joined his swelling lust. "I am."

She looked around again. "You're sure?"

The next register opened up, and she stepped forward and placed her order. He handed his credit card to the cashier. "This is together. Give me a large house roast."

"No, it's not together." The woman handed over her money. The cashier looked between the two for a moment, and then totaled out the first purchase before ringing up Blake's. The attractive businesswoman gave him an unapologetic shrug and set her laptop bag on a nearby table. "I appreciate the offer, but I'm fine. You know this is a coffee shop, not a bar, right?"

He leaned against the chair next to her. She was an entertaining combination of unsure and confident, which did more to wake him up than the coffee would. Some gods had the ability to influence those around them—to change someone's mind with sheer will. His gifts tended more toward weather control and keeping his counterparts from performing tricks, but he didn't mind. The journey was as much fun as the destination for him. "I don't see why mornings should be left out, just because it's not happy hour yet. But if a bar is what it takes, can I buy you a drink tonight?"

She pursed her lips, but the corners of her mouth twitched, a smile threatening to destroy her stern expression. "I'm not much of a drinker."

"You're making this difficult for me." He wasn't annoyed. In fact, he'd rather stay here the rest of the morning, instead of making his meetings. "What do I have to do, to get your number?"

Her brows rose. "You could ask? Or come up with a corny line. I suppose there are a lot of options."

"Would any of them work?"

She took her drink from an employee and set it on the table next to her bag. He grabbed his as well. Pink dotted her cheeks, and her pupils were dilated. "Probably not. But I'm enjoying your efforts," she said.

Too bad. It would have been fun to find out what she sounded like when she was turned on. He didn't have time to keep up the game, though. His first interview was in fifteen minutes, and he still had to walk back to the hotel. He extended his hand. "I'm Blake, by the way."

"Luci."

Two hundred years ago, or even one-hundred, he would have kissed her fingertips and bowed. He settled for focusing on her warm grip when her palm rested against his. Another shock of recognition spilled through him. An image from centuries ago, of a woman in a kimono, black hair flowing around her shoulders. He stowed both the memory, and the pang of longing it dragged with it.

He gave Luci a brief nod. "Thank you for keeping me company this morning, Luci. Enjoy the rest of your day."

She furrowed her brow and studied him for a moment, before stepping back. "Same. Nice to meet you, Blake."

For a moment, when her hand drifted to her bag before snapping back, he thought she was going to hand him her number after all. He was pushy by nature, but he knew when he'd been shot down, and he as a rule he never had to beg. He resisted the desire to glance at her one last time as he strode out the front door. It would have been fun to actually get her information, but it still would have just been a fling, and he could grab one of those somewhere else. A tiny whisper told him it wouldn't be the same, and he shoved the nagging aside.

He stepped onto the street, and pinpricks of electric sparks singed his thoughts, yanking his attention from Luci. Another god was nearby. Caution surged through him. It was an eerily familiar aura. Even before his brain registered a name, his muscles tensed, and his gut churned.

Another zing flooded his head. He scanned the area, and his gaze landed on a woman across the street. Morrigan. Her eyes were so pale, it was evident even with the morning sun casting her in silhouette. She looked up at Blake, smirked, and then faded from sight. The crowds milled in to fill the empty spot, no one even flinching that a woman had just vanished before their eyes. Morrigan being here definitely meant something. But was it fuck-me bad, or was it maybe-he'd-finally-get-his-hands-on-her-long-enough-to-obliterate-her good?

Luci shut her laptop and blew her bangs out of her eyes. So much for getting a little work done before her interview. Normally, she would have worked from home that morning, and then made the hour drive for her appointment. With construction going on, she hadn't trusted travel time. She decided to work in the coffee shop down the street for a few hours, before walking to her meeting spot.

That had been the plan, anyway. The reality was, for the last two hours, her mind repeatedly drifted back to Blake, and not just the eerily comforting sensation of déjà vu that washed over her when they shook hands. She'd almost said his name before he did, but it would have come out Blaine, not Blake, and she had no idea why. Tall, blond... holy hell, she wanted to find out of his chest was as solid under that shirt as it looked. She'd been about two high-speed heartbeats away from giving him her number.

Reality had crashed back in before she made that mistake, though. Gorgeous guys weren't interested in chubby girls unless they wanted something they couldn't get anywhere else. Blake almost screamed, 'I'm hiding secrets.' He was too much like her ex. She wasn't making that mistake again, and not just because she couldn't foot the legal bill. Emotional attachment was a luxury she could live without.

She stepped into the hotel lobby, where her appointment was taking place, and approached the front desk. "I'm looking for Mr. Ugagnkin." Her tongue stumbled over the combination of letters. At least she knew she was pronouncing it right. She'd made his assistant repeat it, to make sure she got it right. She'd tried several times to hint she'd like his first name, but it hadn't been forthcoming.

"He asked that people wait for him over there." Reception nodded at a cluster of chairs across the room. "He'll be with you soon."

"Thank you." Luci had to perch on the edge of the seat to keep from sinking into it and wrinkling her suit. This entire job setup sent a weird vibe through her. Each individual piece was okay on its own. The company was in another city but was hiring contractors nationally, to telecommute, with zero in-office hours. Her interviewer was talking to people in a hotel lobby, because his in-town office reservation had fallen through at the last minute. The pay-scale was at the top end of the industry standard, and she'd been told she would never talk to anyone or need their contact information, during this project, except her direct supervisor or his assistant. All her requirements, changes, and quality-assurance results would flow through Mr. Ugagnkin.

Putting all the components together made her think someone was hiding something. Finding a new contract had been slow going, though, and the pay was good, so she'd stashed her reservations at least until she could talk to this Ugagnkin guy.

The minutes ticked away. She glanced at her phone. Her appointment was almost half an hour ago. This was ridiculous.

"Luci?" A tenor she'd heard before cut through her rambling thoughts and squeezed her pulse back to its high-speed trot from earlier. She looked up to see Blake a few feet away. He looked even better than he had this morning. That wasn't fair. "Lucinda Tansey?"

And he knew her full name. That should have her concerned. Unless... Crap. She'd been hit on earlier by her possibly new employer, and she still fantasized about being pinned under that sturdy frame. She pasted on a smile. "Hello?"

"I'm Blake Ugagnkin. I'm sorry to keep you waiting. The last interview ran over."

Of course it was him. She struggled to push aside the vivid images in her head—him stripping off her clothes a piece at a time, her dropping to her knees and dragging down his zipper—and failed spectacularly. She stood, used smoothing out her suit as an excuse to wipe off her palms, and shook his hand.

The moment she touched him, a flash of images raced through her head. Memories of a dream she'd had most of her life, except this time the other person had a face. Blake's. She wore a kimono, and he stood behind her, untying the pieces one by one and draping them to the side. Sliding the silk down her shoulders.

She pushed the thoughts aside and steadied herself in the now. "No worries. I guess that means you have my number after all." Why had she said that? She hid her cringe. "I mean, I've got time."

His hand lingered in hers, as he studied her face and then shook his head. "I should make it clear what happened this morning doesn't impact this at all. I hope it won't color your decision, if we decide to make you an offer."

If they were going to be working in the same office, he'd definitely have her leaning toward a yes answer. She forced the thought aside—not an easy feat, given the weight of his gaze raking over her. "Of course. The past is in the past," she said.

Except for maybe the occasional after-hours fantasy.

CHAPTER TWO

Blake kept his attention focused on Luci's face. He wouldn't let his gaze fall lower, to the silver locket nestled at the top of her cleavage. "Picasso was as much about commercial mass production as Andy Warhol or any modern clip art collection."

"That's a bit dismissive. Cubism was about taking three-dimensional objects and representing all their facets simultaneously in two-dimensional space." There was no irritation in her voice.

He had no idea how they'd gotten on the subject of art, but he was thoroughly enjoying the conversation. "You talk about it as if you knew the guy. Unless you were there, you can't say for certain."

She rolled her eyes, and laughed. "Because you were good pals with him? Besides, art is as much about interpretation as anything. You might see Warhol as simplistic, but those bright, vibrant representations of pop culture got people to pay attention to the medium."

"I'll agree with that. When it comes right down to it, for you or me, it's about what the eye appreciates." This time he didn't stop himself from looking her over. "A stunning Raphael or Renoir."

She blushed but didn't look away. "Masters of the human form and color and techniques. Definitely beautiful work."

When he'd seen her sitting in the lobby, it would have been so much easier to tell her 'thanks, but no thanks.' Except, in addition to being distractingly attractive, she was also the most qualified middle-tier developer he'd talked to in four cities. That didn't mean he had to cut the conversation short just yet, though.

He needed to stow his lust and hope she accepted his offer. Without the various pieces of this project, he and the other gods supporting this venture couldn't compile a system to record all the gods who had passed, vanished, or turned against the fates. Nor could they identify the vast list of mortals who might be in line to take some of their places and ascend.

Eternity was at stake. "Do you have any questions for me?"

Luci never broke eye contact for more than a few seconds. The uncertainty that had hovered around her in the coffee shop vanished when she launched into her presentation. "I'd like to know a little more about your company. What do you do?"

The truth wouldn't do. "We engineer resource-maximizing convergence, to continually enhance accurate scenarios." His nerves twinged at the meaningless, memorized bullshit. How had he never realized before how terrible that sounded? It didn't matter. Everyone would hear the same information. It was safer that way.

Her lips drew into a thin line. "How long have you been in business?" she asked.

"I started the company when I was in my twenties." That was almost true. He'd started *a* company, and one venture had melted into the next over the centuries, as times and necessity changed. The words still tasted wrong passing his lips.

"I see. So... the company's about five or ten years old?" Skepticism coated her words.

He gave her his warmest smile. "Not as new as you might think, and I guarantee we're stable."

"Of course." Her tone was flat. "I think that's all my questions."

He wasn't ready to stop chatting with her yet, and his desire only had a little to do with not ending the meeting on a sour note. "Listen, I'm really enjoying this, and I think we still have more to talk about. Interview-wise, of course. I was going to grab some lunch before my next appointment. I'd love it if you could join me."

Her frown deepened, and she fiddled with the strap on her laptop bag. "No, thank you. I won't take up any more of your time."

How had that gone downhill so fast? He stood as she did, keeping his voice pleasant and friendly. "This is the part of the conversation where I tell you I'll be in touch, but I'll be honest. I haven't talked to anyone who comes close to your qualifications. The contract is yours, if you're interested."

She shook his hand. Despite the warmth missing from her expression, her touch still lit his senses on fire, and sent vivid images of her and of his past racing through his thoughts. "Thank you," she said. "If you can email me a copy of the offer, I'd like some time to think about it."

That wasn't what she was supposed to say. Not as though he had a choice. "Of course." He pulled a business card from his wallet and handed it to her. He resisted the urge to tease her about having his number now as well. The flirting didn't seem to be working out. "My direct line. Reach out with any questions, and I hope to hear from you soon." As he said the words, he realized just how much he meant them. Because he needed her on board. Not for any other reason.

∞

Luci was glad to be back home, so she could dive back into her job search. She didn't like to be out of work for too long—it ate into her savings. She stripped off her jacket the moment she was inside, and peeled off the rest of her suit as she strode toward the bedroom. Why was she even considering Blake's offer? The money was good, but every time he told her something new about the job or the company, her bullshit meter ticked up another notch.

When he'd invited her to lunch, she almost thought he was interested despite his disclaimers. Even if she did let herself believe the desire in his gaze was real, she wasn't in the mood to pick at a salad in a crowded restaurant, just so no one would ask if she was sure she needed a side of fries with that burger.

She hung her suit in the closet and snagged a pair of her favorite jeans. The ones with the tears right under her ass, because of the way she'd worn the denim out. She grabbed a tank top from her drawer and tugged it on as she made her way back to the kitchen table—the most comfortable spot for working in the one-bedroom.

Time to do some digging and find out if Blake's answers were bullshit, or if she was just being paranoid because of her experience with Craig. She plucked a bottle of iced tea from the fridge and settled in to do her research.

She didn't want to find out Blake was a fraud. Despite everything, she enjoyed the conversation with him. The way they'd flowed from technical questions to pop culture, to music, to art had been the most fun she'd had talking to someone in a long time.

An hour later, her head spun from the circles she'd run in, chasing invisible trails. She'd found several references to Blake's company, all for different functions and businesses, but each time she followed a new link, it dead-ended.

She needed to just tell him no and find a different contract. One that probably wouldn't pay as much and almost definitely wouldn't include the mental stimulation or eye-candy, but it wasn't like she had either of those things before this morning.

Her thoughts ground to a halt when the next website loaded. A phone number and an address. Disappointment nudged her senses. Blake had said he only had one office, and it was in Nashville, Tennessee. This was in Tampa Bay, Florida. Maybe it was just a coincidence, and the two weren't related at all. Best way to find out would be to call and ask if the place had anything to do with Blake. She hesitated with her hand over her phone.

She was being stupid. She needed the answer. Putting off the call wouldn't change what she already knew—taking this job was a bad idea. She sucked in a deep breath and dialed the number.

"F and M Communications." A pleasant voice greeted her.

Maybe she should have thought more about what she was going to say before she placed the call. "May I speak with Blake Ugagnkin?"

Silence greeted Luci. She checked her phone. The call hadn't been dropped.

"Blake—?" The pleasant voice snapped off. "I'm sorry, he's not in this week. Can I transfer you to someone else or give him a message?"

"No. Thank you." Luci disconnected. It wasn't proof of anything. So he worked in an office he'd implied didn't exist. No big deal. Except, combined with everything else...

She couldn't do this. The pros didn't make up for the risk she'd take signing on. That was a practical business decision. The best one she could make. Even if nothing was there, her uneasiness was enough to make the job a must-avoid. She could find another one.

CHAPTER THREE

"Thank you for your time. I'll be in touch." Blake shook the hand of the contractor he'd interviewed. As soon as the man was gone, Blake sank back into the hotel-lobby sofa. He raked his fingers through his hair and exhaled. This guy had looked good on paper, but he'd shown up in a battered T-shirt, cut-off shorts, and reeking of... Blake wasn't even sure. Weed, beer, and sweat. But the job didn't require people to be presentable, just accurate. The meeting had consisted of an hour and a half of stories about past clients, and how stupid they'd been. The best thing about the interview was it had been Blake's last for the day.

His phone vibrated in his pocket, and he grabbed it. The device was set to remain silent, except for priority messages. He dialed into his voice mail and listened to the short message from his brother and business partner, Eli—Byleist, as he'd been known when they were younger. Eli was one of the first impacted by the old myths and curses, and was proof results could vary from the assumed interpretation.

The message was short. "One of your appointments is digging. She talked to Freyr's office. Call me."

Uneasiness danced through Blake's joints like a million tiny jolts. When Eli's fate had played out the way it did, Freyr had become the company's most vocal opposition. In the past few months, his people had become increasingly aggressive and violent in response, hunting down mortals and weaker gods on the list, and eliminating them. It shouldn't matter that one of Blake's applicants had called, though. Given his encounter with Morrigan this morning, Blake's location wasn't a secret, and that would make it simple to figure out who he was interviewing if Freyr cared.

So why couldn't Blake sit still? He dialed Eli's number, and drummed his fingers against his leg while he listened to the rings.

"You got my message." His brother skipped the formalities. After centuries of working together, they didn't usually bother with things like hello.

"Fill me in."

"This woman is on one of our outlying lists, and now they know who and where she is." Papers shuffled in the background. "Lucinda Tansey?"

Fuck. Dread spiked through Blake, and he clenched his empty hand until his knuckles ached. That meant she played a part in the prophecies. A mortal with a destiny, and very susceptible to things like death until her fate came to pass. "I thought we vetted all the applicants against known names."

"We found this reference buried in a filing cabinet from decades ago. We wouldn't have known to look, if your person in Freyr's office hadn't given us a heads-up when Lucinda's name set off their warning bells."

This was why they needed to make everything digital. Exactly the reason he was hiring contractors. Because there was too much to keep track of on paper. "What tier is she?" That would determine if her ties to the myths were significant, minor, or just a remote possibility.

"We're still digging up information about what her fate may be, but she's designated as significant. Could be a clerical error or..." Eli trailed off. They both knew that wasn't the kind of risk they could take. "I can send someone for her this afternoon."

The correct answer was yes. They needed to dispatch a local operative, to start surveillance and intercede as needed. If Luci accepted the contract keeping an eye on her would be easier. Then again, if Freyr decided she was an immediate threat, an operative might not be able to step in quickly enough.

"Helblindi"—Eli's sharp tone carried over the line—"make a call."

"I'll handle it myself." Blake shouldn't have said that. What was he going to do? Follow her around like a stalker? An operative could take care of that. Or Blake could knock on her front door and tell her, *'It's possible you're being hunted by a powerful god because you may or may not be a threat to his future'*?

There was no scenario he could picture in which that went over well. It didn't matter. He'd figure out it. His cock stirred at the thought of seeing her again. Her sarcastic laugh. Her witty comebacks. Her gorgeous curves. Long forgotten emotions he'd locked away—he thought forever.

Since he wasn't one of those gods who could teleport or fly, he had a bit of a drive ahead of him. With any luck, it would be enough time to think up a plan and convince his mind to stop taunting him with graphic fantasies of stripping Luci down, one piece of clothing at a time.

Her pizza was here. The knock on the front door pulled Luci from her job search. She hadn't told Blake yet that she wasn't accepting his offer, but she would. First thing tomorrow morning.

Well, not first thing. Maybe later in the day, to make sure he wasn't busy and...

She shelved the rambling thoughts that had assaulted her since she made the decision not to take the contract, grabbed the money from the table beside her, and crossed the living room. She opened the door. When she registered the sight in front of her, she frowned.

The woman on the other side looked up, pale eyes wide. "I'm sorry. I was looking for Joey?" She trailed her finger along the edge of her collar.

Who? "You have the wrong apartment." Discomfort rolled over Luci. Something about this woman made her grind her teeth. "I don't know him." She pushed the door shut. It was abrupt of her, but her skin crawled, and the urge to bolt surged through her.

"That's all right. You'll do."

The knob was yanked from Luci's hand, jarring her wrist, and the door crashed into her arm before colliding with slammed into the wall. A sharp gust shredded through the room. Her hair whipped in her face and stung her eyes. The slam echoed off through the room, and just as suddenly as the wind kicked up, it vanished. She shoved strands of brown out of her field of vision.

Her visitor stood immediately in front of her, smile in place. Pale blue eyes searched

Luci's face. "It really is you. It's been a long time."

The run-anywhere-but-here instinct pounded inside Luci until her head ached. What the hell was going on? "Morrigan?" She didn't know this woman's, but the name had popped into her head, associated with those pale eyes, and felt as real as Luci's swelling terror.

"You remember me." Morrigan sounded smug. "You're really"—she looked Luci over again—"kind of bland, aren't you? Not that it matters." She held up her right hand, thumb and middle finger pressed together, as if she were going to snap.

"Enough." A roar filled Luci's ears and skull, and Morrigan stopped moving. It wasn't just her snap that froze mid-air, but her entire frame, down to a grotesquely stalled smirk.

Luci blinked, to clear her eyes and thoughts, but it didn't help. A jumble of questions assaulted her mind, mingling with a fear she didn't understand. When she focused again, she wasn't sure she was seeing right.

Blake had Morrigan pinned to the far wall, his hand at her throat. Her feet dangled so her toes only brushed the carpet. "Leave." His voice was low and threatening, rolling on a breeze that didn't have a source.

Terror spilled through Luci. Whatever this was, she wasn't going to put up with it. Her apartment was a wreck, and she had no idea who these people were. This was too much. "What the *fuck* is going on?" she screamed.

Blake glanced back at Luci and then at the blue-eyed lunatic. Morrigan dropped, landing lightly, and dipped her head toward Blake's. "Catch you later, lover boy. Good luck with this." And then she vanished.

Luci shook her head. There was no way a woman had just disappeared from her living room. She looked at Blake. Why hadn't he answered her? Why was he even here? "Blake?"

He frowned, not meeting her gaze. "We need to get you out of here."

"What?" With the strange woman gone, Luci's terror ebbed, leaving room for confusion and frustration. "No. Answer my questions. Who was that? Why are you in my apartment? And why the fuck would I go anywhere with some guy I've only known for a few hours, and don't even trust?"

The creases in his brow deepened, and was that hurt in his eyes? Good. Served him right. He shook his head, and a blank mask slid onto his face. "You come with me, or stay here and the next one who comes for you will kill you. Decide now."

She sank to the couch and rubbed her hands over her face. He was lying. This was some sort of... She didn't even know, but it wasn't real. So why did every inch of her tell her to do what he said?

CHAPTER FOUR

An hour's drive to find this place, and Blake still hadn't figured out what he was supposed to say. Morrigan provided an ice breaker, but seeing her had summoned centuries of demons, rage, and grief. Blake would have ripped her to pieces right then and there if it was within his power to do so.

Despite his ultimatum, no part of him was willing to leave Luci to her fate. He racked his brain for a next step. "You're being hunted by powerful gods, because you may or may not be a threat to their future." It sounded just as crappy and crazy when he said it aloud.

Her raised brows and twisted mouth indicated she felt the same. "You're insane. I don't know what kind of game this is, but I'm calling the cops unless you leave right now. Hell, I'm calling them anyway. Was that even a real job interview this afternoon?"

Her distrust left an ache inside, but he ignored it. "You can't call anyone. Just listen. Morrigan—or someone like her—will be back."

With any luck, it wouldn't be her. He didn't need to see the past repeat itself.

She stood, crossed the room to the kitchen, and grabbed her phone. "I'm calling the police."

"Hear me out." Despite the adrenaline racing through him and the desire to get her to safety *now*, he forced his voice to stay calm. "Please." He had no idea why it was so important to him she listen. With anyone else, he'd have already tossed them over his shoulder and spirted them away to safety regardless of what they thought of him. Mortals were fragile, and he wasn't a god known for his patience. But it was important she trust him, even though he couldn't explain why he was being irrational about that. "If I can't convince you, I'll go." He couldn't though. There was no way he was leaving her.

She clenched her jaw and crossed her arms. Seconds ticked away, and the uncomfortable silence grew. "You have two minutes."

Great. That didn't make it any easier to come up with an explanation. Fuck it. He held out his hand, and with a flicker of concentration, summoned a ball of electricity and let it float about an inch above his palm.

A gasp strangled from her throat, and her phone clattered to the table. She snapped her jaw shut and closed the distance between them.

"Bullshit. That's a trick." She pushed up his sleeves.

When her skin met his, a shock of familiarity seared through him, and images flooded his thoughts. Random snippets he couldn't make sense of. Memories of a woman he'd known almost two centuries ago. A nightgown. A high collar. Her soft gasps, as he stripped away her clothes, mingled with Luci's sigh in the now and dragged him from the vision.

He found his voice. "It's not a trick. It's real." He pulled off his suit coat, draped it over the back of a chair, and rolled up his sleeves. "See? It's just me."

"Can you vanish like that woman did?"

"No. Teleporting isn't in my arsenal."

She made a sound that was half huff, half sniff. "You need better tricks."

Wounded pride swelled in his chest. "I have better tricks." He closed his eyes, bowed his head, and inhaled deeply through his nose. He summoned an image of the afternoon sky, heavy with clouds blocking most of the sun. Electricity and water broiled through the air. Through his eyelids, he saw the light fade. He looked at Luci again, as a clap of thunder rattled the windows and echoed off the walls.

She squeaked and jumped. Her hand flew to her heart, and she met his gaze. "Did you do that?"

That was a better response. He smirked. "We need to go now. I'll explain everything I can, once we're safe, but that requires you to follow me."

Luci looked out the window—rain hammering against it from a sky that had been bright blue seconds ago—then back at Blake. She still had no idea what to believe, but she didn't know of a single magic trick that could make it rain in an instant. The flash of images she'd seen when she touched him... they'd felt like her memories. They couldn't be. Was he doing something to her head? Hypnosis, maybe. That made more sense than a random god having it in for her and Blake coming to the rescue.

Even knowing all that, she couldn't convince herself to send him away. It had to be better than waiting for some vanishing woman who could summon wind from thin air to come back and kill her. "All right. I'll go." Luci expected more anxiety at speaking the words. Instead some of the fight escaped her, and relief sank in.

He pulled a blank card from his wallet, intertwined his fingers with hers, and tugged her toward the closet. What the hell?

"I can't teleport," he said as he passed the credit-card sized object over the knob, "but this always gives me a doorway home." He opened the door, and her eyes grew wide. Instead of coats and jackets, an entryway stretched out in front of her.

He pulled her hand. They stepped into the new room, and the door swung shut behind them. This was too weird. She didn't know if she should freak out or just enjoy the madhouse. She whirled and yanked the knob. The other side was an unfamiliar street, instead of her living room. "How did you....? What...?" She didn't know what to say. Nothing in her scope of experience prepared her for this.

"It's magic." He flashed her a broad smile.

She might have to start believing that or lose her mind.

"You're back." A female voice interrupted Luci's thoughts. A woman tossed her arms around Blake's neck, and he returned the hug. "You're early," the woman said.

Jealousy speared Luci, leaving a sharp pain in her lungs. That was ridiculous. She didn't care who Blake had waiting for him at home, even if the woman was tall, thin, and almost glowing.

"We need to rethink our plans." Blake stepped out of the woman's grasp.

Another man joined them. He looked a lot like Blake but not as broad in the shoulders, and instead of a suit he wore more casual jeans and a T-shirt. He glanced at Luci before turning back to Blake. "You got there in time. I have more information about her relevance."

Luci was a guest, and it was true she had almost zero idea what was going on, but she still didn't like being ignored. She opened her mouth to protest, but Blake rested a hand on her lower back and nudged her forward. The contact sent a jolt of warmth through her and snatched away her objections.

"This is Luci." Even in a few short words, Blake commanded the situation. "She had the distinct pleasure of running into Morrigan, so no, I didn't make it in time. Did we know there were other pantheons involved with her name?" He looked at Luci. "And this is my brother, Eli, and his fiancée, Marley."

Fiancée. The single word soothed Luci more than she thought possible, especially given the last hour or so of insanity. What the hell was wrong with her? She'd known this guy for a few hours, he'd already threatened to uproot her life, and she was crushing on him? She stuffed any further reactions deep down inside, focused on being calm and logical, and smiled at Marley and Eli.

"Fuck." Eli drummed his fingers against his legs. "You still have the copies of the Celtic myths surrounding Morrigan, correct?"

Something resembling a growl rumbled from Blake's chest. "What do you think? And why are you in my house? A phone call wouldn't do?"

"We're here because the old filing cabinets that had the documents with your name are here." Marley looked at Luci. "Goddess in your apartment? You have my sympathy. Are you all right?"

No one seemed to have any issues with this entire bizarre conversation besides Luci. "I'm really fucking confused, and someone promised me an explanation."

Marley reached for Luci's hand and squeezed her fingers. "Don't blame them. They've had centuries to deal with it."

Blake sighed.

Eli wrapped an arm around Marley's waist and pointed her toward the front door. "We'll catch up soon."

Luci's head spun, as silence engulfed her and Blake again. He finally spoke. "Do you want something to drink?"

"I want answers." She hated to sound like a broken record, but the last of her restraint was slowly slipping away, leaving in its place a panic she couldn't define and didn't think she could contain.

He nudged her to the right, toward an open room. It was the embodiment of the term *sitting room* brought to life. A fireplace dominated the far wall, and leather sofas and chairs were arranged to face each other. Blake took a spot on one of the two couches and waved for her to join him.

She couldn't sit. Too much energy thrummed through her. She folded her arms, to keep herself from shaking apart. "I'm waiting."

CHAPTER FIVE

Blake was done searching for the best way to phrase things. At this point there was no reason to try and break the news gently, or ease Luci into things. He hated the worry lines around her eyes, and the way she chewed the inside of her cheek, but something told him meting out information wouldn't ease her expression.

Besides, as gods they didn't keep their immortality and power secret because of things like concern for their safety. Once upon a time, they'd worn the label proudly. It was just that these days, no one believed them anyway. The numbers of people who kept the faith were so small, a god wearing his birthright like a badge didn't make any sense.

Luci stopped her pacing, and started at him. "Well?"

He sucked in a deep breath. Might as well start at the beginning. "Morrigan, the woman in your apartment, is a god. She's not the only one. Eli and I are as well. Marley wasn't, but she is now, and..." He trailed off when Luci's brow furrowed and confusion settled onto her face.

"And at least one of you wants me dead. I get that. But why?" she asked.

"I'll back up." He patted the couch next to him. "Sit. It's going to take a while."

She shifted her weight from one foot to the other, and then dropped into the chair across from him. She drew her mouth into a straight line and watched him, eyes wide in expectation.

"Every pantheon... you would call them mythologies"—he hated that term, but he needed to make her understand this was real, not a children's story about imaginary creatures—"has their own curses, fates, and texts surrounding the end of the world."

She held up her index finger. "Stop. I'm not super up to date on my mythology, but I'm pretty sure there are no gods named Blake. Or Eli."

He resisted the urge to roll his eyes, not at her but at destiny. "It's not our fate for people to know our names."

"Really." Her tone was flat.

"I'm not just saying that," he said. "The text around us specifically says only our brother will be famous. But you're right. Eli's full name is Byleist, and mine is Helblindi."

"I guess I can see why you don't go around calling yourself that."

He scowled. "Thanks. Anyway, besides stripping away our notoriety, our legends say a lot of gods will die, and others will take their place during and after the rebirth of the world as we know it. As you can imagine, not everyone's so keen on seeing that happen. Especially those gods who aren't supposed to survive. None of us took it seriously until a few months ago, when the poems and rhymes we'd recited for centuries started coming true."

"Let's say I believed you." She wrung her fingers together. "Why do any of them care about me? And how did—" She clenched her jaw and shook her head. "Why me?"

He wanted to push her question, find out what else was in her head, but something told him that wouldn't get him anywhere right now. "That's what Eli and Marley are trying to figure out. It's why…" He let out a slow breath. "It's why I'm looking for contractors. All of this information is written down in so many random places, we need to pull it all together. Digitize it."

"But it's not like you can tell someone what you're working on, without them thinking you're insane. So you're having it built in separate modules." She filled in the rest of the thought for him.

"Exactly. Apparently there's a reference to you in one. We'd have known that if we already had the system online."

She flopped back in the chair and turned her gaze to the ceiling. "And it's completely a coincidence that I showed up on your interview list."

The way she said it made the entire thing sound so... conspiratorial. "It is. We still would have found you, but not like this."

"Wow. That makes me feel so much better about the entire thing." Sarcasm dripped from her voice. She dropped her chin to her chest and locked her gaze on Blake. "When can I go home?"

"I don't know."

She rubbed her face, and a tiny whimper escaped from her throat. Her frame shuddered. She dragged the back of her wrist across her cheeks, and looked at him again. "What now?"

"We keep you safe until we have answers and a plan."

"That's swell"—she was on her feet again, pacing—"but it's not going to work for me. I have a life. Things to do. And that doesn't involve sitting around in the middle of—where are we, anyway?—just waiting for the other shoe to drop."

"We're in Nevada. About ten miles outside of Las Vegas." He didn't understand why, but it tore at him to see her so upset. It knotted his muscles and coiled his instinct, making him search for a target he wouldn't find. He stood and stepped in her path. She huffed. When she tried to step around him, he rested his hands on her shoulders and forced her to look him in the eye. He kept his voice low and calm. "It sucks. I get that."

She let out a snorting laugh. "How could you? If this is true, you have no idea how I feel."

"You're right, I can only guess. But I can still tell it sucks. I've had my home, my life, and the people I love ripped from me enough times..." He clenched his jaw at the surge of memories. Grace, in nineteen-twenties' New York. Sayuri, with the flowing dark hair and kimono. Elizabeth, in the silk Victorian dress. An ache throbbed in his chest. "You don't have to just sit down and surrender, but we do need a plan, and we need information first."

"Then let me help."

A compulsion sped through him, and he brushed a thumb over her cheek. The direct contact added another wash of color to the images vying for his mind's attention, blurring her face with others and morphing them together. Except instead of drawing his attention from her, the memories honed his senses in on her presence. On top of it all was heat and desire and the need to protect Luci. "I will. But right now, if we dive into a random spot and start digging, we'll be spinning our wheels. Once Eli has more information, he'll let me know.

She nodded and covered his hand with hers. Lust jolted through him. She licked her lips. "What do we do until then?"

Find out if Luci tasted as delicious as she looked. "I'd still love to buy you a drink," he said.

Some of the lines on her face faded, and the corner of her mouth pulled up. "The last thing I need right now is to be drunk. Though, trust me, it's tempting."

The slightest twist of his hand, and he could wrap his fingers in her hair. A dip of his head, and he could claim her mouth. Ancestors, she was wreaking havoc on his thoughts. "I'll buy you dinner, then." Or make her the main course. Trace his tongue down her chest. Dip between her breasts.

"Dinner. Crap." She frowned and stepped out of his grip. "I completely forgot I ordered pizza before my reality imploded. The poor driver is going to be pissed. I need to call them and apologize."

Desire still skittered over Blake's skin. He clenched his fist, to bring his racing pulse under control, and tried to ignore the strain of his cock against his slacks. He was disappointed at the lost moment, but something about how flustered she looked over a forgotten dinner delivery was still enticing. Flushed cheeks, wide eyes. He laced his fingers through hers. "Calling them will wait."

She caught her bottom lip between her teeth. Did she have any idea how seductive that was? "I feel bad," she said.

He could think of a couple very specific ways to distract her into feeling something else, but the moment was gone. "I don't suspect they'll hold a grudge. If you're that worried about pizza, I can have something more authentic delivered."

"Authentic pizza. In the middle of Nevada. How do you define authentic?"

He knew the perfect place in Naples. Italy. And the goddess who ran the place just happened to be a close friend. "Trust me."

Luci's smile slid back in place. "Oddly enough, I do."

CHAPTER SIX

Luci struggled to wrap her brain around the entire situation. Gods. Myths. Fate. There was no way any of it existed, let alone that she played any part in it. Her logic said it would be just as stupid of her to ignore what was right in front of her as it was to believe it. That included the way Blake kept looking at her. The way his gaze dipped over every inch of her. The flashes of unfamiliar but sharply sensual images every time he touched her. It should be the last thing on her mind, but it consumed most of her remaining mental resources.

She was certain of some things. The pizza he'd ordered had been almost heavenly—hand tossed crust, brick-oven crisp, and like nothing she'd ever tasted before. And she was sure that when she said she trusted him, she meant it. The idea of giving her faith to someone she barely knew terrified her. Now that it was clear what he'd been hiding that morning, the lingering uneasiness vanished. Whatever else happened, she believed him when he said they were working to find answers and keep her safe.

She settled back onto one of the couches after they finished eating, a permanent smile on her face from the conversation that had drifted from one topic to the next with ease. "You really got the pizza from Italy?"

He took the seat next to her, and his thigh brushed hers before he turned to face her. "You meet people when you've been alive as long as I have."

Part of her wanted to know how long that was. Numbers ticked through her head. Five hundred years? One thousand? Her mind twitched at the logic of someone actually living that long. She could only handle so much reality in an evening. "I bet you've seen some amazing things."

He furrowed his brow for a second, but his smile returned so quickly she thought she'd imagined the change. "I have. There are a lot of pluses to being immortal. It gets a little lonely at times, though."

"But you saw so much as it happened. The moon landing, right? Were you there for that?"

"On the moon? No." He winked. "But yes, I remember that. And hearing about the Wright Brothers taking their first flight. And watching large portions of Europe sail to the new world..." He trailed off. "But it all blurs together after a while. There are so many new and amazing things that new and amazing becomes passé." He shook his head, as if to clear away a fog.

The new world. He really was that old. She struggled to place herself in that frame of mind. "It does sound like a lot, but I still bet it was awe inspiring. The world doesn't do incredible things anymore."

"Sure it does." He slid his fingers under hers, where they rested on her knee. "It's not a matter of scope; it's what you remember. The day you graduated high school. Or college. You remember those?"

Should she pull away? No. This was comfortable. Reassuring. But she did wish it wasn't all focused on her. "Of course. But those aren't the kind of things that change the world."

"They change someone's world. Yours, and that's important. Mine, since it's part of what makes you who you are now. You remember your first kiss, right? The anticipation. The buildup. The nervousness?"

His smooth voice glided under her skin and summoned every sensation he described, until her pulse sped through her veins and her lips twitched from the suggestion. "How awkward it was."

He dipped his head in, until his mouth hovered millimeters from her neck, close enough his breath shifted across her skin with every word. "But you had to start somewhere, right?"

Her chest constricted as he traced a line up to her jaw, never making contact. He rested his hand at the back of her neck. Tiny sparks danced through her entire body at the barely-there caress of his lips brushing hers, and she whimpered. He pulled back, but his gaze still lingered on her face, desire darkening his eyes. "It's not about the big things. It's about enjoying those things that are significant to you." His tone was low. Hypnotic.

She wanted more. She licked her lips and tried to make her vocal chords work. "Like meeting a stranger in a coffee shop, who turns my entire world upside down?"

His grin was sinful and hungry. He traced tiny circles along the base of her neck with his thumb. "Exactly. Like that the most gorgeous woman who was in that room is sitting on my couch now."

The compliment nudged a corner of her mind she was trying to keep locked, and her insecurities flooded back in. "You don't have to say that." Damn it, she hadn't meant to let that slip out.

"Say what?"

"That I'm gorgeous." Negative thoughts clawed their way to the surface. She wasn't pretty. She was pudgy and clumsy and plain. Sexy guys like him—he was a god, for hell's sake—didn't look twice at women like her. His gaze said he meant the words, and his touch lit her nerve endings on fire, but her stupid self-doubt screamed in her skull.

"You are." He glided his hand from her neck, to trail a finger down her cheek, gaze never leaving her. He traced her bottom lip. "Every inch of you is stunning." He sounded sincere. He looked genuine.

But her mind still refused to accept it. "I bet that's one of those things you don't forget—the beautiful women you've loved in your lifetime." Why had she said that? There was something wired wrong in her head. Maybe it would take the focus off her, though. Give her a chance to rebuild her walls and stash her uncertainty again.

He intertwined his fingers with hers. "I'm no more likely to tell you that, than you are to tell me about your past love life."

Now he was keeping secrets from her. It was an irrational reaction, but knowing that didn't stop her from feeling it. Her own insecurity was sabotaging an amazing conversation, and she couldn't make herself stop. "I'll tell you about my past loves. I was engaged once. To a handsome, smooth-talking, well-dressed guy, who turned every head when he walked in a room." Shut up, shut up, shut up. It was too late. Blake's frown told her that.

"And madly in love with him, I assume." His seductive tone was gone, replaced with something unreadable. "I suspect a guy would have to be pretty spectacular, to catch your attention like that."

He was making fun of her, wasn't he? Except despite his flat words, there was no malice in his gaze. Not that she was any good at recognizing things like that. "He talked a good game. Even convinced me to go into business with him. Let me handle the accounting. Brought in huge sales." She swallowed the growing lump in her throat at the swell of unpleasant memories. It was good she'd dredged this up. A painful but appropriate reminder she knew better than to lose herself in someone's attention. "Until he skipped town, and I was brought up on money laundering charges." That had been painful, humiliating, and incredibly difficult to clear her name of. If they were talking about moments burned in their memories, the day she testified against her ex was one of the most bittersweet of her life.

"Fuck, Luci." His expression softened. "You didn't deserve to go through that."

"It was my own fault. I let myself be sweet-talked into oblivion and ignored some really obvious signs. I know better now than to trust too-good-to-be-true, all-encompassing lines like 'you're gorgeous.'" A new ache joined her discomfort when Blake frowned. She shouldn't have said that. Her subconscious seemed to know better than her, though. Even if she took the words back, she wouldn't sound genuine.

Blake cupped her chin and forced her to look him in the eye. His voice was firm but calm. "I'm not him. And I mean what I say."

She wanted to believe him, but the mental floodgate was open, and she couldn't convince herself he was sincere. Then again, she also couldn't make herself pull away. "I spilled my guts. Now it's your turn. You must have someone who's left an impact on you. Some stunning beauty from the centuries of your life."

He clenched his jaw and stood. "And if you weren't using it as an excuse to sour the conversation, I might tell you about one of them."

One of them... Of course he'd had eons of lovers. A guy like him, living for as long as he had. She clenched her hand hard enough her fingernails dug into her palm. "That's fine. You have your past, it doesn't impact me. I don't have to know the details, as long as I remember it doesn't have anything to do with me."

"It doesn't." All emotion had vanished from his face and voice.

CHAPTER SEVEN

Luci lay in the unfamiliar bed, staring at the ceiling. Once she'd derailed the conversation with Blake, it was over. He'd backed off, shown her where a guest room was, and handed her a T-shirt to sleep in, if she wanted.

That had to have been at least an hour ago. Sleep eluded her, though. Everything around her smelled like Blake, seeping into her senses and taunting her with whispers of almost-kisses. She hated herself for derailing the conversation the way she had, but at the same time, it was for the best. As long as she kept repeating that, it would sink in, and she'd believe it. He and his brother would figure out why someone wanted to kill her, and they'd send her home, and life would go on.

She rolled onto her side, so she could see out the window. They were too close to the city for there to be anything besides black and the faintest smattering of dots. Light pollution bled into the bottom of the sky. She pulled her knees to her chest and tried to block out her onslaught of swirling thoughts. Life would definitely go on, and she'd be better for the experience once she came out the other side.

The sound of a knock on Elizabeth's bedroom door sent her steadily beating heart pattering at a gallop. She lit the candle on the stand beside her, climbed from her bed—not that she had been able to sleep in this unfamiliar house—and crept to answer.

Henry nudged his way into the room as soon as she cracked the door, and toed it shut behind him. Her tall, blond, strapping Henry. "My beautiful Beth." He placed his hands on her hips and drew her close. He trailed his fingers under her nightgown and over her birthmark. The one shaped like a crow, that he loved to kiss. "Finally, I have you all to myself."

She rested her hands on his chest, intensely aware she wore nothing but the thin shift she slept in. The heat from his palms seared through the fabric and left traces of longing on her skin. "Dinner did seem to wear on for a bit, didn't it?"

He kissed her forehead, then her nose, and finally brushed his lips over hers. "It does not matter. It's over now"—he guided her backward—"and you look stunning." He spun before they reached the bed, dropped onto the feather mattress, and pulled her between his legs.

"What if someone hears us?" Even though they weren't married yet, they'd been together several times, but he had so many guests staying at his home now. All in anticipation of their wedding in a few days.

"Then they will be jealous I've got the privilege of making the most gorgeous woman in the house scream in ecstasy." He kissed her stomach through her nightgown, and her breasts tightened with need.

"My parents won't be impressed."

"Your father has already granted me your hand. No one but you may revoke that honor now."

"I won't scream with so many people here."

In a single fluid gesture, he stripped her clothing off. The cool air brushed her flaming skin and caressed the dampness between her legs. "That sounds like a challenge."

"It isn't," she squeaked out.

He cupped her bottom and drew her close. Her stomach fluttered in anticipation, as he tilted his head in and drew a nipple into his mouth. When he flicked his tongue back and forth over the sensitive nub she groaned and dug her fingers into his shoulders. He worked his hands forward, until he brushed her wet desire.

She gasped at the sensation. Damn being overheard. She leaned in enough to reach the laces on his breeches and fumbled until they were loose. When she worked him free, her fingers wrapped around his hard length, he let out a low groan that penetrated every inch of her.

He grabbed her wrists. "I want to watch you on top of me." He lay back and tugged her with him.

He was so vocal. The words and desire throbbed inside her. She knelt on the bed and positioned herself above his erection. In a single thrust, he pushed inside her, and a cry tore from her throat.

"That's my beautiful Beth." His gaze traveled over her, as they built to a frantic rhythm. He slid his hands up her stomach, to her breasts. Each caress was a feather-light buzz through her body.

She groaned as the soft touches melted into hungry pinches and tugs. He rolled her swollen nipples between his fingers. Pleasure built inside her, dancing along the different sensations of Henry's attentions. Each time with him was more spectacular than the last. Would it be like this forever?

When he dropped one hand between her legs and pressed against a sensitive button, another cry tore from her throat. That was *new. And incredible. Her breathing turned into short pants for air, as he rubbed the new spot and thrust himself inside her. Her thoughts fluttered away, lost in a haze of bliss. Each push from Henry stole more of her reason. Waves of revelry splashed over her, and she ground against him, riding the intensity.*

His grip on her breast tightened, and his grunts became staccato. She recognized the sound of him drawing close to finish. He drove up, filling her.

Luci's eyes flew open, and she gasped. She'd had dreams like that before, where she was someone in the past, but they'd never been so vivid. Her lover had never had a name, now he had two. Henry from her dreams was Blake. The man whose guest bedroom she lay in.

The intensity of the vision still flooded her senses, mingling with faint scent of Blake on everything surrounding her. Need throbbed between her legs, and her nipples ached for attention. She didn't know where the sleeping vision had come from, or why her subconscious had given her the name Elizabeth and placed her in Victorian England. At least, despite all the random unknown variables, her mind had been sadistic enough to still give her that damned birthmark on her hip she hated so much.

Right now, she didn't care. The memory of Blake-as-Henry flowed over every inch of her, obliterating her sense and filling her with an insatiable desire. Still half-lost in the fantasy, she moved her hands to her chest and whimpered at the first brush against her sensitive skin. She squeezed, drawing back the images of his hands on her skin. The pinch of pain and pleasure.

She glided one palm down her stomach, to the pleading need between her thighs. How could a dream be so intense and feel so real, as if she'd lived it? She pushed her panties aside and dipped her fingers between her wet folds. Her clit blossomed in delight when she sought it out.

She rubbed frantic circles, hips pumping against her hand. Climax tore through her, and she had to bite the inside of her cheek to keep from crying out. In her head, she still felt the visions mingling with the present, as if Blake had been buried inside her, stroking her until she came.

Her orgasm ebbed, and she eased off and slumped back against the mattress. Reality slunk its way back in, as the buzz faded, reminding her where she was—what had happened. Pointing out there were voices drifting up from somewhere in the house.

Wait. Voices?

After Luci went to bed, Blake tried to work. He didn't need sleep unless he'd exhausted his power on something, and tonight he wasn't interested in indulging the habit. Instead, he spent a few hours staring at the wall, trying to figure out how the conversation that evening had gone so completely off track.

He hated to see Luci's insecurities rear their head, and that was what he was dealing with. On the other hand, he refused to indulge them. He could only tell her he was being honest so many times, before it wasn't worth the effort anymore.

Except he couldn't make himself believe he'd been right to stop trying when he'd done so. At least sending her upstairs and putting some distance between them had helped him banish the flashes of his past that had haunted him all day.

The past. Something was there... The notion floated just out of his conscious reach. What was it? He closed his eyes, to block out as much external distraction as possible, and honed in on his thoughts. Something about Beth. Grace. This morning.

Morrigan. Of course. Seeing her had never been a good sign. Millennia ago, he and she had dated. When she'd killed Sayuri, he'd assumed it was jealousy. When she obliterated Elizabeth, he suspected it ran deeper than resentment and insanity. And when she went after Grace as well, he knew there was more there.

The words of the legend floated to mind. Words he'd memorized after Grace, hoping he could make sense of them.

The woman who bears her mark will undertake a battle of overthrowing.

He'd never figured it out. It seemed obvious on the surface, given they'd all had the same birthmark, except he had no idea why his past loves would be play a part in overthrowing Morrigan. There certainly hadn't been any battles involved. It had always ended in an instant. He cringed at the vivid memories.

But the women Morrigan had gone after before had been Blake's lovers. Wives. Luci certainly made his pulse race, and he enjoyed her company, but the relationship wasn't the same. Luci wasn't the same as the rest. Then again, there was that sense of déjà vu every time they touched. That flash of memory. That feeling he knew Luci on a deeper level than was possible after such a short amount of time.

And he was reading too much into the situation. Never a good idea.

A soft knock interrupted his painful journey into the past, and he padded to the front door. Surprise and concern filled him when he saw Marley. He stepped aside. "The phone was too difficult to pick up?" What was meant to sound teasing came out as a bark. He gave her a weak smile. "Sorry. Long day."

She didn't seem to take offence. "Tell me about it." She stepped inside and handed him a manila folder. "How's your guest?"

"As well as can be expected, I suppose."

Marley rested a hand on his arm. "You don't know this, but it's not easy being where she is. You just turned her entire world upside down. At least you filled her in quickly and didn't drag it out for several months. But she has to cope."

He didn't miss the hint of irritation that crept into Marley's voice. Even though she said she understood Eli's reasons for keeping his identity secret for so long, Blake knew it still bothered her on some level. She'd gotten immortality out of the entire affair. Was that what waited for Luci?

For some reason the thought left a foul taste in his mouth. Marley seemed to enjoy the newfound power that came with godhood, but Blake wouldn't wish immortality on anyone. Not unless they got to walk into it eyes wide open.

He shook the thought away and held up the folder. "What's this?"

"Can we talk in your office?"

He held out an arm in that direction. "After you."

Seconds later, she closed the door, shutting them off from the rest of the house. "Look inside."

"Just tell me what it is." He opened the folder anyway. His stomach lurched at the contents. Photocopies of documents he'd buried long ago.

"You recognize them, then." Marley's tone was soft.

He should. They were marriage certificates—or at least their historical equivalent. One from feudal Japan, one from Victorian England, and the last from here in the U.S. almost a century ago.

CHAPTER EIGHT

"And?" It took effort for Blake to form the single word.

"Look at the birth dates on them." Marley prompted.

Nothing stood out, except that they'd all been born during harvest season. A whisper of memory tickled his thoughts. A notion from decades ago tensed through his muscles and throbbed in his head. There was a reason he'd shoved that bit of his past aside, though he couldn't recall what that reason was. He didn't have the patience for this. If his past insisted on haunting him so completely, he'd like to know why sooner rather than later. "Just tell me what I'm supposed to be seeing."

She twisted her mouth and raised her brows. "Fine. They were all born on their calendar's fall solstice. They've got other similarities. They were born in foreign countries—to their parents anyway—but raised back home. They were all still single, disgracefully so I'd assume, when they turned thirty. And they all had birthmarks on their hips. Apparently at one point you or someone you knew thought that was relevant, because since Grace, you've been keeping a list of everyone who met those specific criteria."

"It sounds vaguely familiar." It sounded intensely familiar. A ghost he'd chased almost a century ago. An obsession he'd forced himself to abandon, when he realized he could spend the rest of eternity chasing the phantom, and it still wouldn't change the past. A grief-induced dream he'd walked away from, in order to carry on. "But we gave that up."

"You may have, but someone kept searching." Marley's voice dropped in volume. "Look at the last document in there."

He flipped to the photocopy of a more recent birth certificate. From Canada.

Lucinda Beth Tansey.

Born September 23, 1985.

Distinguishing marks: oddly shaped birthmark on the left hip.

He looked back at Marley.

"That's why her name is on a list," Marley said. "And she's the only person in almost seventy years."

Fuck. Damn it. "Fuck it all to Hel". He didn't know how to process the information, but that didn't stop dread and undirected fury from spilling through him.

"There's more." Marley pulled her phone from her back pocket and swiped the screen to unlock it. A paused video waited, and she clicked it to start it playing.

Blake watched, rage growing, as images of Luci's apartment burning played behind a reporter's head. The man droned on about how an explosion had rocked the building early that evening, and while the police weren't releasing any information at this time, there were rumors of a terrorist attack. He said their sources inside the Salt Lake Sheriff's department were certain nothing but a bomb could have caused that level of destruction.

A bomb or a pissed off god. The thought bounced in Blake's head.

The office door creaked open, and Marley's spun on her toe at the same time Blake's head shot up. Luci stood in the doorway, his shirt hanging halfway down her thighs, over her ripped jeans. She looked gorgeous and concerned and so very fragile. How was he going to explain this?

Luci hovered outside the door. From the tour Blake gave her earlier, she knew it led to his office. Two voices floated out—she assumed the two she'd heard through the vents upstairs.

Blake, and if she was hearing right, Marley. There was also a muffled noise she couldn't make out, like conversation coming through a tiny speaker.

"That's why her name is on a list. And she's the only person in almost seventy years."

"Fuck it all to hell." That would be Blake. Even muffled, his voice was distinct.

Should she knock? Walk away? She definitely shouldn't eavesdrop.

"There's more," Marley said.

And then silence. Awkward curiosity trickled through Luci, until she couldn't sit still anymore. She knocked, but there was no answer. She turned the knob and pushed gently.

Blake and Marley both twisted toward her, tearing their attention from a phone in Marley's hand. Marley turned her gaze to the carpet, and a scowl marred Blake's expression.

"Did I miss something?" Luci asked. What was meant to be a light-hearted question, came out as a soft, cautious squeak.

Marley looked at her, brow furrowed and eyes turned down at the corners. "I'm sorry."

"We should do this somewhere else." Blake stepped around her and rested a hand at Luci's elbow.

Luci stepped away from his touch, hating her body for betraying her by reacting to the gentle warmth. "Where?"

"The den."

She followed him down the hall to a room at the back of the house. Unlike the sitting room, which felt sterile and ancient, this entire place radiated Blake's presence. A single recliner sat near the doorway, remotes on the table next to it, and a large screen TV covered most of the far wall. "Have a seat," he said.

She crossed her arms and leaned against the wall. "I'm fine here." If she didn't feel the cold, she was afraid the heat from her dream might consume her. That, and despite her brain's attempts to sabotage her, she wasn't forgetting why she needed to keep her distance from Blake. Secrets. She wouldn't live with secrets.

"Suit yourself." The strain in his voice defied the casual words. He grabbed a remote, and seconds later the TV flickered on. Channels surfed past, until he landed on a news station. The video to the side of the anchorman showed her apartment building, burning bright and spewing smoke into the night sky.

Acid surged in her throat, as the man on TV rambled on about what little they knew. She hugged herself tighter, and her legs wobbled before she gave up trying to support herself and sank to the ground.

"Luci?" Blake's concern barely nudged the edges of her clouded nausea.

"Why is this happening?" She heard her own voice, though she didn't remember saying the words.

Blake crouched in front of her, his face distinct despite the disorientation jumbling her thoughts. His expression conveyed concern, and his tone was sympathetic. "I think a better question is, who are you?"

CHAPTER NINE

"I'm nobody." Luci's voice barely reached her own ears. She didn't mean it in a self-effacing way. She honestly didn't understand why any of these people—creatures?—were interested in her at all. "I'm just a computer programmer, who needs work." In the background, the newscaster droned on about how the blast had been localized but the fire spread quickly. Some tenants were successfully evacuated, but they didn't have a death count yet.

Death count. People had lost their lives because of her? She was going to be sick. She swallowed back the bile and tried to breathe deeply. It didn't work. Her pulse hammered in her chest. What if she'd been there still? At least she wouldn't have to deal with this guilt. What if they—whoever they were—came after her here or wherever she went next? Was this the rest of her life? She gasped, unable to get enough oxygen. She didn't know what to do.

"Luci, stop." Blake's firm words shattered her welling panic. He rested a hand on her arm. "This isn't your fault."

"Bullshit, it's not," she said. He didn't know what he was talking about. He was one of them, and when someone had immortality, how could they care for a human life? The thought added more guilt to the pile growing inside her. That wasn't fair, and thinking it didn't help her feel any better, but she wanted it to.

Marley knelt next to her and draped an arm around her shoulders. "Hey. What can I do?"

"Bring them back. Make that not happen." Luci nodded at the TV. "You're a god, right? Give those people their lives back."

"I'm sorry, that's not something I can do. I'm one now. I wasn't a year ago." The gentleness in Marley's tone overlapped the concern on Blake's face, as he watched, silent. "So I know what you're going through."

She had no idea what Luci was going through, unless she'd watched random people die because of her. Luci swallowed the bitter retort. Reason was slinking past the grief, and pointing this out wasn't going to accomplish anything. "Then no. There's nothing you can do."

"If you're sure..."

Blake stood and offered Marley a hand up. "Thanks for the information. I've got the rest handled."

Marley stepped from the room but returned seconds later. She handed Luci a piece of paper with a phone number on it. "If you need someone to talk to, who understands what it's like to be mortal"—Marley cast a glare at Blake—"call me. Wake me up. I don't care when it is."

"Thank you." Luci forced a smile onto her lips.

Blake didn't like Marley's implication he was incapable of understanding, but he knew why she'd thought it. He let her see herself to the door, knowing she wouldn't be offended. His priority right now was Luci. Except, as with so many times in the last twenty-four hours, he wasn't sure what to say. Luci's grief combined with Marley's revelation—the reminder of what he'd discovered almost a century ago.

When he met Grace, things were too similar to this. Too many pieces clicked into place. He'd figured out before Morrigan got to her that she was a reincarnation of Sayuri, just as Elizabeth had been. His knowledge hadn't been enough to save her, though. When he'd lost Grace, the spiral he slid into almost destroyed him. He'd forced himself to lock away the notion of ever seeing her in another body again, mostly so he could move on with eternity.

This couldn't be her, though. Fate wouldn't give him back the woman he loved a fourth time. He'd lost his chance a little more each time he tried to protect her. Even only knowing Luci for a day, he couldn't imagine giving her up, despite the past, or the logic he tried to force on himself.

So he was either looking at destiny again, or his obsession had reached new, insane levels. Not reassuring, either way.

Luci met his gaze, and her laugh sounded forced. "Do I have something on my face?"

Maybe he shouldn't have stared so long. "No." He helped her to her feet. "Just grief." If it was her, how was he supposed to tell her? And what if he told her, and it wasn't true—or worse, she decided she was done with this insanity and left? That might be for the best. At least she could get out before she lost her life again. "Come on." He guided her toward the recliner, sat in the chair, and tugged her to him.

She hesitated for the briefest moment, then slid into his lap and buried her head in his chest. "This doesn't change *anything*." Her words were muffled by his shirt.

"I know." He wrapped his arms around her and held her. Silence settled in, and they sat like that as the minutes ticked toward an hour. Her weight, her warmth—it all felt so right. "You wanted to know about my past. About the women I've loved before."

Her bitter chuckle shook her entire frame, but she didn't pull away. "I'm responsible for an entire apartment building of people being exploded. They don't even have a body count yet. That happened because of me, and you think telling me about your ex-girlfriends is the best way to take this conversation?"

She had a point, but he was running on instinct, and that rarely failed him. "First of all, what happened to your apartment isn't because of you. You couldn't have predicted or prevented it. Someone else made that decision. Don't let the guilt destroy you. And second, they're not ex-girlfriends; they're wives."

Her entire body froze in his arms. "Excuse me?"

If he overthought this, he'd talk himself out of it. Very little coming out of his mouth sounded rational, but he knew it was the right way to go. "I was married to each of them."

"Oh, of course. That makes it all better. Awesome." She sat up and shifted her weight.

He grabbed her wrist before she could leave, loosely enough she could break free if she wanted, but he hoped with enough force to convince her to stay. "I have a past. Everyone does. Pretending it doesn't exist won't make it go away." She might just be proof of that. He didn't want to hope, but couldn't help himself. "Besides, you wanted to know who I am and who I've loved."

She clenched her jaw and started at the floor, but she didn't stand.

"You don't have to listen," he said. "But you should know, even though I remember them, they're in my past." Mostly. Was he stretching the truth too thin? "I'm here now, not there."

She finally met his gaze. Red rimmed her eyes, though she hadn't been crying, and dark circles lingered underneath. "What were their names? It had to hurt, watching them grow old and die. Except you didn't. Did you?"

Was she guessing or...? "All three of them died within weeks of marrying me." He didn't talk about this with anyone. Even giving her the vaguest information unlocked more of himself than he liked to acknowledged. "Sayuri, Elizabeth, and Grace."

"Beth," she whispered. "That's what you called her."

A jolt ran through him. "Yes." He summoned his restraint and pushed down the surging reaction. It could be a lucky guess. "Beth died because of me—they all did—so I know how you feel right now." That was enough sharing. He needed to close the door on those thoughts before they consumed him with guilt and hope.

"How do you deal with it?" she asked.

Not very well. "I change the subject a lot."

She leaned into him, head on his shoulder and fingers splayed over his heart. "In that case, tell me how Marley ascended. You've both said more than once she used to be human."

He could do that. It might give him the segue he needed to tell her his theory about who she was. It might not, but it was a starting point and a distraction. "I told you there are all sorts of poems out there about the future of the world and the gods' place in it. There's one about my brothers and me, as well."

"What does it say?"

"Eli's stanza comes last, since he's the youngest, but it played out first." He recited the lines with little thought. "As you are, for all of time, to taste neither love nor death. When you find the one worth more than life, she'll draw her last mortal breath."

Luci shivered in his arms. "Creepy."

"Not as much as it sounds, apparently. Marley died and then ascended. She's immortal now. One of the first of the new gods."

"You said brothers. How many of you are there?"

"Three." And he really didn't want to talk about the other one. At times it seemed as if saying Loki's name summoned the asshole, and that was the last thing they needed. What were the odds she'd just gloss over it?

She traced lines over his chest, touch so light he barely felt it. "When do I get to meet the third?"

"I'm sure he'll find a way to introduce himself."

CHAPTER TEN

Luci knew the entire conversation was an excuse to distract her, and she couldn't summon a reason to complain. It was a struggle to push aside how many people had died tonight, even just enough to keep herself sane. Blake's behavior was sweet and comforting and exactly what she needed. He tensed under her when she asked about his other brother. No reason to sour the mood by going down that path. "What about your bit in all of this?"

He trailed his fingers through her hair. "It's a little vague, the way fate tends to be. The world is yours, as you search for your soul. No lover shall bind you to the land. The one you discover, who quiets your might, will bring your journey to an end." His voice had taken on an almost musical tone, laced with melancholy. Each time he spoke, his chest vibrated against her ear and cheek.

"It's pretty." She wasn't sure what else to say.

"I suppose. I've always just seen it as being there."

"It must be disconcerting, though"—she tried to choose her words carefully, as to not derail the calm—"having your future laid out for you like that, from the moment you're born. Or created or whatever."

He paused his hand's attentions on her hair, and then resumed again. "'Born' is as appropriate as anything. And it's not as if it's my entire life—just one portion of it."

"One of the more important portions." Why had she said that? After her past, she'd convinced herself falling in love was a luxury she could live without. Traces of her dream rushed back. Not just the physical sensations it left, but the love Beth had felt when she saw Henry. A pure and complete adoration that still lingered in Luci's chest.

"Maybe." He shifted beneath her, and wrapped an arm around her waist. "Since you're letting me air my thoughts, I meant what I said earlier."

Her entire day was more emotion than detail. "You'll have to be more specific."

"You're beautiful. Not because I'm trying to trick you or manipulate you, but because you are."

Embarrassment heated her face. "Thanks." An empty pit still lingered. A bottomless gaping hole lined with despair. But having Blake there, regardless of the words exchanged, helped her step around it. She couldn't figure out why someone she barely knew was so comforting, but despite the mess that had been her day, sitting with him like this felt familiar and right.

Neither of them spoke. She wasn't sure what else to say, and he seemed to have run out of confessions. She wanted to spend all night talking to him, but at the same time exhaustion was staking its claim.

"Hey." He nudged her gently. "It's so late it's early. You need more sleep."

"I guess." She stumbled, as he helped her to her feet and stood next to her.

He wrapped an arm around her waist again and guided her toward the stairs. She was conscious enough to walk straight. His grip was too tempting to refuse, though. He stopped in front of the guest room he'd set her up in. "Get some rest."

She intertwined her fingers with his. "Stay, please?" It was a selfish, childish request she didn't want to take back. She wasn't ready to surrender that sense of safety yet.

He hesitated, and for a moment she was afraid he'd tell her no. Instead, he guided her toward the bed. "All right."

Still dressed, she lay on her side, and he took the spot behind her. He drew the blanket over both of them, and then rested a hand on her hip. Even through her clothing, she knew he traced circles over the spot where her birthmark sat. The same one Beth had in her dream.

The thought vied for her attention, but she was too tired to grasp and decipher it. With his chest pressed to her back, their breathing falling into sync, sleep took her quickly.

Grace giggled in delight when Blaine swept her off her feet, one arm under her knees and the other at her back. She encircled his neck and pressed her lips to his. Kissing him still felt new. Exciting. She hoped it always would. He stepped into the hotel room, still holding her, and kicked the door shut behind them.

He took a few steps before setting her on the ground, back to him. "Ancestors, you're gorgeous, Grace." He dropped a row of kisses along her neck. Each new touch sent pleasant shivers running through her, and anticipation pooled in her gut.

He dragged down the zipper of her wedding dress, and the fabric loosened around her torso. Nervous excitement joined her jumble of emotions. She'd wanted to wait until their wedding night to be with him. She knew it had been tough on him, but he'd respected her wishes. Now that it was finally happening—

they were married and she was his—a sharp longing ached between her thighs.

"We'll take this slow." He drew her close and rested a hand on her hip. Her skin hummed from the gentle caresses. The soft, teasing touches. He traced her pelvis with his finger, on top of a birthmark she'd always hated. She knew he wouldn't mind when he discovered it. There was no doubt in her mind he loved her as much as she did him.

His breath flowed over her skin, hot and enticing. "I've looked for you for ages. I'm not letting you go again."

Luci's eyes flew open, but the dream didn't leave her. She gasped as it continued to skip forward in her head. That was Blake. Again. And...

Grace lay in the hotel bed, enjoying the breeze on her bare skin. They'd have to return to real life soon, but the honeymoon had been amazing. Blaine stood next to her, gorgeous and naked. Blond, tall, muscular. All hers. He climbed on the mattress and pressed his lips to hers. He sought out her breast and squeezed lightly.

Each new sensation in the dream—memory?—flushed Luci's skin. She struggled to push it away. She saw Blake's guest room, registered the familiar ceiling, and smelled his scent on the sheets, but it overlapped with something else. Visions that were hers but not.

She struggled to move. To pull away from the man behind her, though she didn't know why.

A crash shattered the playful mood, as the door exploded from its frame and clattered into the room. "There you are." A woman stood in the doorway. Her pale blue gaze locked on Grace's, satisfaction and death burning in her irises. "You did a good job hiding her this time."

Morrigan. The name passed through Grace's mind at the same time Blaine said it.

"You remember me." Morrigan's smile radiated destruction.

No. The word repeated over and over in Luci's head. She didn't want this. It needed to go away, whatever this vivid vision was that felt as much a part of her past as waiting in line for coffee yesterday morning. A whimper rose inside, but she couldn't force it out.

There was no way Grace remembered this madwoman. She'd never seen her before. Morrigan raised her hand, thumb and forefinger together, as if to snap. Blaine cleared the short distance between them faster than Grace could blink, and slammed Morrigan into a far wall. He growled. "Never again." A glow radiated out from him, engulfing both bodies.

Morrigan looked over Blake's shoulder, smirked at Grace, and snapped her fingers.

Agony shredded through Grace, as if she were yanked apart in a million different directions. She tried to scream, but her vocal chords didn't work.

"Luci." Blake's concern cut through the foul memory. She focused on him leaning over her, concern painting his face.

Her entire body still screamed in agony, though part of her knew she was fine. She struggled to draw in another breath.

"Love? Are you with me?" He brushed a strand of hair from her face.

She sucked in another desperate gulp of air, more grateful than she should be that it was an option. Reality displaced the memory and left confusion in its wake. "I was..." She didn't know. What was that?

"It's okay." He helped her sit, shifting so he could support her. "You're here, not somewhere else. It was just a dream."

Except it wasn't. She looked at him and saw the face of a man who had worn four different names. But they were all him. She dropped her hand to her hip. "You knew." Her voice rasped out past dry lips.

He furrowed his brow and studied her. "Knew what?"

That was a good question. If those men were all him, and what she'd dreamed was real, how did she know it as though she'd lived it? And why was she so convinced it wasn't just a waking nightmare? A voice whispered in her head. An insistence she not write this off like she always had in the past. That meant she *was* those women. She always figured it out too late. Just as Morrigan killed her. But that didn't make any sense.

No more sense than the fact she was sitting in a god's guest bedroom, wondering how much he'd kept from her. She wrenched away from him and stood. "You knew who I was."

"No." Even the single word had a waver to it. He held her gaze. "I didn't."

Except he did, because he knew what she was talking about. Rage and betrayal roared inside, carried on the lingering agony of remembering her own death three times over. "You did. And you lied to me about it."

CHAPTER ELEVEN

Blake didn't know what Luci had seen, but for several minutes it hadn't been him. He'd awoken to her whimpering and shivering, but couldn't shake her from her glass-eyed gaze. Whatever had been in her head, she knew something now. He could feign innocence and try to draw the details out of her, but he had a pretty good idea what she was talking about. "I didn't know until tonight. And even then, I wasn't certain. It's what Marley came to tell me."

Luci stepped back from the bed, fury and confusion warring for dominance of her features. "It's true, then. I'm the living embodiment of those women you were married to."

How much did she know? He wanted to sit and talk it through with her. Find out what she'd seen. That probably needed to wait. "Maybe. Probably. Apparently. I wasn't sure, even after Marley showed me. I wanted to find out before I said anything to you. You're already dealing with enough discovery."

"Maybe it should be my decision what is and isn't enough. You sat there and prodded me. Feeding me names. Nudging me, to see how I'd respond to stories about your past."

"That's not what I was doing." Or maybe it had been. "I wanted you to know who I was. And if it's true, if you're them, I need to figure out how to stop this from happening again." He kept his voice firm.

"I'm not *them*." She clenched her fists. "I'm me! I refuse to be a walking memory, so you have something to cling to rather than move on with life. So your fucked up associates have another ghost to hunt down. You want to know how to keep me safe? Stay away from me. Maybe they'd have lived to see forty if you'd done that."

"You have the birthmark, don't you?"

She rolled her eyes, jerked up the hem of her shirt, and tugged down the waistband of her jeans. A splotch of a crow glared back at him, distinct against her pale skin. "Really? That's what you care about right now? Do you even like me, or do you just see shadows of your past every time you look at me?"

"That's not a fair statement." Now probably also wasn't the time to argue the logistics of reincarnation with her and point out she was them, even if she had a different face, name, and childhood. "I was attracted to you before I knew.

While you were a stranger in a coffee shop, not a mysterious link to the gods."

She didn't want to hear reason. "I'm done with this bullshit." She backed toward the door. "With hiding and whimpering and waiting for you to find a way for me to be safe. Seems to me the safest place I can be is where you're not."

The words burrowed deep, slicing at his core. She had a good point. "I shouldn't have brought you here, but you can't go home. It's not safe."

"I don't have a home, remember?" Hysteria surged into her question. "Some psychopathic bitch who thinks I'm part of an ancient prophecy blew it up."

Right. "I mean you can't just go wandering out into the streets."

"I won't. I'm calling a cab and checking myself into a hotel long enough to figure out where to go next, but with any luck, not long enough for any of them to get hurt because I'm there. I need to be anywhere that's not near you. Someplace *they* can't find me until they realize I'm not a part of this."

Was it really that simple? He hated to think so, but if she wasn't a part of his life, his fate wouldn't impact her. "You're right."

Her shoulders slumped, though fury still spilled from her. "Of course I am."

He nodded toward the door, hating what he was about to say. It was the best way to do this, though. He hadn't known with Sayuri or Elizabeth, but he'd been selfish with Grace, thinking he could hide the truth from her and keep her to himself. Letting Luci leave was the only solution. "I won't look for you. We'll do whatever we can to keep Morrigan away from you. Go live your life."

She worked her jaw up and down, shook her head, and spun away. Seconds later his front door slammed shut, rattling the entire house.

He dropped back onto the bed with a grunt. Every inch of him ached over watching her walk out. From her perspective, he barely knew her, but that wasn't true. He'd already lived three lifetimes for Luci.

This was the best solution, though. The only way to keep it from happening again. He lay there, replaying everything in his head, as the sun crept into the sky and light spread across the room. Empty longing grew inside. Emotions he'd locked away ages ago and never intended to let free again played on an endless loop in his head.

He bolted straight up. Fuck, he shouldn't have let her leave. Morrigan already went after her once, and that was before Blake had any idea who Luci was. Even if Luci never forgave him, he wasn't going to let this happen again. He'd move heaven and earth to save her. He sprinted to his study and grabbed his phone.

"What's up?" Eli picked up the other end.

"How long to tell me if Luci's used her credit card to check into a local hotel today?"

"Ten minutes, tops. You let her leave?"

"'Let' is a strong word. Call me back when you have an address."

Blake paced. A million solutions jockeyed for his attention, each discarded as quickly as it formed. He needed to get to Luci now.

Luci sat at the desk in her hotel room, staring at the wall. Take a flight back to Utah or rent a car? Either way, she would be paying for this unexpected trip for a few months. She'd better find work as soon as she got back. And a new place to live. The deposit on another apartment wouldn't be cheap either.

She used her irritation with Blake to suppress an onslaught of memories that weren't hers, but her resolve grew weaker with each new image that slipped through the cracks. She wanted to hate Blake for lying to her, but she understood his reasons. 'Hey, you might be the fourth reincarnation of my dead wife,' wasn't exactly casual conversation.

Or she was just getting sucked into someone else's life too quickly, and was guilty of the same thing she'd accused him of—seeing his past instead of her present. The longer she thought about it, though, the more she realized it wasn't that simple. Grace, Sayuri, and Elizabeth weren't separate people; they were all her. They knew things about Blake, and now she did too. They'd fallen for him, and she could see why.

A pit echoed inside her and resonated with a painful combination of longing and realization. She'd loved him, more than once. It pinged in her chest and twitched in her fingers and filled her thoughts. And she wanted to find that again. Was it possible? Marley had gained immortality. Maybe all Luci needed to do was stay alive long enough for that to happen. Death obviously wasn't the right course in her case, but survival might be.

She should call Blake. Or maybe she should wait until she was back in Utah. The distance would give them time to know each other.

"Boo," a female voice said in her ear.

Luci jumped to her feet and whirled, heart hammering in her chest. Her pulse increased several more notches when she saw Morrigan standing in front of her, a smirk on her face.

"How'd you shake the bodyguard?" Morrigan asked.

Luci tried to swallow past her fear and couldn't. "I left." She finally managed to speak.

If she could convince Morrigan she didn't care about Blake, would the goddess leave her alone?

"Aww…" Morrigan gave her an exaggerated pout. "Lovers' spat?"

"We're not lovers." Luci dredged up more resolve. "We're not anything."

"See, that's where you're wrong. You may have convinced yourself of that, but your heart knows otherwise."

"How do you know?"

Morrigan stepped closer, mouth hovering near Luci's ear. "A goddess can tell." She pulled away again and studied Luci. "The question is, what's it going to take to keep you from coming back again?"

"Not killing me?" Luci needed a weapon. She didn't know if it would do her any good, but trying to figure out what she could grab made her feel better. "Let me life a long, fruitful life away from all of you, and destiny will be done with me forever?"

"No. I don't think that's the answer." Morrigan's smirk grew, until she showed teeth. "Nice try, though. I'm looking for something a little more immediately permanent."

CHAPTER TWELVE

Morrigan never turned her attention completely from Luci, as she wandered the room. "How long do you think it will take Helblindi to get here?" The goddess's voice was sing-songy, set to a rhythm Luci couldn't hear.

"Blake's not coming for me." Even as she said it, Luci realized exactly how true it was. Why did she walk away from what little security she had?

Because this wasn't supposed to happen if she left.

"Oh, Lovely... That's what he calls you, right? Lovely Luci? He's coming." Morrigan picked the remote from the nightstand, turned it over in her hands, then whirled and threw it.

It flew at high-velocity toward Luci's head, and Luci ducked just in time to hear it whistle past her ear. This was worse than being killed instantly. Or maybe it wasn't. This was different from every time in the past—she remembered that. Morrigan had never talked before. Was this how she kept Luci from ever coming back?

Maybe Morrigan intended to talk her to death this time.

"He'll always come for you, Lovely." Morrigan picked through the far end of the room, ruffling her fingers over the curtains and glancing out the window. "That's why I need to figure out how to stop you from coming back. You're his obsession. As long as you keep showing up, he'll keep pursuing you. Even the first time, he mourned you for over a century."

The idea warmed Luci more than she wanted it to. "Why do you care?"

"Hmm..." Morrigan tapped her chin. "Because I don't like him. That's strictly personal."

"So you keep killing me?" Luci's fingers brushed something smooth and cold. The phone. Would clocking this madwoman in the head buy Luci even a few seconds? She was willing to find out. She inched her fingers over the device, a few millimeters more every time Morrigan turned away.

"Oh, that. No. I keep killing you *in front of him* because I don't like him. That's why you're still alive right now. But you're in more than one fate, Lovely. You're destined to be my downfall, and the idea anyone is capable of replacing me is a load of horseshit. I'm not going anywhere, but you are until you stay dead."

"It must suck to be you." Luci meant the bold words to be a distracting taunt, but something about them rang deeper. What would it be like to spend an eternity always looking over her shoulder, wondering when her life would end? Maybe she didn't want immortality after all.

"It doesn't." Morrigan wiggled her fingers in the air, and the phone was wrenched from Luci's hand. It slammed into the far wall with a sickening clang and left a dent in the plaster. Pieces of plastic clattered to the ground.

Luci stretched her fingers, panic surging back again. Morrigan had to be wrong. Blake didn't know where she was and wasn't coming for her. That meant she was safe until Morrigan got bored and offed her anyway. Instinct told her that was a very imminent possibility. Luci gripped the back of the chair next to her. Could she use that as a club?

Morrigan's mouth stretched into an exaggerated yawn. "The problem with waiting for someone who can't move quickly is not knowing if he's on his way and just slow or if we're going to be here all afternoon."

"You can leave. I won't mind." Luci tried to keep her tone light, but terror gripped more of her thoughts every minute. She remembered what it was like to be torn apart by Morrigan's magic and wanted very much for it to not happen again. Her heart hammered in her chest, and her stomach turned in on itself.

"Nah." Morrigan perched on the edge of the bed and crossed her legs at the knee. "We'll give him thirty more minutes, and then I'll just obliterate every last inch of you. Or maybe only ten. I have other things to accomplish this year."

Luci tightened her grip on the chair, forced all her strength into her arms, and swung. The furniture shattered before it reached Morrigan. Splinters bigger than Luci's forearm flew at Luci, some slicing her skin, and others slamming into her bones and bruising.

"Or we'll do it now." Morrigan stood, brushed invisible dust from her clothing, and stalked toward Luci.

Shit. Panic, fear, and the distinct desire to live at least a few more years spilled through Luci. She threw a wild punch, and Morrigan knocked her hand aside. Luci stepped back, but the desk was in the way. What was she supposed to do now?

"I never figured out what he likes about you." Morrigan's sing-song voice returned. She drew a line in the air, following the curve of Luci's neck. Though Morrigan never made contact, Luci felt the skin slice and warm blood trickle down. "You've always been odd." Morrigan continued a downward path, and a tear split Luci's shirt above her right breast. This time she saw the ugly red gash appear. "You're fat. You're boring. You're whiny." She dragged her nail past the waistband of Luci's jeans and over her hip.

Luci couldn't hold back her scream, as the cut sliced through denim and her birthmark. Her legs threatened to give out from the pain.

"And you're not suited to wear my mark," Morrigan said, "let alone take my place."

Blake heard Luci scream halfway down the hall, and his sprint turned into a flat run. He slammed through the hotel door in time to see her drop to her knees, red splattered around her.

Morrigan spun with a smirk. "You took yo—" Her taunt ended in a gurgle when Blake pinned her to wall by the throat. He summoned his power from within and forced it out. His gift was unique among gods. No one else but Marley had the ability to stop another immortal from accessing their power, and unlike in the past, he had enough warning and experience to keep Morrigan incapacitated. As long as he held her in place, she couldn't do anything.

The problem was, neither could he. She wasn't mortal like this, just powerless.

"You're here." Morrigan's voice held too much glee.

Blake wanted to check on Luci. To see if she was all right and to figure out how to stop the bleeding. But if he let his attention shift for even a moment, he and Luci were both fucked.

"Stalemate," Morrigan said, her tone taunting. "What are you going to do now?"

CHAPTER THIRTEEN

Blake lifted Morrigan off the ground by the throat, hoping to find enough leverage to cut off her air and stop her babbling. She didn't need oxygen to survive, but she did need it to talk. He couldn't squeeze her windpipe tighter, though. Her energy pushed against his. Mentally, he shoved back. He was vaguely aware of Luci climbing to her feet, but he didn't dare give her more than the barest recognition.

He summoned more from within, pushing harder against Morrigan. This wouldn't happen again. He wouldn't let it. Out of the corner of his eye, he saw Luci stumble toward the bed.

A surge slammed into him and threw him back from Morrigan. The goddess dropped softly to her toes, grin sliding back onto her face. The expression vanished when Luci brought a framed print down on her head. Glass shattered, dropping in shards around Morrigan. She snarled, whirled toward Luci, and flung her into a far wall. Luci landed with a loud slap. A crack rent the air, and she screamed as her arm snapped to an unnatural angle. The cuts on Morrigan's scalp were already healing.

Blake reached inside and grabbed everything he had. He pushed it all toward Morrigan in a single burst, building a bubble of helplessness around her. He dragged up the last bits of what he had and then scraped further for more. He poured every bit of power he'd ever known into keeping Morrigan from accessing her own.

Her smugness vanished, and she dropped to her knees. The cuts in her head re-opened, and blood flowed freely. Still he pushed harder. He wouldn't let Luci die. He refused to. Pain seared his veins, burning through his muscles, ravaging his joints, and he forced out more energy.

The edges of his vision blurred and then grew black. Spots danced in front of his eyes. He was vaguely aware of someone screaming. His name maybe. He wasn't sure. Morrigan collapsed on the floor, and the persistent glow of her aura vanished.

Blake's world went dark.

Luci cradled her arm to her side and bit the inside of her cheek to keep from screaming. Blake and Morrigan both lay on the floor, unmoving. The cuts on Morrigan's scalp had reopened, and blood matted her hair. They needed to leave before the goddess woke up, but Luci had trouble standing. There was no way she could drag Blake out of there. She pulled herself onto the bed, doing her best to avoid broken glass and wood, grabbed her phone, and dialed Marley's number.

"Hello?" a tentative voice answered.

"We need help." At least talking didn't hurt. She gave a brief rundown of what had happened.

"Shit. We'll be right there," Marley said.

Luci slumped back against the wall, exhaustion flowing through her. Every movement hurt, and she didn't dare take her eyes off the bodies on the floor. It felt like an eternity before her doorknob rattled, but was only a few minutes according to her phone. Seconds later, a jolt bounced off her eardrums and the door swung open. When Marley and Eli rushed into the room, Luci let out a breath she didn't know she held, and let the pain muddy the edges of her vision.

The scene around her passed in a blur. Eli was on the phone, barking orders for cleanup and containment. Marley knelt next to Blake and then was by Luci's side. Someone else appeared in the middle of the room and vanished just as quickly, taking Morrigan with them.

"Hey." Marley nudged her leg. "Look at me."

Luci forced herself to focus on the other woman's face. "Is he...?" Dead wasn't the right word. Gods didn't die. Except he'd said they could. That was part of the legends.

"Mortal." The syllables rolled off Marley's tongue, but they didn't make sense.

Blake groaned, and Eli helped him sit.

"I... What?" Luci stared at Marley, looking for some indication this was a joke.

"Let me see your arm." Eli rested his palm on her shoulder.

A frantic dance of sparks raced through the limb, until she thought her head might burst in a tower of sparks. The pain amplified and then vanished. She gasped at the contrasting sensations.

Blake rubbed his face and wobbled to his feet.

"Better?" Eli asked.

Luci nodded. She wanted to ask what he'd done, but she needed to know something else first. She looked at Marley. "Go back to what you said."

Blake joined them on the bed, despite how crowded it had grown, and flopped onto his back next to Luci. "She said mortal."

"Take it from someone who knows," Marley said. "Never think you can guess what the legends actually mean, until they play out."

Luci wasn't sure if she wanted to laugh or cry.

"Hey." Blake reached up and laced his fingers through hers. A smile played on his face, instead of the negativity Luci expected. His voice was calm, and soothing, despite the fact he sounded exhausted. "It's all okay. I'm all right, and so are you."

Hot water sluiced over Luci's head and down her back. She leaned forward in the shower and pressed her forehead to the cool tile. She couldn't help but smile. She'd only been here at Blake's for a week, and especially if she ignored the insanity that had been their first twenty-four hours together, it had been an incredible week. She was still adjusting to the memories of three other lifetimes, but she knew now they were all hers. Not overlapping time lines or conflicting ideas, but experiences she'd lived in another time and place.

The shower door slid open, and the cool air chased steam around her before vanishing again. Blake rested his hands on her hips, pressed his chest into her bare back, and traced his lips up her neck. "Good morning, *Elskede*."

The word filled her. He'd told her it meant beloved. Despite the jumble of past lives, it was hers and hers alone. She leaned against him. "I'm pretty sure you already showered."

His hard length pressed into her ass. He traced along the scar on her hip. Eli had been able to heal the slash through her birthmark, but not hide the wound. She didn't mind. It felt right that the symbol was scarred over now. "But I'm feeling dirty again," Blake said.

"I know a solution for that." She plucked the shower gel from the shelf in front of her and handed it over her shoulder. After the incident with Morrigan, they'd determined Blake had exhausted his power and completely neutralized the goddess's, leaving them both mortal. They'd stuck Morrigan with local police, amid protests that she was a goddess and threats that she'd make everyone pay.

Luci heard a squirt, and seconds later, something cold hit her stomach. She squealed at the sudden jolt.

"Sorry." Blake sounded anything but. His touch warmed quickly, as he soaped his palms up her torso. Her giggles faded into a moan when he brushed the underside of her breasts. His tight grip, combined with the slick surface, sent shudders of pleasure through her.

She squirmed under his touch. "Do you really want to do this in here?"

"Here. The bedroom. Anywhere I can have you." He dipped a hand between her legs. His touch was light at first, caressing her outer lips and teasing the wetness from her.

She ground against his erection. "Anywhere?"

"Pressed against the glass, moaning in pleasure. Bent over the dining room table." He parted her folds and sought out her clit. "Anywhere."

Water cascaded over them. The soap rinsed and pooled at their feet before vanishing down the drain.

He rubbed her aching button. "I have a lot of catching up to do."

Anticipation built inside as he stroked. Her senses soared. Her gasps became short pants for breath. He dug his teeth into her shoulder, and she sucked in sharply through her teeth. He eased off and then pressed harder. Her head threatened to float away, as blood rushed downward, toward her swollen bud. The sharp scents of citrus soap and Blake filled her nostrils. Luci swam through all of it—the heat of the water, his skilled touch, the sound of his grunts. It all crashed over her when she came, carrying her on a wave and drawing her through ecstasy.

She pushed against his hand, until she couldn't take anymore and shuddered away.

"See?" His deep voice drilled into her thoughts, and he nipped at her earlobe. "Now, we take this into the other room."

CHAPTER FOURTEEN

Luci reached for a towel, and Blake grabbed her wrist to stop her.

She struggled halfheartedly. "We'll get water everywhere."

"Oh, no." He traced his nose up the side of her neck. "Then everywhere might have to dry out. Besides, I'm impatient." He steered her away from the shower and toward the bedroom. He'd be the first to sing the praises of mortality. It had been centuries since the world around him was so intensely vivid, and part of it was seeing things through Luci's eyes. Everything felt and tasted and smelled more distinct now, as if a filter had been removed from his senses.

She hesitated at the foot of the bed, and he propelled her forward, urging her to lie on her back. He crawled toward her, visually drinking in every curve and nuance of her body as he moved. "They're sheets. Water won't kill them." He kissed her navel and followed a path up her chest, until he claimed her mouth. She tasted like toothpaste and smelled of oranges and felt like satin sliding against him.

His fingers slid easily between her folds, and she groaned. The teasing in the shower had been fun, but his cock ached for attention. Especially after the way she'd ground her generous ass against him. He'd been tempted to bend her over then and there, and thrust inside her.

He wanted to see the expression on her face when she came. Another thing he didn't think he'd ever get tired of. He rolled onto his back and tugged her on top of him.

She smirked and hovered inches from his dick. The heat of her pussy taunted him, warm and tempting and just out of reach. "If you can tease me, I can tease you." Her velvet voice tickled his senses.

She reached between her legs and grabbed his shaft. A guttural groan tore from his chest. Her damp opening met the swollen purple head, and he thrust up with a grunt. "Ancestors, you're tight."

She rose up almost to the tip, then dropped down against him again. The slow build-up raised the friction between them. He wanted to memorize every touch. Every whimper that drifted from her throat. He gripped her thighs, digging in his fingers, and increased the speed. When she closed her eyes and leaned back, driving him deeper inside, he knew he'd hit the right spot.

"Fuck, *Elskede*." He liked the way the endearment rolled off his tongue almost as much as he liked the way she squirmed when he licked her to orgasm. He drove one hand up her chest, pinched a nipple, and rolled it between his fingers. She gasped and pushed harder against him.

His balls tightened at the feeling of her squeezing him, but he wasn't ready to come yet. He wanted to draw this out as long as possible. See the flush flood her body. Watch the tiny circles her full mouth formed as she drew close to climax.

He dug his fingers into her thigh, as their pace grew more frantic. Her lips parted, gasps blurring together. He found her clit, swollen and peeking from its hood, and drew tight circles around it.

She leaned back with a cry, and she raked his legs with her nails. Her gorgeous, full chest heaved when she came. Her pussy clenched around him, milking him. Breaking down his resistance. Ancestors, she was incredible. He couldn't hold back any longer. He spilled inside her, hot and frantic, thrusting until he was spent.

They both struggled to catch their breath, as they slowed to a stop. She shuddered, smile never leaving her face, when he pulled out of her. He tugged her forward, so her head rested on his chest, and trailed his fingers up her spine.

"Are you going to miss eternity?" Her question was muffled by his chest.

He'd wondered when she was going to ask about that. So far, she'd danced around the issue, inquiring in the vaguest terms if he was all right but never mentioning it directly. As if she was terrified he might change his mind. "No. Even if I had a choice. If someone came to me right now and told me I could have godhood back, I'd tell them no."

"Are you sure?"

"The only other thing I've ever been as certain of is how much I love you." He lifted her head so he could look her in the eye. "And if I can have you by my side for the rest of my life— no matter how short or long it is—that's all I care about."

She dropped her head back onto his chest, but not before he caught a glimpse of her smile. "I love you too." Her words were distinct this time.

From here on out, he was happy to help his kin with their fate however he could, but he was never going back to that life. This was his fate, and he couldn't have asked for a better one.

~*~

About Allyson Lindt

USA Today Bestselling Author Allyson Lindt is a full-time geek and a fuller-time author. She's found her own happily ever after, where she and her spouse call their furbabies their children. Coffee is her task-master and Whimsy is her muse. When she's not writing, she's fangirling over the latest superhero movies. She likes her stories with sweet geekiness and heavy spice, and loves a sexy happily-ever-after. Because cubicle dwellers need love too.

Learn more about Allyson's books, including signing up for her newsletter, by visiting http://www.allysonlindt.com.